WHEN HE WAS BAD

When He Was Bad

SHELLY LAURENSTON

CYNTHIA EDEN

BRAVA

KENSINGTON PUBLISHING CORP.
http://www.kensingtonbooks.com

BRAVA BOOKS are published by

Kensington Publishing Corp.
850 Third Avenue
New York, NY 10022

All Kensington titles, imprints and distributed lines are available at special quantity discounts for bulk purchases for sales promotion, premiums, fund-raising, educational or institutional use.

Special book excerpts or customized printings can also be created to fit specific needs. For details, write or phone the office of the Kensington Special Sales Manager: Kensington Publishing Corp., 850 Third Avenue, New York, NY 10022. Attn. Special Sales Department. Phone: 1-800-221-2647.

Brava and the B logo Reg. U.S. Pat. & TM Off.

ISBN-13: 978-0-7582-2726-3
ISBN-10: 0-7582-2726-4

First Kensington Trade Paperback Printing: June 2008
10 9 8 7 6 5 4 3 2 1

Printed in the United States of America

CONTENTS

Miss Congeniality

Shelly Laurenston

Dear Reader,

All I'd asked was, "Do you think I'm pretty?" And I was a little offended by the silence on the other end of that phone. Is it really that hard for an editor just to tell her writer what she needs to hear? Especially when all she has to say is, "Of course you are!"

Instead, her response was a much more vague, "What does that have to do with what we're talking about?" And boy, is there *tone*.

"I don't want to talk about that," I say with a dramatic flair I'm quite proud of. "For I am an artist. And artists don't explain their art. Their art just *is*."

I hear a loud noise on the other end of the phone and it sounds as if my editor has accidentally banged her head against her desk . . . several times. Funny how strange things sound through a cell phone, huh?

"Please, Shelly," she says after a few moments. "Do this for me."

"But I'm an—"

"Artist. Yes. I got that. But do this for me because I'm your editor . . . and I have no problems killing you."

I frown, convinced I misheard part of what she said. "I'm sorry? I missed that last part."

"I said, because I'm your editor and I care so much for you."

And honestly, how can I turn such a loving statement down? I actually had to wipe tears it touched me so deeply.

So here I am, dear reader, to explain that the story you're about to read is set in the far distant past of 1984 when leg warmers were a fashion choice; *Terminator* was in the theaters for the first time; and a synthesizer was actually considered a musical instrument. So, break out that Devo or Flock of Seagulls cassette tape and the all-important hair gel (this is of über-importance if you're from Long Island, New York) and settle back for a little *Miss Congeniality*.

Shelly

One

"Where do you get those stockings from, doc?" growled Niles Van Holtz, Van to his friends and family. Those stockings, with that one sexy line up the back of each leg, were like something out of a 1940s movie. He bet she wore garters too. Man, the woman drove him absolutely crazy and she didn't even notice.

Cold, brutally pale blue eyes turned and locked on Van. "Ah, yes," she sighed out. "Niles Van Holtz. My night at these charity functions wouldn't be complete without your biting wit and continual obsession with my underclothes."

"Why else do you think I'd drag myself to the science building, of all places, except to see you?"

Van had known a lot of mean women in his time. Coming from a wealthy background filled with lethal predators, he was more surprised to find a nice female than a mean one. But Irene Conridge, PhD several times over and Rhodes Scholar by the time she was fifteen, made mincemeat of them all.

Irene Conridge was what one would call a child prodigy. At least she had been. But at a luscious twenty-five she'd left her "child" anything long behind.

From the time Irene had walked onto the university campus, Van had locked onto her scent and had hunted her relentlessly ever since. She'd been eighteen at the time and Van twenty. He'd thought she was just another freshman. Or, as his buds had liked to call them, freshmeat. But he'd found out quick enough—when she'd coldly laid into him, leaving him standing speechless in the middle of the Square—that she was actually a guest professor. And a big deal. Ivy League universities all over the country and Europe had fought for her. But, for some unknown reason, she'd taken the job at this small but elite university on the border of Seattle, Washington. She'd turned down Harvard, Yale, MIT, Berkley, Oxford . . . all of them.

No one understood it, but Van did. Why go to a big university with a bunch of other former prodigies when you can go to a smaller one and be Head Shit in Charge? Because Irene had gone "small," she ruled. They denied her nothing, gave her whatever she needed, and strove hard to keep her happy. In return, Irene kept the university's name alive in academic circles, had students begging to get into the school so they could enroll in her class—until they actually had to get *through* one of her classes—and kept the money flowing in. The woman wasn't charming but somehow she dragged money from some of the richest families in the Northwest. His included.

"Besides, I'm only obsessed with *your* underclothes, doc." He knew she *hated* when he called her that. "Tell me, do you wear garters under those clothes?"

"Yes," she replied plainly. "I don't like pantyhose. I find them too binding."

Van couldn't help himself; he growled again. Enough that she turned and looked at him directly. "Did you just growl at me?"

"It was much more of a purr."

"Fascinating."

"Am I?"

"No. You're not. But the fact that a grown man would growl over garter belts is fascinating. I'm sure the psychology department would find you a fascinating test study."

"Sweet talker."

She frowned, and it wasn't a frown of annoyance or concern, but one of deep thought. "Am I? I've been told I'm cold and quite removed."

Van had to try really hard not to laugh. To be honest, he didn't know a colder woman on the planet. Female cavewomen who had been frozen in blocks of ice for millions of years were warmer than Irene. And yet . . . he simply couldn't leave her alone.

His sister, who currently floated around the party avoiding anyone who annoyed her, didn't understand his obsession over that "plain girl," as she often called Irene. He'd heard it before. Irene called "plain" or, his personal favorite, "not hideous." But Van didn't know what they were talking about. The woman was absolutely adorable. Black shoulder-length hair that had an out-of-control curl thing going that made him, for some unknown reason, think constantly of sweaty, rough sex. Full lips he'd seen in more than one wet dream over the years and a regal nose. A long, curvy body she constantly hid behind boring prim and proper power suits in the dullest colors, but she always wore those sexy stockings and killer shoes. It was the eyes that did him in though. He saw eyes like hers on arctic wolves. So pale blue he didn't really even think of them as blue at all. He'd heard more than a few people call her eyes freakish or disturbing, but he could stare into those eyes forever.

"I bet you're not really cold, doc. Not underneath it all."

"Actually, I am. Oh. And Jackie and I have a bet going." She motioned to her roommate, Jaqueline Jean-Louis, a former child music prodigy. The two women had known each other for years and Jean-Louis taught in the university's prestigious music department. What Van found fascinating about the whole relationship was the fact that Jean-Louis was a shifter. A jackal, specifically. He always wondered if Irene knew. If she did, she absolutely never showed it. But it wouldn't be unusual for her not to know. Many shifters went through their entire lives successfully hiding who they really were from the full-humans close to them. It was important to their kind to hide who they were. In fact, hard choices were sometimes made in order to keep their secret.

"Is that right?" he asked, taking a glass of champagne from the tray passing by.

"Yes. I'm convinced you believe I'm a virgin and all this time you've been hoping to defile me."

No matter what he did, he couldn't keep from choking that champagne right back up.

She simply didn't understand. For nearly seven years now, the man had sought her out. At every charity event. Every university function. Anything she had to go to in order to fulfill her responsibilities to the university, Niles Van Holtz was there. He wouldn't pounce right away. He'd wait until she'd finally entertained the thought that he'd decided not to attend and then *boom*. He'd be there. Usually easing up behind her and asking her something rather inappropriate in her ear. You could almost say she'd come to expect it.

Irene looked up into Van Holtz's handsome face. And he was handsome. Gorgeous, in fact, if you followed the normal societal standards. Dark brown hair that had streaks of white, black, and gray nearly covered those oddly colored eyes of his. Kind of a gold amber or something. She wasn't really a color person; she left those sorts of decisions to Jackie. Even now the gown Irene wore—a pale silver . . . thing—her friend had picked out for her.

Van Holtz also had a rather square jaw and a nose she bet once had a deviated septum, based on the way it went crooked right below his brows, and a rather abnormally large neck.

Yes, a very handsome man. And, perhaps, one of the most arrogant beings she'd ever come across. Truly, if she had any emotional investment in this man, she'd be forced to have him wiped from the planet. But Irene had very little emotional investment in anyone. Jackie and Jackie's boyfriend, Paul, pretty much covered her emotional investment. And she was quite okay with that.

More than okay.

Van Holtz cleared his throat. "Um . . . and why do you think it would matter to me if you're a virgin?"

Irene shrugged. "You have that demeanor. I imagine you probably like it when the virgin tells you, 'Ow! You're too big. Please, we have to stop!' And you say"—she lowered her voice several octaves to match Van Holtz's—"'Don't worry. I'll make it good for you, sweet little virgin girl.'"

Van Holtz stared at her for at least a full minute and Irene began to wonder where Jackie had wandered off to. She brought the woman with her to stop Irene from doing things like this. Saying something that would cause huge repercussions financially. The Van Holtz family gave the university a lot of money and with a stupid attempt at honesty, Irene may have caused that money supply to dry up.

But then Van Holtz threw his head back and laughed, shocking Irene and causing everyone in the room to turn around and stare at them. Not surprisingly, Jackie suddenly appeared at her side.

"What's going on?" she immediately asked, a lovely fake smile on her face.

"I'm unclear as to whether I'm being laughed at or laughed with," Irene told her friend.

"Laughed with, doc," he finally managed. "I promise. You just never fail to amuse me."

"Knowing that, my life is now complete."

Jackie tugged a lock of her hair. A signal that she needed to shut up now.

As it happened any time Irene found herself in a conversation with Niles Van Holtz, two people always showed up if they were around. His older sister, the less than pleasant Carrie Van Holtz. And Farica Bader. A woman clearly interested in Van Holtz for herself. The two women surrounded them while eyeing each other cautiously.

"Did I miss something?" Carrie asked her brother.

"Yeah. But I'll tell you later." Those amber-colored eyes glanced at Irene. "I was just spending some time with my favorite biophysicist."

"Why?" his sister asked, and Irene had to appreciate her honesty. Of course, Jackie didn't. And she gave a little warning snarl that almost made Irene smile. Except Irene didn't smile. When she did it felt weird and uncomfortable. So she never bothered unless caught off-guard.

"Van," Farica breathed huskily, going up on her toes to kiss him on the cheek, "I missed you at last week's get-together."

"Sorry, Farica." Van Holtz swiped a quick kiss across the back of her knuckles, but his eyes stayed focused on Irene. "I had to go to San Francisco to check on the new restaurant."

"I thought your father handled that sort of thing."

"Normally he does," he murmured, his eyes traveling down Irene's dress and back up again. "But lately he's become quite the demanding prick."

"Perhaps he's considering retirement." And even Irene could hear the hopefulness in that cold, cultured voice. The Baders were a small family but clearly had hopes of becoming more powerful among the Seattle elite. Connections with the Van Holtzes would ensure that. Especially marriage. Although from what Irene had heard these past seven years, getting Niles Van Holtz down the aisle would take a team of oxen and many chains. The man never stayed with one woman for any length of time, although he may go back and forth between his favorites.

Sex. It all had to do with sexual intercourse. Something Irene actively avoided if at all possible. As she'd told Van Holtz, she wasn't a virgin. Two years at MIT ensured that. But she'd never enjoyed it and she'd tried it with several different partners. She found the whole process rather revolting. She had the distinct feeling she'd one day have to explain that to Niles Van Holtz so he could stop looking at her like his next conquest. As handsome as he was, the idea of getting naked with him and writhing around did nothing but make her feel slightly ill. It wasn't him per se. It was the physical act itself.

Irene shuddered a bit merely thinking about it.

Van Holtz stepped closer, invading her personal space. "Are you cold?"

"No," she answered plainly. "Just disgusted."

"Why? Did you look in a mirror recently?" Farica commented.

Irene didn't even blink. She'd been insulted by Farica before and she never worried about it. The woman had her own painful insecurities to deal with, lashing out at Irene gave her little satisfaction, and Irene refused to be baited. But Van Holtz turned on Farica Bader so fast, the woman took several steps away from him only to crash into his sister. The unholy smile on that woman's face made it clear Carrie Van Holtz would happily throw Farica into a pool of sharks if the opportunity presented itself.

But Jaqueline, Irene's self-appointed protector, moved forward, her hands curled into ready-to-fight fists.

With a sigh, Irene grabbed her friend's arm and dragged her back. "Come on, Jack. I want to show you my new computer. In my office." Irene walked off, Jackie stomping behind her.

She didn't bother to turn around and look at Van Holtz or his sister. As with most human beings, she'd already forgotten about them as soon as she stepped out into the hallway and headed up the stairs to her office.

"Don't ever speak to her that way again," Van snarled. If they were on a hunt, he'd have Farica Bader on her back, belly exposed, with his jaw wrapped around her throat.

If she thought knocking down Irene would somehow endear her and her tiny Pack to Van, she was sadly mistaken.

"I didn't realize you were so attached, Van."

"I'm not attached. It was mean. Unnecessarily so. Do you beat up kittens, too?"

"How dare—"

Carrie stepped between the two of them. "Go away, Farica. My brother is not interested in you. And I'd hate for us to have to wipe out your Pack for, ya know, amusement."

With a last glare, Farica turned on her overpriced shoes and stormed away to lick her wounds.

"Tell me you never slept with her."

"Are you high?" Van slammed his now-empty champagne

glass on another tray moving by. The fact that those trays were attached to actual human beings, he rarely noticed. "That woman wants one thing. And that's to be marked and mated to a Van Holtz. I'd rather chew off my own arm."

"I'm glad to hear that. But"—and Van knew he was about to have one of those painful conversations with his big sister— "I want to see you mated and happy one day to someone. Like I am. But preferably not to Irene Conridge."

Van snorted. "Mated? With Irene? Wait. Let me rephrase that. Mated? With *anyone*? Not going to happen, big sister."

"You have no intention of marking anyone as your own?"

"Christ, what a load of shit Mom and Dad handed you. And you've bought into it. I thought you were smarter than that." The idea that biting a female made her yours forever to the exclusion of every other pussy available seemed beyond ridiculous. Van didn't believe any of those old She-wolves' tales. He simply had too much sense. Not only that, but he'd never give up having access to an array of females. Why should he? If they were there, wet and ready, he would fuck them. He kind of saw it as his civic duty . . . yes, he *was* that good.

"To answer your question, no. I don't plan to mark any-one"—he used air quotes here—" 'as my own.' I have way too much sense to do that to myself."

"Okay. But you'd get Dad off your back if you mated with somebody."

Both siblings had noticed their father had been much less pleasant in the past year. Grouchy didn't do his recent temperament a lick of justice. Constantly the man pushed Van, and Van didn't know why. Maybe the old wolf wanted to retire. And that would be fine. Just hand over the business and the Pack and Van would be more than happy to take over. But life was too short and insane to start playing these barbarian games of the young wolf taking down the old. They were Van Holtzes, goddamnit. They were civilized, cultured, and damn good-looking. If the old man wanted a fight, go hang with the Magnus Pack or, even better, the Smiths. That Pack only breed Alpha Males and, not surprisingly, in-fighting went on constantly.

Van, however, liked his life just as it was. A wonderful business, the ability to shift into wolf whenever the mood struck him, the opportunity to travel whenever he wanted, and a plethora of available females at his disposal. Why would he change that for anything or anyone?

Actually, he wouldn't change it.

"Well, whatever you do, maybe you should stay away from Conridge. She doesn't exactly seem interested."

"True, she's resisting me. But I'll wear her down. Like the time we ran down that elk in Canada. Took us two days but we did it."

His sister sighed. "I'm starting to become concerned about your taste, little brother. She's . . . odd."

"She's odd because she's brilliant." He motioned to the exit where the female had disappeared. "At this moment, she's discussing things you and I could never even comprehend."

"I *absolutely* could create a lightsaber."

"You could not create a lightsaber."

"I could too. It's all science."

"I thought being a Jedi was mystical?"

Irene snorted. "Mystical, my butt. It's all about science."

Unlocking the door to her office, Irene walked inside with Jackie following. She walked around her desk and threw herself into her office chair, feet up on the wood. Her friend sat in the chair opposite.

"Sorry about that, sweets." Jackie sighed.

Irene blinked. "Sorry about what?"

"About what went on with Farica Bader."

Frowning, Irene stared at her friend.

"You know," Jackie went on, "Farica Bader? Who only moments ago insulted you?"

"Oh, yes. Her."

"How do you do that?" Jackie asked with a smile.

"Do what?"

"Not let stuff get to you? I mean, I hate that woman."

Irene shrugged. "Why hate her? It requires emotion that takes time out of my schedule. The Farica Baders of the world can say what they want. But in the end, they go back to their small, petty lives while people like us go on to perform for the kings and queens of Europe or produce life-changing creations. She is meaningless to us. They all are."

Jackie gazed at her for several moments and Irene marveled at how truly beautiful Jackie was. Stunning, in fact, with almond-shaped brown eyes from her mother's side of the family and naturally blond-brown hair from her father's.

"I love you, Irene," Jackie finally said.

Surprised, Irene asked, "You do?"

"Of course I do. You're my best friend and you're amazing. I don't know what I would have done without you these last few years."

"That makes two of us, my friend. But now you have Paul."

"Yeah. I guess. But he's been acting weird lately."

"He's madly in love with you and trying to figure out how to handle it. Give him a week or two."

Jackie laughed. "That sure, are you, Dr. Conridge?"

"Of course. When am I ever wrong?"

Still laughing, Jackie stood up and headed out the door.

"Where are you going?"

"Bathroom."

"Use the one down the other hallway. The one right here is blocked off by the construction."

Jackie stood in the doorway, staring at the near-destroyed hallway. "When are they getting that done, anyway?"

"Not soon enough," Irene said while booting up her computer. The chances of her returning to the cocktail party became distinctly remote as soon as her new machine powered up. "I've had six fights with the foreman about noise. How they expect me to get any work done with all that banging, I'll never know."

Jackie stepped back into the office. "Hey. This was in your inbox." She handed Irene an envelope from the dean's office.

"Great," Irene muttered, afraid of another student complaint about being made to cry. Weakness. She detested weakness.

Tearing the envelope open, Irene took a quick look at the letter, took it all in, and processed it. She felt the color—what color there was—drain from her face. "Uh-oh."

Again Jackie came back into the office. Poor thing, she couldn't quite make it to the ladies' room. "What's wrong?"

"They need access to the labs next week."

"So?" Then Jackie's eyes narrowed. "Irene, tell me you took care of that little issue we discussed."

"Um . . ." Irene let out a breath. "Not quite."

"Irene!"

She held her hand up. "Don't worry. I'll take care of it tomorrow. It's perfect. It's Saturday. Very few students will be here and I can get them to go away if necessary." When Jackie only glared harder, Irene continued. "I promise. All of it will be gone by tomorrow."

"It better be." Jackie stormed out and this time wasn't suddenly forced to come back in.

Irene turned back to her computer, went to her C: prompt, and called up all her files on the Terminate Project. She'd foolishly kept these files, concerned she might need them later. It was hard to get rid of something one had worked so long and hard on. But now that she knew what it could do . . . Jackie was right. It all had to go. She typed in "DEL C:\Project8" and hit ENTER.

Letting out a sigh that at least that much was now gone, Irene sat back in her chair, but the creak outside her door had her sitting up again. Okay. Now she was being paranoid . . . wasn't she?

She heard another sound and Irene stood up, walking to her door. She glanced both ways but didn't see anything. Another sound from the end of the hall that led out had Irene's entire body tensing. She glanced around and realized she had nothing to defend herself with should it become necessary. Moving quickly, she went over to the construction supplies lying on the floor and grabbed the first thing she saw.

Slowly, she stepped closer to the construction area, trying her best to make no sound. It could be her imagination, but she sensed someone there. Behind a pack of piling. Ridiculous, of course. It had been several years since her government or any government, for that matter, had followed her. They'd begun to lose interest in her as soon as she went into teaching rather than working for some government-funded bioweapons company. Still, if someone had found out about her little creation, Irene had no doubt they'd go through their usual measures to get just a sample of it.

Irene stopped. Government agents always had guns. She had a two-by-four . . . exactly when had her legendary logic escaped her? True, she had her own homemade weapon in her backpack, but she still wouldn't use that against a gun. No, she needed to get Jackie and go. Although it was most likely all her imagination anyway, better safe than sorry.

As it was, no one knew about her project, and no one would either. She would make sure of that.

"You okay, doc?"

Without thinking, only on instinct, Irene turned and swung, slamming the two-by-four right into Niles Van Holtz's head. She hit him so hard, his head hit the other wall and then he hit the floor.

"Oh . . . oh, that can't be good." She'd killed a Van Holtz. As she crouched beside him, Irene's mind quickly zipped through all the law books she'd read over the years, looking for any way she could prove this was self-defense.

"What the hell . . . Irene, what did you do?"

Irene looked up at her friend. "He snuck up on me," she replied calmly.

Jackie crouched beside Van Holtz's prone body. "You split his head open."

"A few stitches. Perhaps some slight brain damage, but none that we'd notice." She put her fingers to his throat. "He's got a pulse. Chances are high he'll live."

Sighing, Jackie glared at her. "The emotions you should currently be experiencing are regret, tempered with a little guilt."

Since they'd met so many years ago, Jackie remained the "emotional one" and Irene the "logical one." Jackie had artist-like sensibilities. She had no control over her spending habits or her tendency toward rage. Irene didn't understand human emotion and had long given up trying. When most little girls fell in the park and scraped their knee, they cried. Irene analyzed what had made her fall and why, exactly, her knees should hurt so much. Then she would analyze the momentum it took for her to actually do the level of damage she'd done.

"Guilt?" she asked. "For what? It was self-defense."

"That'll never play to a jury."

"Damn." She'd really hoped it would.

"Tell me what happened."

"I thought I heard something."

"You did hear something. I heard it too."

The two friends stared at each other, then Jackie took Van Holtz's arm and pulled it around her neck. "This is what we're going to do. I'll take him back to his family. *You* get that shit out of here tonight."

"Yeah, but—"

"No buts, Irene. Take it out of here tonight. Okay?"

Irene nodded, realizing she had to put her ego aside when it came to this. "All right." She didn't need to help her friend lift the still-unconscious Van Holtz.

"Do you know what to do with it?"

"Leave it to me." Irene headed back to her office. "I have my backpack in the car and extra clothes here. I'll change and then I'll move that stuff out."

Jackie headed down the hall. "See you at home in about an hour?"

"Yeah. Perfect."

Irene closed her office door and pulled out a bag she kept for emergencies or seriously late nights. Nothing fancy, just a T-shirt, jeans, and sneakers. But the perfect ensemble for what she needed to do.

Still, the question remained . . . did she get rid of *all* of it?

Could it really hurt just to keep a smidge? Just for testing purposes only, of course.

Before Van opened his eyes, he realized two things. First, he was sitting against a car. Second, his sister was *pissed off*.

Hand to his poor abused forehead, Van forced his eyes open and looked around. As he'd guessed, his back rested against the family limo while his sister ripped the head off the She-jackal.

"Where is the little bitch? I'll kill her myself!"

The jackal seemed unimpressed by his sister's tirade. "You go near my friend, I'll rip your throat out myself."

"Oh, really?" Carrie stepped into the jackal's space and Van knew he had to say something before things went from bad to worse.

"Carrie. Cut it out."

Immediately his sister was by his side. "Are you okay?"

"I think you should get me home. I think Dr. Vasquez may need to sew up my head for the night." Leave the stitches in longer than twenty-four hours, though, and the skin would heal right over them. The dilemma of having a seriously amped-up metabolism.

"Okay." Carrie grabbed his arm and helped him stand.

"How long have I been out?"

The She-jackal shrugged. "I'm not sure. But I've been arguing with her for at least fifteen minutes."

"*Her?*" his sister snarled.

"Need stitches," he reminded Carrie, before she could blow something else out of proportion.

With a grunt of annoyance, Carrie helped him into the limo and got in after him. She slammed the door shut, glaring out at the jackal's retreating form.

"Where's Irene?" he asked.

"That bitch wouldn't tell me. But trust me when I say I tried to find out." His sister turned in the seat and looked at him. "You're not mad, are you?"

How could he be mad at a woman with such great instincts? "I scared her and she reacted. Don't blow this out of proportion."

His sister gave an annoyed sigh and leaned back into the seat. "Fine. I won't. You want to let this go, that's on you."

Irene pulled her car over to the side of the road and got out. She grabbed hold of her backpack and slung it over her shoulders. She'd headed out to one of the richest neighborhoods in town, about fifteen minutes from the university. It made the most sense because of all the open property and, thankfully, she didn't have to worry about the flora and fauna. What she'd created did damage to only one thing . . . the human body. For everything else—animals, plants, trees, insects—it remained a nourishment. How her good intentions had gone so horribly wrong, Irene still didn't know.

Setting off, Irene walked straight into the woods and she kept walking. She knew the area a bit but only from maps. The three families who lived in this area, including the Van Holtzes, didn't have any events that involved the university staff. Irene had never been inside any of their homes, but she'd never really cared.

Irene walked until she neared the ocean by the Van Holtz property. A perfect location. Kind of that midway point between the Van Holtz property, the Löwes', and the Dupris', one of the creepiest families Irene had ever met. But their money was green and beneficial, so she schmoozed when necessary, even while her skin crawled.

Deciding she'd walked enough, Irene stopped by a big, sturdy tree. She pulled on rubber gloves and carefully removed her concoction from her backpack. She had it in a special titanium container and took great care in unscrewing the cap and dumping the liquid on the tree. Irene waited, and she couldn't help but smile when she saw the blooms burst to life on the branches. Out of season, no less.

She screwed the cap back on the container and returned it to her backpack. Then she took out a thermos of tap water and dumped that on the spot and on her rubber gloves. That would wash away any additional remnants. Irene shook her head. The government couldn't ask for a better weapon.

Ignoring the bit of guilt lurking in the back of her mind about the two ounces she had safely hidden in her office, Irene tossed the thermos back in her backpack along with the rubber gloves.

Zipping up her backpack and placing it back on her shoulders, Irene stood but she froze in her tracks when she heard the crack of a tree branch.

Squinting, she stared into the darkness but couldn't see anything. She could, however, feel something. Something had cut off her way back to the car. Scanning her memory, she pulled up the map she'd looked at about seven years ago when she first moved out here. About a mile away was the Löwe house. She couldn't risk going to the Van Holtzes with her being the potential murder suspect of their firstborn son.

Controlling her fear and desire to run like a girl, Irene took a slow step back and then another. Moving purely on instinct, Irene knew she had to make a run for it . . . from what, she really didn't know. But she knew she had to.

So she spun on her heel and ran into the clearing, but came to a sliding halt as her feet touched the wet dirt.

Irene watched as it lifted its head from the elk carcass before it, face covered in blood. It stared at her and she quickly searched her brain to identify it.

Hyena. Irene swallowed and took a careful step to the left. She would be heading into Van Holtz territory, but she'd face Niles Van Holtz's family and manslaughter charges over this any day.

Irene took another step and another, carefully moving. She gripped the straps of her backpack, ready to yank it off. There was only one. She could fight off one. *There's only one*, she said to herself again.

At least that's what she thought until the second one slammed into her from the right, taking hold of her backpack and swinging her around like a doll. Then it tossed her, and that tree it aimed for came up excruciatingly fast. . . .

Two

"Pull over," Van snapped.

His sister patted his back. "You going to be sick?"

"No." The limo pulled over and Van stepped out.

"Van, what's wrong?"

Wiping the still-oozing blood from his eyes, Van stared at the very old Pinto.

"Well?" his sister demanded.

"This is Irene's car." He remembered it clearly. She'd almost run him down with it once. At the time, she'd said it was an accident but he hadn't appreciated her smirk when she'd said it.

Van looked around, sniffing the air.

Carrie shrugged. "And? So it's her car. What? You want to set it on fire?"

Ignoring his sister's question, Van glanced at her. "Look where we are."

Carrie glanced around and then she looked off into the woods. "Oh, God. The Rubicon."

He was already moving, parts of him shifting as he crossed the road. "Call to the Pack."

"But Van—"

"Do it!" was the last thing he could tell her before he'd

shifted completely and charged into the woods after Irene. If she'd already crossed the Rubicon, he might already be too late. But he couldn't think about that. He had to get to her. At the very least, he had to try.

Irene hit the tree hard, but she turned in time so it was her side that slammed into it as opposed to her face. She landed on the hard, unforgiving ground, and jaws, stronger than any other like-predator on Earth, tore the backpack off her, flinging it aside. Then it came for her.

Short, blunt claws slapped against her back, tearing past her T-shirt and ripping into soft human flesh. Focusing on one goal, Irene tried to pull herself out from under but its fangs grabbed firm hold of the remaining bit of her T-shirt and yanked her back, tossing her into the middle of the feeding ground.

More of them came out of the woods toward her. They made a strange laughing sound, calling to each other. They didn't run toward her. They didn't have to. They all knew she'd never outrun them.

Irene crawled backward and pressed up against the remains of the elk they'd been feeding on, her mind racing with a way out of this that would leave her face and most of her limbs intact.

Quickly scanning the ground, Irene saw her backpack. If she could only get to it . . .

But the hyenas must have seen what she was looking at. One of them ran toward her, jaws wide open. But before it could get to her, a blur of gold tackled it from the side. The hyena rolled away and scrambled up, trying to avoid the charging male lion. The male wasn't having it, though. He slapped at the hyena casually, seeming to enjoy the "little chase" around the clearing. Another male joined in and Irene saw her chance. But before she could move, nine lionesses came out of the other side of the woods and ran straight for her.

Again, Irene scrambled back, panic trying to set in. She

wouldn't let it, though. She needed her mind clear to get out of this. To survive. Her only goal was to survive.

More hyenas came and they charged the female lions, keeping them away from Irene and, apparently, their food source for the evening.

She knew she had only one chance and she either took it now or ended up finding out if so many religious belief systems were correct about there being an afterlife.

On hands and knees, Irene made a mad dash for her backpack. She'd just gotten hold of it when fangs gripped her side and flung her back into the midst of the fight. She landed hard, rolling to keep any of her bones from breaking in the process while maintaining a death grip on her pack.

They were still toying with her. She knew that because the lioness that grabbed her could have broken her spine but strategically dug into her side. They didn't want to kill her too soon. Where would the fun be in that?

Focusing on her task, Irene tore open the zipper on the bag, spraying her papers, files, and computer printouts everywhere. She ignored all that and took hold of what she still had buried inside. Her fingers wrapped around the metal as sharp teeth sank into her thigh and dragged her back.

Somehow knowing this would be her last chance, Irene waited until it had dragged her off into a corner, away from the current battle between lifelong enemies, and then it released her. Before it could get another grip on her or tear into something vital, like an artery or her brain, Irene turned and slammed her homemade weapon against its throat.

Amazing the things one could come up with when bored and reading an electronics magazine. At the time she'd figured if someone named Jack Cover could create the device, why not her? So she'd created three nonlethal ones exactly like his, the one some police stations around the country were using. But she found the nonlethal devices boring. So she'd increased the voltage on the last three as much as she could. Still she'd never used them before but merely kept one in her bag for those long, late-night walks to her car across campus. Until now.

Irene pressed the side buttons she'd added to the device and squeezed. Those increased volts now tore through her attacker.

The hyena's entire body jerked in surprise—until it began to smoke. The smell of burning fur didn't deter Irene from keeping her weapon against its throat. She sat up when it started to stumble back and fall over, never stopping the charge or allowing the device to move away from the hyena's neck.

After sixty seconds, she figured enough had been done and she stood and stumbled away, the hyena remains nothing more than a charred and bloody mess.

Irene quickly remembered there were more, and she spun around with the weapon held up in front of her. Rough breaths came out of her and she could feel blood trickling down her back and thigh, coating the inside of her jeans. As one, they all looked at the hyena's remains and back at her.

Trying to control her shaking but knowing that with any animal a show of weakness would be her undoing, she yelled, "Well? *Come on!*"

At first, they didn't move at all, staring at her with those cold eyes. She thought for sure they'd seen through her. That they could see and smell her fear. But she never looked away and slowly they stepped back. All of them.

They kept their eyes on her as if they thought she was as dangerous as they, and they took another step back. And another. And another. When they had a healthy distance between them, both lions and hyenas turned and trotted off back into the woods, heading to their own territories.

Irene waited until she could no longer see or hear them, then she turned and froze again, briefly wondering how much more she could take. They watched her with eyes much less cold but no less frightening.

It had to be an entire pack of wolves. She lifted her weapon, unable to stop her shaking this time, and waited. The one in front trotted forward and she watched it, waiting for it to make its move.

It did, shifting from wolf to human. And suddenly Niles Van Holtz walked toward her. Irene raised the weapon higher, where his big neck would be if he stepped any closer.

Van Holtz stopped and stared at her. "It's all right, Irene."

"I have to go." Irene ignored the fact that her entire body now shook with fear and panic and pain. "I have to work. I need to go back to my lab. I can't stay. You can't make me stay."

"Irene, I won't let anyone hurt you. I promise. But you've gotta trust me and come with me, baby."

"No. I'm going back to my car. Stay away from me, Van Holtz." She kind of jerked the homemade stun gun and a few of the wolves stepped back. But not him. "I'll do to you what I did to him," she warned, motioning toward the charred hyena. "So stay away from me."

"They won't let this go, Irene. They'll come back for you. You'll never make it to your car. You have to come with me."

He sounded so reasonable. He sounded like he cared. But no one cared about her. They cared about her brain and what she could do for them or what she could create. But no one—except maybe Jackie—cared about her at all. Especially Van Holtz.

She had to give it to the man, though. He was persistent.

"Irene, I know you're scared, baby, and I can explain everything to you. But I need you to come with me."

"Explain? Explain what?"

"About what you just saw. About me."

She shook her head. "You don't have to explain anything. I know all about you, Van Holtz."

"Because of Jaqueline Jean-Louis, right?"

Irene nodded, but one of the wolves moved and she pointed her weapon again, taking a quick step back.

"Irene." The snap in Van Holtz's voice drew her attention back to him. "Tell me what you know."

"What?"

"About us. About the Van Holtzes. Tell me what you know."

So she did.

"The Van Holtz Pack are descendants of the Holtzes from Gaul. Barbarians used by the villagers to stop the advancement of Caesar's armies across the Rhine River. They used pagan rituals to force this"—she motioned to the Pack—"on you. Used your kin as war dogs of a sort. But once it was over, they couldn't control the Holtzes. No one could. You finished with the Romans and turned on the locals, using them as cattle to feed on until the Christian church took power and went after anything remotely pagan. That's when the now *Van Holtz* Pack, due to a marriage involving Dutch wolves, broke apart. Some left Germany altogether and went to other parts of Europe. Eventually, they ended up on the shores of North America and briefly settled in a small town called Smithville."

By now, almost half the Pack had shifted to human and they stared at her. She wondered how many of them didn't even know this background information about their own Pack. Probably all of them.

Finally, Van spoke up. "That was amazing, Irene. How did you know all that?"

"I found a book in the library of an old German monastery. Buried in the back and under a ton of other books. It was in Latin, Greek, and some old German."

"And you understood it?"

"Latin and Greek I already knew. I had to do a little deciphering to figure out the rhythm and structure of the older German. It was quite fascinating," she added.

"Is that how you found out about Jackie?"

"No. I knew about her first. It was an accident. Her puberty hit early, while we were at a camp for gifted children. She was only twelve when it hit her one night. She must have shifted six or seven times in less than an hour. She couldn't control it. She told me everything and I never told. I never would."

Van nodded. "I know that, doc. I really do."

Irene realized she'd lowered her arm to her side and her body no longer shook. She took another deep breath and it no longer went in or came out shaky. Somehow Van Holtz had calmed her down, simply getting her to focus on the one thing she loved. Knowledge. And that's when she finally realized Van Holtz was right. She *had* to trust him, because the hyenas would want her dead for killing one of their own, and the lions, the more pragmatic of the shifters, would want her dead for seeing too much.

"I'll come home with you," she told him. "I can call Jackie from your house; she'll be worried."

Appearing relieved, Van Holtz nodded and held out his hand.

Irene took a step—with absolutely no intention of taking the man's hand—and quickly found herself face down on the ground. Before everything went black, she thought, *Ah, yes. Blood loss. I should have accounted for that.*

Her wounds worried him. A meaningless scrape on her forehead, but deeper gouges in her torso and thigh. A lovely, still-bleeding gash on the side of her face, a black eye. Her fingers were torn up from dragging on the ground when she was trying to get away. *You put up quite a fight, didn't ya, my little PhD?*

"Are you sure about this?" Carrie asked close to his ear.

"Yeah. I'm sure."

"The hyenas are going to want her blood and the bitches will just want her dead," Carrie needlessly reminded him.

"Call a meeting with the Pride and the Clan. We'll figure this out, but I'm not letting them kill her."

Carrie nodded as Van stood with Irene tucked safely in his arms.

"And get Vasquez for me," he ordered while they walked back into the woods and onto Van Holtz territory. "I'd prefer she not bleed to death in the middle of the night."

It was that brutal snoring that woke her. How could any human being sleep through all that noise? As it was, Irene wasn't much of a big sleeper anyway. So any additional noises she found simply annoying.

Irene lay in a wonderful bed on her left side, naked, and she immediately knew why. The slightest movement sent a shock wave of pain through her system. Turning her head slowly, she looked down the length of her body, barely covered with a single white sheet. Some parts were bandaged up and she guessed that was to protect the stitches she could feel every time she moved. The rest that hadn't been bandaged had lovely black and blue marks. Good thing she didn't have an ego about her looks; otherwise she'd probably be sobbing right now.

Irene turned her head toward the snoring. Damn. Van Holtz. Had he really stayed by her side the whole night? She wouldn't put it past him to sleep in his own room and then stroll back here around five a.m. trying to give that impression.

Still, he'd saved her life last night and she couldn't ignore that. He'd taken a risk by bringing her to his home and not letting the others kill her. As Jackie would say, "This is one of those times where your emotion should be one of gratitude." And Irene was grateful. Few people ever helped her and she was quite loyal to the ones who did. Although the thought of being loyal to Van Holtz made her butt itch. She knew the man well enough to know he'd take any advantage he could get. So, she'd be loyal but she didn't need to announce it. Quiet loyalty had its benefits as well.

She stared at him, asleep in that chair. In sleep, he almost looked innocent. Yet he wasn't innocent. Far from it. Because even in sleep he still had a smirk. Who smirked in their sleep?

He wore only a pair of jeans and nothing else. Since he'd graduated from the university seven years ago, Irene normally only saw the man in a tuxedo. Sometimes a casual dinner jacket. But half-naked except for jeans . . . yes, this was quite new.

And, if she were to be brutally honest—and when was she *not* brutally honest?—she'd have to admit the experience was not entirely unpleasant. He had an exceptional body. Perhaps a tad unnecessarily big but his muscles were lean and extremely well-defined.

His body was quite perfect, even by her standards. Long and powerful.

Glancing around the room and seeing that they were alone, Irene allowed her eyes to stray lower, wondering if he were big all over. Clearly he was. And, even more fascinating, it seemingly had a mind of its own. She watched as it grew before her eyes. Then it hit her—he hadn't been erect in the first place. Well, exactly how big did that thing get, anyway? Was that normal, even by shifter standards? And why did she suddenly care?

"Uh . . . doc?"

Horrified but not willing to show it, Irene looked into Van Holtz's face. And yes, the smirk was decidedly worse now.

"Looking for anything in particular there?"

"No," she answered honestly, "just fascinated by the size. It seems inordinately large."

Van Holtz shut his eyes. "By sheer will, I'm going to ignore you said that because . . . well . . . it's killing me. And, instead"—he leaned forward in his chair, his eyes examining her body closely—"ask, how are you feeling?"

"Like I've been mauled by a wild animal."

"You're gonna be bragging about that for years, aren't you?"

"Pardon?"

"How often does a full-human get to say they not only survived an attack by lions and hyenas but that they actually took out one of the hyenas?"

Irene grimaced. "I'd prefer not to . . ." She shook her head, slowly rolling onto her back, pulling the sheet with her to continue keeping her naked body somewhat covered. "Killing something or someone who was human at least part of the time is not a situation I'd run around bragging about, Van Holtz."

"You're right. Sorry."

"No need to apologize. Based on what the staff and students say about me, I'm sure you thought I'd happily kill another being and mount them on my wall."

"Haven't you?"

"Only the students who dare cross me."

The bed dipped and Irene slowly turned her head to focus on the man stretching out on the bed beside her. "What are you doing?"

"Getting comfortable."

She glanced at him, took in the way he lay on his side with his head propped up with one hand, and frowned. "Why?"

"Because I can." He lifted the lone white sheet and peeked down the length of her naked body. "You don't mind, do you?"

Irene frowned again while he stared under that sheet. "Am I now supposed to have sexual intercourse with you?"

The sheet dropped back into place and Van Holtz's eyes slowly looked up to focus on her face. "Sorry?"

"Am I supposed to have sexual intercourse with you because you saved my life? Like a form of medieval payment for services rendered?"

Something in her voice stopped him from trying to snag another peek under that sheet and had him looking directly into her face. She wasn't joking. Nor was she being insulting. She really *had* asked him if she had to have sex with him as a form of payment.

"Of course I don't expect that."

"Oh."

He waited for more but more, apparently, was not forthcoming.

"Perhaps we should understand each other, Irene. I want you. I have for a long time. But I want to have sex with you because we'll both enjoy it. Not because you owe me anything."

"Oh. I see." She looked up at him with those intense blue eyes and spoke as plainly as any woman ever had before. "The problem is, Van Holtz, I detest sexual intercourse. I don't mean I don't enjoy it. Or I've had bad experiences and the thought of it makes me uncomfortable. I mean, I detest it. I find the whole passing back and forth of bodily fluids repulsive. And I'm not talking merely semen. I mean sweat and saliva." She grimaced and it clearly wasn't forced. "The number of germs passing between two people during those moments would boggle your mind. Besides, I really hate sweating. And I hate being distracted. Because one should pay attention when involved in intercourse, I've found past partners noticed when I wasn't and they were always so offended. Anyway, depending on who I'm with at the time, that could be anywhere from ten minutes to an hour where I'm forced to focus on the needs of one person and, to be quite honest, there are much more important things I should be doing."

Van stared at the naked woman lying in his bed. "Do you like living like that?" he had to ask.

"Yes. I do. Personally, I don't understand why people involve themselves in relationships. They're complicated and often very unsatisfying. Then the only way to get rid of the person is through legal means."

"Relationships are one thing. I agree with you there. But I'm talking about sex. Don't you have . . . uh . . . needs?"

"Yes. But I take care of those by myself. I have a very handy vibrator."

Van laughed. He'd never met a woman who openly admitted, in general conversation, she liked to get herself off.

"Look, I'm a feminist, Van Holtz. I feel there's absolutely nothing wrong with a woman physically taking care of herself."

"I see."

She glanced at her bandaged side. "I can feel so many stitches. You know, I saw an open-heart surgery once and let me tell you—"

"Irene," he cut in, before she could run off on some tangent, "I'm still back on the detesting-sex conversation."

"Oh. All right."

"Is this conversation bothering you?"

"No."

"Okay." Van got comfortable next to Irene Conridge. Normally, a woman told him she had no interest in sex and he had no interest in her. And although his sexual interest in Irene had gone far, far away, he still found talking to her kind of . . . well . . . to quote her, "fascinating."

"Do you ever miss sex?"

"No."

"Do you ever miss being around people?"

"I am around people. I live with Jackie."

"True, but I mean, someone in your bed. Holding you. Or do you and Jackie . . . uh . . ."

She stared at him blankly and he realized that he could get rid of those kinky fantasies, too. Apparently Dr. Conridge didn't like "sexual intercourse" with anyone. Male or female.

"If you mean lesbianism, then no. I have no interest in women either. But you shouldn't feel bad for me," she calmly insisted. "I'm not frigid in the clinical sense and I like the way my life is. Except for being mauled, it's relatively simple and calm. And that's just how I like it."

"Then that's all that matters, doc."

"That's how I feel." She gazed up at him. "What you did tonight . . . I do really appreciate it. I know enough of shifter politics to know you didn't make any fans this evening."

"I'll handle them. You just get better. And any chance you'll tell me why you were out there in the first place?"

"No. And you know I don't have to stay if I'll be in the way."

"Yes. You do have to stay, Irene. I've got to work something out with the Löwes and the Duprises to ensure they don't come after you. Until I have that, you can't leave."

"Jackie—"

"Is completely safe. She's spending the night here and she's more than welcome. She just went to bed about an hour ago after watching every move our doctor made."

Without thinking, he carefully tucked the sheet around her body. "I'll make sure you're safe, doc. I promise."

"I'm sorry," she said after several moments.

"For what?"

Irene shrugged, then grimaced, probably regretting the move, considering the pain it most likely caused. "For always thinking you were an asshole."

Van grinned. "I am an asshole. And you're a cold bitch. But that doesn't mean we can't be friends, doc."

"Friends?" She nodded. "I don't mind being friends. I have so few of them."

"Really? With your natural charm?"

"Ha, ha, Van Holtz." And she gave what almost looked to be a smile.

Van slipped out of bed and headed toward the door. "I'll send one of the She-wolves in to get you to the bathroom and I'll make you some breakfast."

"You? Make me breakfast?"

"Of course. Just wait until you taste my waffles, doc. You'll see God."

"Considering my personal belief system, I somehow doubt that."

Van stepped into the hallway and closed the door. As he made his way past his family's rooms, he caught sight of one of the She-wolves and motioned for her to take care of Conridge. The look on the girl's face was how he'd imagine she'd look if he'd ordered her to stand in front of a firing squad. As he walked down the stairs, he saw his sister sitting on the bottom step reading the newspaper. He sat next to her and shook his head in disbelief.

"You're right."

"I'm right about what?"

"About Conridge. I don't think anything will be happening between us anytime soon."

Carrie patted his shoulder. "Shut you down, did she?"

"You could say that."

"She reminds me of the computer from *Alien*."

"Huh?"

"You know, 'This ship detonates in T-minus five minutes and counting.' That's her."

Van chuckled. "She's not that bad. She's just different. I like her. We'll probably be friends. Which means I'll never have sex with her."

"You're pathetic."

"Yeah. Yeah," he said, standing up to head to the kitchen to make breakfast for the entire Pack and Irene. "I love you too, sis."

"Oh, and Dad's looking for you."

Van stopped but immediately shook his head. "I'll talk to him later. I can't deal with him right now." He again headed toward the kitchen, his sister following right behind him. "And get on the phone. I want that meeting with the Löwes and the Duprises set up as soon as possible."

He went to the industrial-size refrigerator and began pulling out eggs and flour for the batter. "I mean, if I'm not going to fuck her, why have her in my house?"

Carrie sighed. "That's lovely, little brother. You make us all so proud."

"Well, ya know . . ." Van grinned. "I try."

Three

Irene looked up from the book in her lap and out the open giant glass doors leading to the big lawn on the Van Holtz estate. For nearly seven days she'd enjoyed the luxury of the wealthy. And, to be quite honest, she could see herself easily getting used to it. Although no one was exactly friendly—besides Van Holtz himself—they were polite.

For the first time Irene could actually remember, she felt relaxed. She couldn't really afford to go on vacations, so usually if she traveled, she often had work to do once she arrived at her destination. But due to her injuries, Irene didn't do much of anything. And, to be honest, Van Holtz wouldn't let her. When he found her on the phone with her teaching assistant during her second day at the house, she thought his head might explode. "Is this you resting?" he'd demanded while pulling the phone from her hand. They'd even had a minor scuffle over it, but when he started to pull up the T-shirt she wore, she released the phone. Then he'd had the nerve to look triumphant as he hung up the receiver.

She would have been extremely angry if she didn't find the man so humorous.

Irene watched a squirrel creep down from one of the big trees littering Van Holtz's property. She'd always found squirrels quite fascinating. The way they moved always kept her quite entertained. This one picked up something from the ground and quickly moved back to his tree. But, unfortunately, he simply wasn't quick enough.

Irene grimaced when the first wolf pounced, tossing the squirrel in the air. Another wolf leaped over the first's head, snatching the squirrel from midair, and took off running, the other wolf right on its heels.

"Hey, doc." Van Holtz squeezed in next to her on the oversized chair. The man simply had no concept of personal space. "What are you doing?"

"Oh, merely sitting around being horrified."

"Horrified? Why?"

The two wolves came back into view, now playing tug with what was left of the squirrel.

Van Holtz laughed until she stared at him and then he choked it back. "Sorry." He leaned forward. "Hey, guys." The two wolves stopped and stared. "Go play somewhere else."

They trotted off and Van Holtz leaned back, comfortably resting against her. Since he always did this to her unwounded side, Irene didn't bother arguing. She knew he'd only ignore her.

"Sorry about that. Those two just hit puberty and figured out how to shift."

"I see."

Grabbing the book out of her hands, he glanced at the cover. "So I'm off to meet with Löwe and Dupris. I can't believe they made me wait this long for this meeting, but I'll argue that point once I'm assured of your safety. I'm thinking you'll be heading home today."

"That's fine." She took back the book, relatively confident he couldn't read ancient Arabic. "The doctor should be here soon to take out the stitches. And Jack will pick me up to take me home."

"I can have our driver take you home."

"No, thank you."

"Fine," he teased, "be difficult."

"I will."

Van pushed himself out of the chair and scratched Irene's head affectionately. "Talk to you later, doc."

"Good luck," she said while opening her book. "You'll most likely need it."

Van had the front door open when his father's voice stopped him and his sister.

"Where are you going?"

Van motioned his sister out and turned to face his father. "Meeting with the Löwes and Duprises."

"Over the full-human?"

"Yes."

His father stepped toward him, staring him straight in the eye. "Do you think that's a wise thing to do, son?"

"It's the only thing to do."

"Are you attached to her?"

"No. I'm not." Van grinned. "She's a friend."

His father raised one eyebrow. "A friend? Since when are women, not blood relations, your friends?"

"Since her."

"Well, hurry up. When you get back we need to meet about the business."

"I've actually got to—"

"Was there anything I said that actually led you to believe that was an option?"

Van gritted his teeth, the hackles on the back of his neck rising. Lately he couldn't shake the feeling his father was goading him, but he couldn't figure out why. "No, sir."

"Then I'll see you when you get back."

Nodding, Van took a step out onto the porch.

"And don't do anything stupid."

Van made a fist but decided to keep walking before he did something he'd regret for the rest of his life.

Irene felt those eyes on her long before she lifted her head. When she did, she briefly wondered if *all* Van Holtz males had that smirk. Did the women, too?

"Dr. Conridge."

Tamping down her sudden nervousness at having the head of the Van Holtz family and the Pack's Alpha Male speaking directly to her, she answered, "Mr. Van Holtz."

"Please, call me Dieter." He sat down in a chair across from her. "So how are you feeling?"

"Much better, thank you. I get my stitches out today."

"Good. Good. I hope my family has treated you right."

"Yes. They're quite polite."

He grinned. "Polite?"

She shrugged. "Polite is satisfactory for me. I really don't expect or want much more than that."

"I see. And my son? Was he . . . polite?"

"I wouldn't call him polite . . . but he was definitely pleasant."

"Do you like my son, Dr. Conridge?"

Irene closed her book and stared at the older Van Holtz. "I don't dislike him. But that was recent. I used to not like him but he's been very kind since I've been here. So now I like him. I'd almost say we are friendly . . . but perhaps that's too big a leap at this stage."

He gave a soft laugh. "I see. Are you always this . . . uh . . ."

"Brutally honest?"

"I was going to say direct, but brutally honest works as well."

"Yes. I am. And I know—it's a character flaw."

"Not at all. I love honest people."

"Everyone says that . . . until I say something they don't like. Then I'm a bitch."

"Perhaps you haven't realized it yet, Dr. Conridge," Van Holtz said, that big grin still firmly in place, "but this is the one place in town where being a bitch is not only accepted but expected. So . . . it seems to me that you fit right in here."

Dieter Van Holtz stood. "I'll let you get back to your book. And I truly hope this isn't the last we see of you, Dr. Conridge."

"Not at all. There's a charity holiday gala in December. I expect you to be there with checkbook in hand."

"Of course." And there went that smirk again. "But we both know that's not what I meant."

"Uh . . . we do?" But the strange man was already long gone.

"Genetics," Irene muttered while opening her book. "Clearly the insanity flaw is in their genes."

Van rubbed his forehead and tried to rein in his temper. It wasn't easy when all he really wanted to do was pop one bitch lioness right in the mouth.

"So what are you saying?" he snarled at Melinda Löwe.

"I'm saying she can't be trusted."

"Melinda, she's been living with a jackal since she was thirteen. She's kept her secret all this time; do you really think Irene Conridge is suddenly going to snap and tell the world?"

"Friends are one thing. But she has no real stake in protecting us. And you know my feelings on jackals. They're like the African wild dogs. I don't really even count them as one of us."

"That's nice."

"Don't give me your bullshit, Van. Like you're so above it all. You only took the woman 'cause you were hoping to fuck her."

"I took her because I didn't think it was right you wanted to kill her because the hyenas decided to have some fun with a full-human."

Clarice Dupris glanced up from her cup of tea. "Why are you all looking at me?" she asked innocently.

"This is your fault," Melinda accused. "But that doesn't change the fact that Irene Conridge can't be allowed to live. She knows too much and she has no reason to protect any of us."

Nibbling on a piece of Scottish shortbread, Clarice said softly, "What if she were marked? As a mate?"

Once a shifter marked and mated with a full-human, the human was considered "one of us." They were protected the same as all shifters, but they had to be ready to take on any challengers to their territory or to protect their pups or cubs.

Melinda frowned. "Who'd mark *her*?"

It took Van a minute to realize they were all staring at him. He grinned. "What? Is that a challenge, Clarice? You don't think I would?"

"Uh . . . Van?" He waved at his sister to keep her quiet.

"Well?" he pushed.

Clarice shrugged rugged shoulders. "All I said was maybe someone could mark her. I didn't say it had to be you."

"Marking anyone is bullshit and you all know it."

"I wouldn't know if it was bullshit or not," Melinda admitted. "It just seems like something you wolves like to do. Personally, I like keeping the males at a distance until I'm actually in the mood to breed."

"We mock ours relentlessly," Clarice added, "until they cry or turn on each other. It brings us joy."

"But," Melinda added, "if it keeps your precious full-human alive—"

"—and you don't believe in marking anyway—"

"—then who could it hurt?"

They didn't think he'd do it. And, if he believed even a modicum of the crap his parents tried to shove down his throat for the past twenty-seven years, he wouldn't do it. But Van didn't believe. If they wanted Irene Conridge marked, he'd mark her, all right. And then he'd walk away.

"Done." He stood up. "Always nice to see you two," he lied.

As soon as they stepped outside the tea shop, his sister latched on to his arm. "*Have you lost your mind?*"

He pried her fingers off. "Stop panicking. This is nothing. I bite her and send her away."

"You are such a . . . why do you . . . oh!"

He put his arms around Carrie's shoulders. "Stop. It's okay. I know what I'm doing."

"No, Van. For once you don't know shit." She glanced back at him. "And what, exactly, makes you think Irene Conridge will let you mark her?"

"Because the woman couldn't care less. If the means to an end keeps her breathing, she'll agree."

* * *

"Not on your life, Van Holtz."

Irene stormed into the kitchen, Van Holtz right on her heels.

"You're being unreasonable. If this is all I have to do to keep you alive, what does it matter?"

Normally she'd agree with him. Normally, she'd turn around, pull her hair out of the way, and let the man have at it. Then she'd go on about her life and hopefully never see him again. But something, she didn't know what, kept telling her that would be a mistake. A mistake she would never recover from.

"No."

"I thought we were friends now."

"We are. That's why I can be clear and concise without fear of reprisal. And the answer is definitely no."

Van Holtz let out one of his dramatic "look what I have to put up with" sighs and leaned against the kitchen counter. "Irene, don't you want to go home?"

"Of course I do."

"Then you give me two minutes and you can be out of here."

"Or I can just leave."

"And not live through the night."

"And that affects you how?"

"I made a commitment."

"Yes. You did. And I do truly appreciate it. But I'm not going to do this. Nor am I letting you do this. I'll just go."

Irene stepped away from him and that's when his fingers closed around her wrist, halting her. She tried to pull her arm away, but he wouldn't let her go.

"I'm not joking, Van Holtz. Get off me."

"I'm not joking either. I won't be responsible for you dying."

"You aren't. I am. I absolve you of all wrongdoing in this matter. Now get the hell off me!"

She yanked her arm again and, with a growl, the presumptuous bastard yanked her back against his chest. Slamming her foot into his instep and her elbow into his face, she distracted him enough to release her and she tried to scramble away.

But he was fast. His big arms wrapped around her waist and dragged her toward him. Irene gripped the sink and held on.

Van Holtz wasn't giving up, though. He pulled her back and her fingers slipped. Spotting a frying pan in the drying bin, Irene reached for it. He'd already taken a two-by-four to the head; a frying pan would probably cause just enough damage to get her free and away. Her fingers slid across a metal handle and she grabbed blindly for it. Van Holtz swung her around, and Irene lashed out but only hit him in the leg.

Then they stared at each other in shock before they both looked down at his leg . . . and the lovely chef's knife protruding from his denim-covered thigh.

Horrified, Irene stepped back. "Oh, my . . . I mean . . ." She looked up to what had to be the angriest face she'd ever seen. "I swear, Van Holtz. I swear that was an accident."

Van Holtz didn't say anything, but he didn't have to. The expression on his face called her a liar, and the way his eyes shifted from human to wolf in a heartbeat told her she needed to run—now!

Irene made a wild leap for the door but she didn't even get near the opposite counter before she heard that snarl and the loud clang of the knife hitting the kitchen floor, then those big arms wrapped around her one more time. He slammed her against the wall with her back to him, using his body weight to hold her in place.

She tried to push herself away from the wall but his knee pressed between her thighs, throwing her off balance, and he used his chest to force her back against the wall.

Irene knew she could have begged him to stop. Pleaded with him. Or simply asked him nicely. But, for some unknown reason that until the end of time she'd never understand, she decided fighting would be a better route.

Growling, she slammed her hand down onto his open wound and dug her fingers in. She'd apparently shoved that knife in far, because her fingers sank in deep and Van Holtz roared in pain. He didn't let her go, though. Instead he grabbed her by the hair and yanked her head to the side.

She made one last-ditch effort to get him off her by pushing back, but the big bastard wouldn't budge. And then those fangs sank deep into her shoulder and Irene cried out in pain.

In retaliation, she dug her fingers in deeper but those damn fangs locked into her flesh even harder.

After several agonizing and rather physically painful moments, Van Holtz unhinged his jaw and released her while she unhooked her fingers from his wound.

With both of them panting, Irene rested her forehead against the wall and Van Holtz rested his against her shoulder.

For two people who prided themselves on always being in control, she considered this a rather tragic moment.

At what point had he lost control? When she'd stabbed him with that knife? Yeah. He had gotten a little angry there. Or when she'd tried to run? Yeah. That had annoyed him a bit.

Yet none of that had pushed him over the edge. Niles Van Holtz had lost control when she'd told him no.

It wasn't ego either. It was something else. He could almost say he had been kind of hurt when she'd said no with so much finality and a wee bit of vehemence. As if he'd suggested something so horrendous.

And then when she'd stabbed him . . . accident or not, it had snapped his remaining bit of control. The wolf in him had taken over and all Van could think about was marking her. And he did.

Christ, he hoped she didn't suddenly think this changed anything. Like suddenly they were dating.

But clearly Van momentarily forgot whom he was dealing with.

"Are you done?"

The coldness in that voice hit him like thirty-below-zero weather when he'd just shifted from wolf to human.

He stepped away from her. "Yeah. I'm done."

"Good." She stepped away from the wall and walked to the sink. She rinsed his blood off her hands, calmly dried them with a paper towel, and adjusted her clothes. "I assume now I'm safe."

"As safe as you can be as long as you don't step on their territory or talk."

"No. I won't talk. I've kept the secret to myself all these years. I'm not going to change now."

"I tried to explain that to Melinda Löwe, but she refused to listen."

"Not surprising. She's never liked me anyway." She looked up at him and those ice-cold eyes said absolutely nothing. "Well . . . thank you for everything. I appreciate all your help in this matter."

Van's eyes narrowed. He felt a growing rage in his gut he didn't much like. He especially didn't like that a woman put that rage there. "You're welcome," he said as lightly as possible.

She took a step away but stopped and looked at him. "Do you mind if I borrow your sweatshirt? I'll make sure it's returned to you in the next day or two. At the moment, I'm simply not in the mood to discuss this with Jackie and the scent from your sweatshirt should keep her off my back for at least a little while."

"Yeah. Sure." Van reached back and gathered up some of the shirt, before pulling it over his head. He shook the hair out of his face and handed it to her. She stared at him for a moment but, once again, he couldn't read anything from her.

"Thank you."

She pulled the way-too-big red sweatshirt over her head but for a few seconds she seemed to lose her way and he stepped forward, helping her get her arms and head through all the appropriate holes.

"Thank you," she said again. And it was something in her voice and the way she suddenly wouldn't meet his eyes that caught Van off guard. Putting his fingers under her chin, he lifted her face so she had to look at him.

"What is it?"

"Nothing."

"It's definitely something. Tell me."

She frowned in confusion. "Why . . . why did you do it?"

"Do what? Mark you?"

"Yes."

Van shrugged. "Because it'll keep you alive."

"Is that the only reason?" *Uh-oh.* Just as Van feared, Irene seemed to be thinking this had more meaning than it really did. Time to dissuade her of that immediately.

"It's the only reason." He cleared his throat. "Irene, you know a lot about our people but all that stuff about marking mates and making them yours forever is all folklore. Fairy tales. I didn't believe it when I was a kid and I don't believe it now."

"Really?"

"Yeah. Really." God, he felt like shit. Maybe he could beat up on some puppies later, too. Maybe kick a kitten. He had to be breaking this poor woman's heart. . . .

"Whew!" She let out a gasp and, for the first time ever, smiled. "Thank the DOS gods for that."

"What?"

"I thought you'd start hanging around my house like some stray dog I'd accidentally fed. But now I don't have to worry. Correct?"

Van nodded, that rage he'd experienced only a few minutes before roaring back to life. "Yeah. That's correct."

"Good. Now I can relax." She let out another deep, relieved breath. "Well . . . again, thank you for everything. Although I think I've been mauled enough to last me a lifetime." She kind of, sort of chuckled. "Oh. And give your parents my best."

Then she was walking away from him. Not even doing that backward-glance move. Without thinking, he followed her. She already had her backpack sitting beside the front door, ready to go.

"Are you leaving now?"

"Jackie's waiting outside. Didn't you see her car when you came in?"

"Must have missed it."

"I told her to come in but you know you guys and territory." She opened the front door and Van wondered how he could have missed that two-door, cherry-red Mercedes and the pretty woman sitting on top of the hood reading a book.

The She-jackal looked up and smiled. "Ready to go?"

"Yes." Irene picked up her backpack and swung it onto one shoulder, wincing as the weight of it landed on her newest fang marks.

She looked at him over her shoulder and shrugged. "Well . . . goodbye."

Van stood at his front door and watched Irene Conridge get into her friend's car, placing her backpack in her lap like a small child, and then drive off.

He didn't know how long he stood there before his sister came to his side.

"That was . . . really . . . odd," she said softly.

"I know."

"Are you okay?"

He shrugged. "Yeah. I'm fine. It's over."

"This is true, but—"

"No, Carrie. No buts. No nothing. Even if I did care, which I don't, *that* woman is like a polar ice cap. Thank you but I like a little more heat in my bed."

"Okay."

"So let's just forget it."

"Okay."

"It's over."

"Um . . . okay. And Conridge—"

"Couldn't care less. Trust me when I say, Irene Conridge feels nothing for no one."

"I hate him."

Jackie glanced at Irene in surprise. "What?"

"I. Hate. Him."

"But you don't hate anybody. You said it required emotion that took time out of your schedule."

"That was before I met the biggest . . ." She struggled for the right word and her friend helpfully provided one.

"Asshole?"

"Yes! He *is* the biggest asshole. And I hate him."

"Did something happen I should know about, sweets?"

"I don't want to talk about it or him ever again. I just want to put this whole horrible time behind me and get back to work."

"Okay." Jackie stopped at a red light. "How about we get you home and changed and then we catch a movie?"

She definitely needed to change. The bright red sweatshirt she wore stunk of the man's scent. And although it wasn't a horrible smell—in fact it was quite nice—she was clearly too angry to not let it annoy her. In fact, she regretted promising to return the sweatshirt to him. She'd rather burn it in effigy.

"Irene?"

"What movie?" she asked.

"*The Terminator* is supposed to be good. And there's lots of killing."

Irene crossed her arms in front of her chest and felt as if she was possibly pouting . . . a truly horrifying thought. "You sure there's lots of killing?"

"Vicious cyborg from the future goes on killing rampage searching for one woman to destroy. At least that's how Paul described it to me. So, yeah, I think there's lots of killing."

"Fine." Because she refused to sit around thinking about Niles Van Holtz . . . the asshole. "I'll go."

"Good." Jackie started driving again and her hand reached out and patted Irene's leg. "And don't worry. As soon as you get back to work, you'll feel like your old self again."

"I better," she growled. Because if she had to keep "feeling" things for much longer, she might have to kill that man on principle.

The asshole.

Four

When her thirty-three-year-old master's student burst into tears, Irene felt like maybe she'd crossed the line a tad with "Pass you? You're lucky I haven't killed you."

Annoyed more with herself than anything else but unwilling to show it, Irene reached her hand back and her teaching assistant handed her a box of Kleenex. She slammed it down in front of the student, ignoring the man's increased sobs, and stalked back to her desk.

"I expect all lab work completed by the end of next week." With her back to the students, Irene quickly shuffled the recently handed-in bluebooks into an orderly alphabetical pile for her TA. "I won't accept any excuses because, mostly, I really don't care. Short of ending up in a casket, any student with unfinished work will automatically fail the course. And please don't test me on this."

She handed the stack of books to her TA and turned to face her class. "Why are you still here? Get out." They ran like she'd unleashed live poisonous snakes on the floor.

"Is it my imagination or are you a little . . . uh . . . *terser* than usual?"

Irene glanced back at her TA, Mark. She'd gotten over seventy submissions to be her TA last year but Mark was the only one she'd felt qualified for the position. She wasn't an easy teacher to work for, but she made it worth the trouble. Almost all students who survived one of her internships went on to super-hot jobs at some of the most important labs or installations in the country. For top dollar. So she had no regrets putting them through the Conridge Gauntlet, as many called it. Only Mark didn't seem remotely intimidated by her. She kind of respected him for it, but on days like today, she really was only looking for a victim to take out her recent bout of anger on.

"If you really want to see how terse I am, keep annoying me, Marcus."

"Gotcha." He picked up all her papers and headed off to her office. She grabbed her briefcase and followed.

Why she ended up crashing into his back, she didn't know until she looked around him and saw the two men sitting in her office.

Perfect, she thought.

Stepping around Mark, she leveled her gaze on the first male she saw. "And what brings you here, Agent Harris?"

"Just came to check on you, Professor Conridge."

Irene moved into her office, dropping her briefcase on the floor beside her desk. "Is there a particular reason you can't call me Dr. Conridge? Or is it just your general insecurities as a man speaking for you?"

Mark grabbed his backpack from a corner and nodded at Irene. "Uh . . . Dr. Conridge, I'm going to head off to the library and get through these papers for you tonight." Then he practically ran.

"Another pussy-whipped male, I see," Harris murmured.

Irene sat down at her desk. "Is there any other kind?" She placed her feet up on the worn wood and relaxed back into her chair. She'd learned a long time ago how to fake a relaxed posture when that was the last thing she might be feeling. But Agent Phillip Harris wouldn't be here unless he had a reason. The FBI rarely wasted time with fishing expeditions.

"So, Agent Harris, what brings you to my humble little office?"

"You do, Professor."

"Really? And why is that?"

"There's been a lot of talk about you lately."

"I'm very well-known among the biochemical and computer technologies communities. You know that."

"These aren't articles about your work, Professor. I'm talking about intercepted conversations between known Soviet agents."

Irene blinked in surprise. Russians? Why the hell would Russians be chattering away about her?

"I would ask you what they've been saying but I'm sure if you knew, you'd have moved on it by now. So you're here hoping I tell you something fascinating."

"Perhaps this is a game you shouldn't play, Professor. Treason—"

"Is not the issue here and we both know it. I'm the wrong person to play chess with, Agent Harris. You can't scare me into thinking you're worried I'm a Russian agent." She chuckled. "Although with my complexion I'm sure I'd fit in quite nicely in that country. But sorry to disappoint. I have no idea what they or you think I have and I'm not about to start worrying about it now."

"I could take you in for your own safety." And she knew it was a threat.

Irene smiled and the agent standing behind Harris looked like he might make a run for the door. "Do you really want to do that, Agent Harris? Do you really want a repeat of what happened when that was tried before?" Irene put her hands behind her head, interlacing her fingers. "Tell me, did they ever repair that city block? Or is it still a sunken hole?"

Harris didn't answer, but he glared awfully well. Irene rolled her eyes and swung her legs off her desk. "I'm done talking to you, Agent Harris. I have work to do and, to be quite blunt, you simply aren't that interesting."

Turning to her computer, Irene flipped on her monitor.

She could hear Harris getting to his feet, and his partner moved quickly to the door.

"I'm sure we'll talk again, Professor."

"I live for the day, Agent."

Irene waited until the door closed and she'd given them a minute or two to walk away before she let out a sigh. Okay, so she did have a rough idea of what the Russians wanted. And what her government would love to get its hands on. But no one, absolutely no one, would ever touch it. She'd never unleash that stuff on the world. But sitting around obsessing over it wasn't going to help either. So Irene called up her latest work and thought about other things.

Unfortunately, those other things turned out to be Van Holtz. Three days had gone by and she still thought about him. Why? Most people she could stop thinking about in minutes, if not seconds. But every time she allowed herself a moment to think about something other than equations and formulas, her poor belabored mind always went back to that idiot.

She glanced across the room at the poster of Einstein one of her students had put up to, in his words, "Make this office a little more . . . friendly." But she wasn't seeing brilliant Albert. No. Instead, she kept wondering how many women the bastard had slept with by now. Probably hundreds. She'd bet cash he was a sexual glutton. An any-hole-will-do sort of man.

And here she sat . . . *thinking* about it. Putting portions of her million-dollar mind toward that boneheaded idiot. How pathetic. How ridiculous. How . . . human. Jackie promised it wouldn't last. This sudden surge of emotion. And Irene had begun to count the days until these "feelings" would go away. Far away. How normal-IQ people lived with this sort of thing from day to day, she'd never understand.

Irene Conridge using her extraordinary brain power thinking about a man. Absolutely tragic.

"Someone shoot me now."

Except for a few students, she didn't think many would take her up on the offer.

"And the bastard has probably slept with thousands," she griped before sending one of her favorite pens flying across the room.

Van paced restlessly behind the boutique shop owned by Athana Löwe of the Löwe Pride. Although Van found Athana's older sister Melinda a real pain in the ass, he liked Athana a lot more. Plus the lionesses were great for the occasional "get together." Lions mostly bred only with their own kind, which meant they were great for no-strings-attached sex. Exactly what Van needed at the moment. Simply so he could prove his parents horribly, horribly wrong.

For three days he'd been going to work and back to either his apartment or the Van Holtz estate and not once, in all that time, had he brought a female with him. Only this morning he'd been standing in the kitchen, chatting with his sister, when one of the newest She-wolves walked in. She had on shorts and a T-shirt and nothing else. From what he'd heard, she hadn't shown much interest in anyone so far. But she'd looked at him with avid interest. She was adorable and surprisingly petite for a She-wolf. But what had he done? Smiled, nodded at her, and gone back to talking to his sister.

To quote one of his cousins, "What the fuck was that?"

When he'd realized what he'd done, Van had been absolutely horrified at himself. Where had the old Van gone? The "if she's cute and stops long enough, I'll fuck her" wolf that had such a reputation? Had that evil woman, with her cold eyes and cute, curvy body given him one of her experimental drugs to see if she could rid men of a sex drive? He wouldn't put it past her.

Hell, even his sister noticed. Mainly because more than once he'd walked away from her in the middle of one of their conversations to chat up a girl. But this morning . . . nothing.

When he complained to his parents, they only snorted and gave each other that *look*. The one every parental unit had down to a fine art. The "let him suffer until he learns a lesson" look.

In the end, though, Van refused to believe it. Irene Conridge, PhD, had absolutely no hold over him whatsoever. And she never would. If he wanted to sleep with a cold fish, he'd have the mob cut his throat and toss him into the Pacific Ocean.

The back door to the shop finally opened and Van turned around to see the lovely lioness poke her head out. When she saw him, her expression went from welcome to sultry.

"Hey, handsome."

See? Now *that* was warm and friendly. From a cat, no less. Christ, Irene Conridge was colder than a cat? Was that even possible?

"Hey yourself," he replied gruffly. "Now come here."

She smirked and sashayed over to him. Athana pretty much sashayed everywhere. He'd always liked that about her.

Gold eyes looked up at him from beneath pitch-black lashes. "Yes?"

Suddenly, out of nowhere, a strange feeling of guilt washed over him simply because he stood alone with a female in a back alley. He'd never felt it before and to say he wasn't happy about it would be a drastic understatement.

Snarling, he grabbed Athana's arms and yanked her close. Startled, her lips parted and he swooped in, kissing her hard.

After almost a minute, he finally pulled back and Athana stared up at him.

"Wow," she finally said. "Kind of like kissing my Aunt Gertrude when she comes over for Thanksgiving."

Van held her at arm's length. "*What?*"

She actually pouted but didn't seem really upset. "Damn. And you are so good too. The hyenas were running around saying you'd mated with a full-human but I kept hoping the rumors weren't true."

"It doesn't mean anything."

Athana giggled. "Come on, Van. You're a wolf. You might as well accept your fate."

He shoved her away and paced over to a Dumpster. "No. I refuse to be trapped by this."

"Sweetie, it's too—"

Before the word "late" could come out of her mouth, Van spun around and said, "Let's get a hotel room and fuck."

Rolling her eyes, Athana headed back to her store. "Forget it, Van. I've never fucked around with another female's mate, and I'm not about to start now. Even if she is full-human."

"But I'm not interested in her." Oh, God! Did he just whine that?

She pulled the door open. "If you're that convinced it's a mistake, go to her and find out."

Go to her? His healed but scarred thigh automatically tensed at the thought . . . then other parts of him tensed for an entirely different reason.

"Trust me," Athana sighed. "If you kiss her the way you just kissed me, you are definitely not interested."

"How do I look?"

Irene looked up and nodded at her friend. "You look amazing."

"Thanks, sweetie." A car horn blew and Jackie grabbed her wrap. "Sure I can't talk you into coming? These university events are so much more tolerable when you're there to mock with me."

"I can't face it. Not tonight."

"Agent Harris freak you out?"

"Well, he didn't make me feel at ease."

"Should we stay?"

"No. You and Paul go. Have a good time." Irene tossed her lopsided ponytail off her face for the eighteenth time. "I'm going to work on these papers and watch some television."

"Okay." Jackie started to walk out but stopped. "Do not, Irene, take apart my Macintosh."

Irene looked over at the newest "thing" in computing. A three-thousand-dollar Steve Jobs joke, if you asked her. An overpriced toy. Still, Irene wanted to take it apart to see what Jobs had done. Damn Jackie for knowing her so well.

"I mean it."

"Yes. Yes. Isn't Paul waiting?"

Jackie narrowed her eyes in warning one more time before swooping out.

Irene glanced at the off-white box sitting on her friend's desk and forced herself to focus on the student papers before her.

A few minutes later the doorbell rang and Irene didn't move. She wasn't expecting anyone, so she wouldn't answer the door. She dealt with enough people during the day, she'd be damned if her nights were filled with the idiots as well.

The doorbell went off again, followed by knocking. Irene didn't even flinch. In a few more minutes she would shut out everything but the work in front of her, a skill she'd developed over the years. Sometimes Jackie would literally have to shake her or punch her in the head to get her attention.

But Irene hadn't slipped into that "zone" yet and she could easily hear someone sniffing at her door. She looked up from her paperwork as Van Holtz snarled from the other side, "I know you're in there, Conridge. I can smell you."

Eeew.

"Go away," she called back. "I'm busy."

The knocking turned to outright banging. "Open this god-damn door!"

Annoyed but resigned the man wouldn't leave, Irene put her paperwork on the couch and walked across the room. She pulled open the door and ignored the strange feeling in the pit of her stomach at seeing the man standing there in a dark gray sweater, jeans, and sneakers. She knew few men who made casualwear look anything but.

"What?"

She watched as his eyes moved over her, from the droopy sweatsocks on her feet, past the worn cotton shorts and the paint-splattered T-shirt that spoke of a horrid experience trying to paint the hallway the previous year, straight up to her hastily created ponytail. He swallowed and muttered, "God-damnit," before pushing his way into her house.

"We need to talk," he said by way of greeting.

"Why?"

He frowned. "What?"

"I said why do we need to talk? As far as I'm concerned there's nothing that needs to be said."

"I need to kiss you."

Now Irene frowned. "Why?"

"Must you always ask why?"

"When people come to me with things that don't make sense . . . yes."

"Just let me kiss you and then I'll leave."

"Do you know how many germs are in the human mouth? I'd be better off kissing an open sewer grate."

Why did she have to make this so difficult? He hated being here. Hated having to come here at all. Yet he had something to prove and goddamnit, he'd prove it or die trying.

But how dare she look so goddamn cute! He'd never known this Irene Conridge existed. He'd only seen her in those boxy business suits or a gown that he'd bet money she never picked out for herself. On occasion he'd even seen her in jeans but, even then, she'd always looked pulled together and professional.

Now she looked goddamn adorable and he almost hated her for it.

"Twenty seconds of your time and I'm out of here for good. Twenty seconds and I won't bother you ever again."

"Why?"

Christ, again with the why.

"I need to prove to the universe that my marking you means absolutely nothing."

"Oh, well, isn't that nice," she said with obvious sarcasm. "It's nice to know you're checking to make sure kissing me is as revolting as necessary."

"I'm not . . . I didn't . . ." He growled. "Can we just do this, please?"

"Twenty seconds and you'll go away?"

"Yes."

"Forever?"

"Absolutely."

"Fine. Just get it over with quickly. I have a lot of work to do. And the fact that you're breathing my air annoys me beyond reason."

Wanting this over as badly as she did, Van marched up to her, slipped his arm around her waist, and yanked her close against him. They stared at each other for a long moment and then he kissed her. Just like he had Athana earlier. Only Athana had been warm and willing in his arms. Not brittle and cold like a block of ice. Irene didn't even open her mouth.

Nope. Nothing, he thought with overwhelming relief. This had all been a horrible mistake. He could—and would—walk away from the honorable and brilliant Irene Conridge, PhD, and never look back. Van almost smiled.

Until she moved slightly in his arms and her head tilted barely a centimeter to the left. Like a raging wind, lust swept through him. Overwhelming, all-consuming. He'd never felt anything like it. Suddenly he needed to taste her more than he needed to take his next breath. He dragged his tongue against her lips, coaxing her to open to him. To his eternal surprise she did, and he plunged deep inside. Her body jerked, her hand reaching up and clutching his shoulder. Probably moments from pushing him away. But he wouldn't let her. Not if she felt even a modicum of what he was feeling. So he held her tighter, kissed her deeper, let her feel his steel-hard erection held back by his jeans against her stomach.

The hand clutching his shoulder loosened a bit and then slid into his hair. Her other hand grabbed the back of his neck. And suddenly the cold, brittle block of ice in his arms turned into a raging inferno of lust. Her tongue tangled with his and she groaned into his mouth.

Before Van realized it, he was walking her back toward her stairs. He didn't stop kissing her, he wouldn't. The last thing he wanted was for her to change her mind. He managed to get her to the upstairs hallway before she pulled her mouth away.

"What are you doing?" she panted out.

"Taking you to your bed."

"Forget it." And Van, if he were a crying man, would be sobbing. Until uptight Irene Conridge added, "The wall. Use the wall."

Five

Van slammed her against the wall. He'd been trying to be gentle and patient, but fuck, he was losing control fast. Losing it to this woman who didn't, according to her, like sex. Of course, this same woman reached down and took firm hold of his cock through his jeans. She squeezed and more of his control slipped. He wanted to reach for her bedroom door, but he couldn't bring himself to let her go. The wolf in him wanted to claim this woman before she did something stupid like change her mind. She'd be his because she was meant to be. As annoying as the whole thing was—and Christ, was it annoying—he wouldn't let her go now. Couldn't. Hell, he couldn't even bring himself to release her body so he could get her to a bed.

With surprising skill, she unzipped his jeans and wrapped her hand around his cock. Van shuddered. Who was this woman trying to fool? Detest sex? There was no way this woman could detest sex. More like she simply hadn't met her match . . . until now.

Her long fingers ran along his cock, causing a pretty devastating effect on a man who rarely had those anymore, while she kissed him with as much passion as he'd ever felt with anyone.

Forget it. He'd never make it to the bed. Not until they got this first one out of the way.

"Back pocket," he gasped against her mouth.

"What?"

"Back pocket."

Her arm slipped around his waist and her hand dug into the back pocket of his jeans. She pulled out the strip of condoms he'd put there before leaving his apartment. Of course, that had been for Athana, but no reason to ruin the moment with ugly little truths that didn't mean anything anymore.

"Little sure of yourself, huh?" she asked, holding the condoms in her hand.

"Damn right." And he knew she'd have him no other way. "You're not on anything, right?"

"On anything?"

"Birth control. The Van Holtz men could impregnate a tree stump. So unless you're ready to get knocked up—"

Apparently she wasn't, because she had that condom on him in seconds. Which was good because Van wasn't certain how much longer he could hold on. The wolf in him wouldn't be satisfied until his mate had been taken, their claiming final. At least by wolf standards. He knew Irene would take more convincing than that. Not only because she was human but because she was a pain in the ass and didn't do anything easily or simply. But no problem. He could concentrate on that once the beast in him had been satisfied.

Van hitched her up higher, pushing her hard against the wall to hold her steady.

"This one's gonna be fast, doc," he warned her. "But I'll make it up to you."

"Do me a favor, Van Holtz. Stop talking. You keep reminding me you're in the room."

His head snapped up from the heady sight of his cock about to enter her to glare into those strange blue eyes. But he quickly realized she was teasing ... well ... for Irene it was teasing.

"You gonna keep testing me, doc? You gonna keep trying to push me over the edge?"

"I thought I'd already done that. If you were any more out of control, your hair would be on fire."

"Speak for yourself, baby." He pushed his cock against her but still didn't enter her. "You and I both know that, at the moment, I *own* this beautiful ass."

Damn him! He was right. She'd give anything—absolutely *anything*—to have this man inside her.

Irene had never felt this way before. She'd never wanted anyone the way she wanted one of the most obnoxious men in the world. Hell, she'd even consider begging if it meant he would fuck her. And she knew that's what they were about to do. He would fuck her. Not sexual intercourse—except in the most technical terms. Not making love. There'd be no soft sighs or moans. No entreaties of love or promises of tomorrow. He'd fuck her and that's exactly what she wanted.

Clearly she'd taken too many intellectuals to bed. Men who *thought* they knew what a woman like Irene would want sexually. Everyone had missed the mark.

But it wasn't until Niles Van Holtz shoved himself deep inside her, brutally slamming her back into the wall, that she realized he would give her exactly what she'd always wanted. Needed.

He pressed his still-dressed body against hers. He'd torn her shorts and panties off on their way up the stairs. But she still had on her T-shirt and bra. He didn't even try any basic foreplay. He didn't touch her breasts or caress her body. And he didn't need to.

Leaning in, he whispered hoarsely into her ear, "I do own this ass, don't I, Irene? Just admit it."

Irene had no doubt other women would scream "yes" and keep screaming. Unfortunately, Irene had never been like other women. If she'd been like other women, she wouldn't have suddenly dug her teeth into his neck and bit down hard. She tasted blood and Van Holtz yelped in pain seconds before he began to viciously pound into her.

For the first time ever, Irene couldn't think. She couldn't reason. Logic and theorems flew out of her head like water from a fallen drinking glass. All she could focus on, think about, was the way Van Holtz fucked her. He wasn't a tender lover and she didn't want him to be. Even though there was definite pain—her last sexual experience being almost three years before and Van Holtz being unnaturally large, in her estimation—there was even more pleasure. She lost herself in that pleasure. Lost herself to the man who did—at the moment—own her ass.

He growled and she pulled handfuls of his hair trying to make him move faster, harder. They were beyond words now. Beyond playful or even vicious banter. For once, all Irene could do was feel . . . and she loved it.

The tingling came first. Low in her belly, deep inside her womb. Then it burst out, spreading through her limbs, exploding through her system. She'd never felt anything like it and the small part of her brain still functioning told her she was coming. Hard, based on the way her muscles became rigid and how she completely lost the ability to speak.

Irene held Van tight as he groaned against her neck, his body draining completely as he came like a freight train.

His knees almost buckled and he held them both up by sheer willpower. The woman had nearly killed him.

They clung to each other for several minutes, harsh breaths the only sound in the hallway.

"Which . . ." Van swallowed, his throat dry and raw. "Which room is yours?"

"That one." One hand finally released the death grip she had on his hair to point out the door with the biohazard emblem painted on it. *No kidding?* Van thought, wanting to chuckle but unable to. The woman was a lethal toxin. Deadly. No wonder none of the men she'd been with had ever done it for her before. They were full-humans. Women like Irene needed more than a normal DNA strain.

Hands still gripping her ass, Van walked them both to her bedroom and laid her out on the full bed that didn't look like she slept in it much.

Pulling out of her slowly, gritting his teeth when she moaned, Van ran his hand down her bare legs.

"Bathroom?"

"Next door over."

"Don't move. I'll be right back."

Don't move? Irene felt pretty confident that wouldn't be a problem. She *couldn't* move. It was called paralysis and she seemed to have it at the moment.

For the first time in her life, Irene understood why people insisted on having sexual intercourse. And why women insisted on having sexual intercourse with Van Holtz.

Good thing she hadn't discovered this much earlier in life. She'd never have become a Rhodes Scholar or gotten her third PhD. Instead she'd have spent more time "boning like a madwoman," to quote Jackie.

Perhaps it was a shifter thing. Something built into their genetics. She'd always wondered exactly what antics went on over in Jackie's room anytime Paul spent the night. She loved her friend because she didn't try to make a lot of noise, she didn't flaunt her relationship with Paul. But there were nights where things seemed to get seriously out of hand. On those nights, Irene went back to her office or labs to get work done. But in the back of her mind, she always wondered what exactly Paul did to her friend to make Jackie so . . . happy.

Well, now she knew.

Irene sighed, her eyes drifting closed. Finally. It was done. They were done. Van Holtz got what he wanted and so had she. Now she could focus on her work and forget about him.

Her bedroom door opened and Irene didn't bother to open her eyes. She didn't need him to give her excuses for why he needed to leave.

But he didn't leave. Instead a warm cloth wiped across her vulva, carefully cleaning it. She forced herself not to frown, not to even acknowledge what he was doing.

"Sorry about that," she heard him mutter. "I didn't mean to startle you."

Irene began to respond to that when Van Holtz suddenly buried his face between her thighs.

She gasped, her eyes flying open and her hands grabbing the back of his head.

"What . . . what are you doing?"

He looked up at her from between her legs. "I'm eating you out. No one's ever done that for you?"

All she could do was shake her head while watching him, her eyes wide.

Van Holtz grinned. "Cool. I'm your first." Then he dived back in.

Irene leaned back, her hands still dug into his hair, and stared up at the ceiling. The man licked and sucked, taking his time. Irene kept hearing whimpering and finally realized it was her.

"God, Irene. You taste so damn good," he groaned.

Irene frowned. "In what sense?"

Van looked up at her again, one eyebrow raised.

"What's that look for? I'm just asking. Seems an odd thing to say."

"You think too much."

"Yes, well—"

"We need to put a stop to that." Van grabbed hold of her ankles and bent her legs back to her chest, then pushed them wide open and went back to what he was doing. Another orgasm, more powerful than the last, tore through her and Irene cried out, incoherent words and some ancient Greek spilling from her lips. She didn't pass out but there were definitely some nonsensical moments there.

When she could think again, she realized Van Holtz had taken off all her clothes and had removed his as well. Now he lay next to her, his head resting in the palm of his hand, while he stared down at her.

"You okay?" he asked, his free hand idly tracing circles across her stomach and chest.

"You need to go."

Van Holtz tensed but he didn't leave. "Why?"

"I've got so much work to do," she admitted honestly, even if it still was an excuse to outright panic. Now that the passion had died, Irene didn't feel comfortable with the whorish creature she'd become only minutes before. She had responsibilities. Commitments. She couldn't shirk them simply to have mindless, useless intercourse with this man and his perfect body.

"I see," he said simply. "How about we do this." He reached down and pulled the comforter over their bodies. "Let's take a quick nap."

"And what will that do exactly?"

"You look burned out, doc. A few minutes' sleep will do you good. And I'm still a little too wound up to drive. Okay?"

Irene turned on her side, away from him. "Fine. Although your twenty seconds were up ages ago."

"Duly noted, doc." Van Holtz chuckled as he settled in behind her.

Irene woke up and immediately glanced at her clock. Not even eleven o'clock yet. Perfect. She could get a ton of work done now. She stretched and Van Holtz moved beside her. Although she might be tempted, she wouldn't rush him out into the night. Instead she'd leave him to get some sleep while she went back downstairs and . . .

Grabbing hold of the big hand slipping between her legs, she turned and faced a wide-awake Van Holtz.

"What are you doing?"

He didn't bother answering her as he latched onto her nipple and sucked while a probing forefinger slipped inside her and began to stroke in and out.

"Wait—"

Two fingers were enthusiastically pushed inside her and Irene's back arched, her hips desperately rocking against his hand. Then his thumb pressed against her clitoris and she exploded, her entire body shaking and heaving against his.

By the time her head fell back on the pillow, she'd fallen fast asleep.

Irene opened her eyes and realized that Van Holtz had turned off the lights. No matter, she often moved around in the dark. Moving slowly so as not to wake him up again, Irene carefully threw her legs over the side of the bed but she froze when her foot slid over a warm, and standing, moving surface.

"Uh . . ."

"Going somewhere, doc?"

"Wait," she begged. But he already had her flat on her back and was inside her, fucking her while he kissed her neck and licked and stroked her nipples.

"Van Holtz, you bastard! You're doing this on purp . . . on . . . oh! That feels very nice. Do that again."

She'd just come out of the bathroom and was about to sneak downstairs when he caught her around the waist and carried her back to the bedroom. Setting her at the foot of the bed, he used his legs to push her thighs apart. Then he took her from behind, his teeth gripping her shoulder while his hands played with her breasts. His weight kept her pinned in place and she wished she could say she didn't like it. But she kind of did.

He released her shoulder, pulled her head back by her hair and kissed her while he continued pounding away inside her. But the way he kissed her always seemed so tender. Even when things went out of control, his kisses never seemed brutal or vicious. Just . . . determined.

The bastard.

* * *

Irene yawned and turned over, snuggling back under the covers. Big hands pushed her onto her back and she groaned. "No, no. I'm not awake. I swear! I was just getting comfortable!"

"So am I," he gasped, embedding himself deep inside her yet again. And dammit, but it felt wonderful.

Van pushed her hair off her face and Irene groaned in defeat. "No. Not again. I can't."

He grinned, almost ashamed of himself—but not really. She'd tried to throw him out. Like he'd ever let that happen.

"Not again. I have to go," he whispered and she finally opened one eye. And who knew a person could glare out of one eye.

"Good."

He'd be angry if she didn't sound so cute . . . and worn out.

"I'll be back tonight. We'll go to dinner."

"I can't," she said simply, closing her eyes. "I have a previous engagement."

Overwhelming jealousy washed over him. "Previous engagement? With who?"

"It's 'whom' and that's none of your business. I had these plans weeks ago. I'm not changing it for a wild romp in the hay." She pulled the comforter up to her chin. "You got what you wanted, Van Holtz. Now you can go back to your regular life and I'll go back to mine. After last night, you must have gotten what you needed." She turned on her side, shutting him out. "So go back to your supermodels and your country club elite. And I'll go back to men who actually know what the Algorithmic Information Theory is."

Van gritted his teeth and stared at the back of Irene's head. Fuck if he knew what goddamn Algorithmic whatever whatever was. And fuck if he cared. Because in the long run it didn't matter. Not to him. And it shouldn't matter to her. But did she really think she could make him walk away that easily? Did she really think it would be that easy to get rid of a Van Holtz?

Yeah, the Romans thought that too in 52 B.C. True, Irene Conridge was a hell of a lot tougher than a battalion of well-trained Roman soldiers, but he was a descendant of barbarians . . . he'd get what he wanted.

And he wanted her. So he'd have her—and she'd better be goddamn glad about it, too.

Six

"What?" Irene asked again, turning her office chair around to glare at her TA. He'd been getting on her nerves all day.

"I said do you need anything else from me before I leave?"

"No."

Irene started to turn back around but stopped and asked, "Were you on my computer earlier?"

Mark nodded while pulling his backpack together. "I had to pull your latest draft on Sharkovsky's theorem for your publisher."

"Well, be careful when you use it. I keep finding all my files mixed up."

"I was trying to organize—"

"Well, don't. Don't organize. Don't move. Don't touch my files, Marcus. Understand?"

Mark stood up and for the first time Irene noticed how tall he was. Not in a skinny, awkward way either, but in a well-developed, "I've played football all my life" way. "Sorry, Dr. Conridge. I didn't mean to cause any problems."

Irene shook her head. "Forget it, Mark. Go. I'll see you on Monday."

It was one thing when she picked on her students for her

own amusement, but picking on them because of one man simply disgusted her beyond all reason.

How had she allowed this to happen? How had she allowed one man to eat his way into her brain like a vicious virus? All day she'd thought of nothing else and it horrified her. She'd always prided herself on being able to block out nearly everything so she could focus on a problem or a task. Jackie actually had access to Irene's bank accounts because she made sure to pay all the bills. When Jackie went on her European tour two years ago, they'd almost lost their home and poor Jackie came back to a dark house because Irene had forgotten all about the electric bill. Now if Jackie wasn't around, Paul took care of it.

But, for the first time in her life, Irene wasn't completely focused on one theory or mathematical problem. For once she wasn't focused completely on inanimate objects or thoughts. Instead, all she could think about was having sex with Niles Van Holtz.

Her weakness disgusted her. Irene's flesh and bones had never been more than a device to haul her brain around in. Now they were alive with needs and feelings.

Bastard.

A knock on her door jolted her and she had to calm her breathing before she said, "Yes?"

The door pushed open and one of her grad students stuck her head in. Jenny Fairgrove. Or, as Irene privately called her, the Perfect Jenny Fairgrove. Long blond hair and warm blue eyes, Jenny was everything Irene was not. And, unlike Irene, she'd never have to fight for a damn thing. Because pretty people never had to.

"Hi, Dr. Conridge."

"Miss Fairgrove."

"I just wanted to drop off my paperwork for the TA position for next year. I wanted to get it in early."

Irene was one of only eight professors in the university who handled their own TA program. Students submitted for the position directly to her and she chose however many students she wanted or needed. The other professors who had to share TAs or couldn't choose their own hated her for it, too.

"Put it in the bin over there."

Jenny walked in and dropped the forms in the basket. Irene watched the girl from the corner of her eye. Jenny had on a short denim skirt with leather boots and a tight T-shirt and short denim jacket. She actually looked her age of about twenty-three. Irene always felt like she looked forty. Hell, she felt forty. Until last night. Last night she'd felt her age for the first time in her life.

"Wow. Is that the new IBM PC AT?"

Irene glanced at her computer. She'd practically had to put a gun to the dean's head for him to authorize the damn thing. "Yes."

"Wow," Jenny said again, with annoying enthusiasm. "I heard it had a color screen but that looks great, huh?"

Perky and blond. Any more annoying a combination, Irene didn't know of.

"Yes."

The girl stood in front of her desk. "Um . . . Dr. Conridge, I just wanted to say that I would love the opportunity to work for you. I've really kept up with your career and I think you're just amazing."

Irene turned back to her computer and started to run her programs. "You all say that . . . in the beginning."

"Wow, Dr. Conridge!" If the woman said "wow" one more time . . . "Is this your boyfriend?"

Irene's head snapped around. "What?"

Jenny handed her a picture frame and Irene gazed into the smugly grinning face of Niles Van Holtz.

"Where did you get this?"

"Right here on your desk." Jenny wiped her brow. "He's gorgeous, Dr. Conridge. How lucky are you?"

When did the man even get into her office? Then it suddenly occurred to her that he'd put a framed picture of himself on her desk. Like somehow his big, gorgeous, worthless face *belonged* on her desk.

Irene gripped the sterling silver frame in both hands and snarled, "Bastard!"

By the time she looked up again, Jenny Fairgrove was long gone.

"Is that the best you could do, Reeny?"

Irene smirked and stared after the retreating form of her date, Bradley St. James of the Boston St. Jameses. "He's quite knowledgeable on art history and has tenure."

"Oh. Well, there you go." Paul snorted. Irene had cared for Paul since Jackie brought home his drunk hide after a Devo concert one night. Jack said she couldn't just leave a shifter lying in the middle of the road like that. The next morning, Irene found them huddled up on the couch having one of those painfully long personal discussions over coffee that people liked to have. Irene knew then they'd be together forever. Because he was so good for her friend, Irene actually allowed him to refer to her as "Reeny." He was like the big brother she'd never had or even wanted. But if she'd been forced to have a brother, she'd have wanted Paul.

"You know what I just realized, Reeny, my love?"

"What, my sweetness?"

Paul motioned around the enormous room packed with people in their finest clothes and jewels, waiting for the lights to signal that the concert was about to begin. "All these people are here to see *my* woman."

"Yes, they are." Irene glanced at him. The man had been in an awfully good mood all night. "Your woman, eh?"

Paul shrugged, but he couldn't stop the grin. "She is now." He leaned in and whispered, "I marked her last night."

Irene clapped her hands together before throwing her arms around Paul's neck. "I'm so happy for you!"

"Thanks, Reeny. I was so nervous she'd say no."

"Are you insane?" Irene leaned back to look into his face. "She loves you. Of course she said yes." She kissed his cheek. "I'm very happy for you both. And I'm glad you *asked* her first."

"Of course I did. I've gotta make it right for *m'lady*."

Irene stepped back and readjusted her dress. She hated it but Jackie had picked it out for her and insisted it looked good on her. She felt . . . exposed.

"How much do you hate that dress?"

"A lot."

Bradley returned from the men's room just as the lights flickered twice, letting them know the concert would begin soon. Together they all walked into the hall and took their seats. Because of their connections, Irene and Paul got to sit in the ridiculously overpriced box seats.

As the accompanying orchestra tuned up, a page stepped into their box and whispered into Bradley's ear.

"I'll be right back," he said and squeezed her hand. *Eeew*. Sweaty palms. She *hated* that.

Once he'd left and she'd wiped her hands on her dress, she turned back to Paul. "Okay. So just tell me straight. When are you two moving out? I need to know so I can set up some overly elaborate system to remind myself to pay my bills and eat."

"Perhaps you failed to remember that I live in a house with four other guys." He stuck his hand out. "Say hello to your new roommate."

Irene let out her breath. "I have to say I'm relieved." She teasingly slapped his hand away.

"This is you relieved?"

"Yes. Can't you see that I'm brimming with emotion?" she asked flatly.

Paul laughed. "Sure. Your brimming emotions are crystal clear. And why are you relieved?"

"I thought you two were going to leave me alone."

"No way. You're her best friend. And one of the few people she actually tolerates . . . besides me, of course."

The lights dimmed and the conductor stepped out on the stage. The audience applauded loudly since he was quite famous, but it wasn't until Jackie walked out onto the stage holding her Stradivarius violin that the entire theater erupted into applause, including Irene and Paul.

Jackie grinned and nodded, waiting for the applause to stop. As it did, Bradley came back to his seat.

"Where did you—" Irene stopped speaking when she realized it wasn't Bradley sitting next to her but Van Holtz—in a full tux, no less.

"What the hell are you doing here?"

"Sssh." He pointed at Jackie. "She's about to start," he whispered.

She leaned in and hissed, "Where's Bradley?"

"I had my driver take him home."

Irene blinked. "Alive?"

Van Holtz shook his head, apparently refusing to be goaded.

Jackie began to play and Irene forced herself to listen and enjoy the incredible talents of her friend, rather than notice the idiot sitting next to her. Five minutes into the concert, when he took her hand and then wouldn't let it go, she didn't even throttle him.

Although she really wanted to. Especially when she noticed that *his* hands were dry and damn comfortable.

Van almost felt guilty for scaring off Irene's date, but pudgy, middle-aged men named Bradley were not for her. Besides, it really hadn't taken much. If he were worthy of her he'd never have let anyone buy him off. But Bradley took that cash and followed Van's driver out the front door. *Prick.*

And, more important, could she be any cuter than when she silently seethed? He thought for sure she'd tell him off during intermission, but she didn't. She just drank her scotch on the rocks and fumed. But Van took the time to learn he didn't have to worry about the jackal hanging around her. He belonged to her friend Jackie and that was all that mattered to Van. He'd been a little worried when he saw the two of them hugging before the concert started. Van's eyes had narrowed and he wondered how hard it would be to twist a jackal into a pretzel.

Pushing through the mob of people hanging around backstage after the concert, the trio made their way to Jackie's dressing room. Another mob of people stood there as well and they decided not to push their way through until Jackie had finished greeting her fans and well-wishers.

"Fuck," Paul muttered, turning toward them.

Irene glanced up. "What's wrong?"

"That old professor of Jack's is here. And his flowers are bigger than mine."

Both she and Van leaned around Paul to see an older man kissing Jackie's cheeks and holding a dozen roses.

Irene snorted. "I don't know why you worry about that. It happened a long time ago and that prick doesn't hold a candle to you."

"He was her first love."

"Not even. Besides, she was only eighteen at the time, which is creepy and disgusting all on its own. He took advantage of her. Trust me when I say she's definitely over it."

Paul glanced at his little bouquet of a half-dozen roses. He acted like he'd grabbed weeds from outside the building.

Eventually Van couldn't take that pitiful jackal look anymore. "Don't worry about it." He motioned to his driver, who walked forward with the two dozen roses he'd told him to pick up after dropping off Bradley. Van plucked off the card from his bouquet and put the one from Paul's on it instead. "Give her these."

Shocked, Paul took the heavy display from Van's driver. "Are you sure?"

"Yeah. Go ahead." Van grabbed the half-dozen roses Paul had and put his card on top. He had a feeling Jackie wouldn't care either way, but he knew men well enough to know Paul would be obsessing all night.

Paul shrugged. "Thanks, man. I owe ya."

"No problem. Besides," Van added, "I don't like the look of that guy."

"Yeah. Me either."

Irene sighed and rolled her eyes. "Just give her the flowers so we can be gone." She glanced at Van. "I grow tired of the company."

Paul walked away and Van leaned against the wall, staring down Irene's cleavage. "You know, Irene," he said low, so only she could hear, "when you're mean to me like that . . ."

"Yes?"

"It makes me so horny."

Well, did she really think she would get rid of him that easily? He had to be the most determined man she'd ever known. Why he felt so determined regarding her, Irene had no idea. He'd gotten what he wanted, so Irene didn't quite grasp why the rest of this was necessary.

"Mind telling me what you did with my date?"

"I told him he wasn't right for you and if he left quietly with no fuss, I wouldn't snap his neck like a twig."

Irene looked up at Van Holtz. "Are you serious?"

"Very."

"I don't understand," she said, shaking her head.

"Don't understand what?"

"Why you're here." She leaned in closer and so did he. It almost felt as if they stood completely alone rather than boxed up with a room full of people. "I'm very honest with myself, Van Holtz. I'm not beautiful. I'm not nice. Most people go out of their way to actively avoid me. I don't have much of a sense of humor. I'm not charming and if people suddenly disappeared off the planet, I probably wouldn't even notice. You, however, are cultured, wealthy, and blindingly arrogant. You have more than enough beautiful women who are convinced you are as amazing as you believe yourself to be and would have no problem telling you how amazing you are every day until the end of time. Plus you never have to worry they'll say something inappropriate or rude. Or that they'll ever be smarter than you. We have nothing between us except surprisingly good sex, but based on what I've been told, the allure of that won't last very long. So, then . . . what is it? What are you expecting from these little romantic displays?"

Irene stared at him, waiting for his response. And she kept staring. Finally, she snapped, "Well? Aren't you going to answer me?"

"Answer you about what?"

"About everything I just said to you."

"Oh. That. I stopped listening and just stared at your lips instead, which are quite beautiful, by the way. But I could tell you weren't going to say anything I wanted to hear, so I just ignored you."

She had absolutely no idea what to say to the man. For once, someone had left her speechless and . . . slightly amused.

"Is ignoring me supposed to endear you to me somehow?"

"No. That's the job of my thighs and my get-lost-in-them-forever dreamy eyes." He leaned in even closer and blinked his eyes several times. "Mesmerizing, aren't they?"

Irene couldn't hold it back anymore. It flooded out of her and she couldn't stop it. Even when everyone turned and stared at her, including Jackie and Paul, she couldn't stop. And she tried.

Because laughing this much really would only exacerbate his ego even more.

He knew he wasn't playing fair but he didn't have a choice. If he'd asked her to go to dinner with him, she would have automatically said no. So he invited her friends and assumed she'd come along. Which . . . she did.

If he'd asked her to come home with him, she would have said no. So he used the fact that Paul and Jackie were just mated by arranging for them to get a night in the honeymoon suite at his cousin's five-star hotel downtown before they took off for a few days in Mexico. Then he had his limo driver take them to said hotel. Which kinda, sorta left Irene stranded.

Van waved at the limo one more time before turning

around. She stood there in that scintillating red, full-length gown, one foot tapping, arms crossed over her chest, not looking nearly as annoyed as she probably wanted to be.

"Well?" she snapped.

"Well, what?"

"How am I getting home?" She held up her tiny purse. "I have all of five dollars in this bag because Paul was going to pay for the taxi."

"You should always carry more money on you than that." Her eyes narrowed and Van held his hands up. "Sorry, sorry." He shrugged. "I thought maybe you'd want to see my apartment. It's just down the street."

"Why would I want to see your apartment? Are there zoo animals there?"

She asked the strangest questions. "No. No zoo animals." He grinned. "Except me, of course."

"Would I have to pretend I like it even if I don't?"

"Why would you ask that?"

"Because my first response is usually my most honest but I've actually lost the university charity money because my first response insulted someone important. Your family gives a lot of money to the university; I need to know if I should plaster on that fake smile that makes my face ache."

"No. I always want you to be honest with me, Irene. Even when the honesty sucks."

"Will we have sex again?" she asked the same way someone might ask if the IRS was about to give them an audit.

"If you want to."

"Do you want to?"

He groaned. "You have no idea."

She glanced around the empty street. "I have work to do."

"You always have work to do. It can't be healthy, Irene. You have to take some time for yourself."

"Well . . . I would like to have sex with you again." She looked at him with that brutally honest face and said, "It was much more enjoyable than I thought it would be."

Knowing she wasn't in any way joking, Van replied, "Yes. I

enjoyed it a lot, too. Maybe you could spend the weekend with me."

"I should work."

That definitely wasn't a "no."

"You can work in the afternoon."

"And the rest of the time we'll have sex?"

Van cleared his throat. "Yes, Irene. The rest of the time we'll have sex."

After several long moments, she nodded. "All right, then. Which way is your apartment?"

"That way."

Irene started walking west and Van called after her, "Irene?" She turned around and looked at him. He held his hand out and she stared at it for several more long seconds. He could almost see her brain sifting through the appropriate responses. Finally, she reached out and placed her hand in his.

Van interlaced their fingers and headed home with Irene right next to him.

And he'd never been happier.

Seven

"Do you actually need all this room or is this the only place you could find where you could fit your head?"

Irene accepted the glass of wine Van handed her.

"My, my, we certainly are rolling with the jokes this evening."

She shrugged. "I guess. I find myself surprisingly comfortable around you. Well . . . as comfortable as I can be with anyone remotely human. And you are somewhat remotely human."

"Such compliments." He took her hand, and it felt strange to her to not automatically want to pull it away again.

Van led her through the apartment. Apparently he owned it and the entire building. The furniture was tasteful but useful. She actually felt like she could sit on the couch. Each room was tidy and well kept. But his kitchen . . . she'd never seen such a sparkling kitchen outside of a cleaning-fluid ad.

"This is very . . . clean."

"It's the kitchen. Of course it's clean. Would you prefer to think your food is coming from some place with roaches?"

"No. But this does seem to be above and beyond the standard clean."

"Not at all." Van turned to take a beer from the refrigerator.

With him facing away from her, Irene shifted the big knife block on the counter slightly to the left.

"I grew up around chefs," he continued, turning back around and immediately shifting the knife block back to its original position. He probably didn't even realize he'd done it. "You always keep your kitchen clean or you hear about it. And my uncles can be mean. Usually fangs are involved."

Irene nodded, surprisingly enthused to find a little obsessive-compulsive behavior in the always-controlled but perpetually laid-back wolf.

He stared at her and Irene didn't know what to make of it. To get things moving she said, "So are we going to do this or what?"

She already had the straps of her gown halfway off her shoulders when he left his unopened beer on the pristine counter and grabbed her hands.

"Hey, hey. What's the rush?"

Irene sighed in annoyance. "Look, I've got responsibilities. Things to do. I'm not some rich kid who can do whatever I want. In other words, I need to get this done and then get back to work."

"Are lives being lost because you're spending some time in my kitchen?"

"Lives? Of course not, but—"

"Then relax, Irene."

Irene realized he had a point and frowned in concentration as she tried to force herself to relax.

Van Holtz released her. "Is that you relaxing?"

She growled. "If you keep talking I won't be able to. I need to focus to get myself to relax. Focusing is the key."

"All right. That's it." Van Holtz grabbed her hand and dragged her out of the room.

"Where are we going?"

He didn't answer but dragged her into a bedroom. She briefly thought, *Oh, good.* But then he kept walking into a bathroom that could have housed the entire Foreign Legion. He released her and closed the bathroom door.

Irene shrugged. "A shower? Do I not smell fresh?"

Van Holtz snorted a laugh. "Doc, you smell wonderful."

"Then why are we in your bathroom?"

He went over to the obscenely large tub that looked more like a pool and turned on the water. It began to fill up quickly. "I thought we'd take a bath."

"A bath? What am I, eight? Will there be bubbles, too?"

He snapped his fingers. "Good call, doc." He walked over to one of the cabinets and popped open the doors. "One of my cousins from Germany stayed here about six months ago and she has three daughters. I think they left . . . yes!" He turned around, holding a plastic bottle. "Pink bubbles."

"I don't understand. Is this a prelude to sex?"

"Everything with me is a prelude to sex," he muttered, checking the temperature of the water before pouring in the entire contents of the bottle. "But this isn't only about sex. I've decided."

She didn't like the sound of that. "Decided what?"

"That you're staying the weekend."

"I haven't agreed to that and why would I?"

Van Holtz stood and walked over to her. "Because you and I are going to hang out. We're going to watch TV, eat delicious food that I make, maybe go shopping for shit we don't need, and neither one of us is going to do any work of any kind."

"Again . . . why would I do that?"

"Because we're going to spend the weekend getting to know each other."

"I thought we did know each other. And we'd come to the conclusion that we were friends . . . only."

"We are friends. And friends hang out doing nothing."

"Forget it." Irene headed toward the door. "I've got a ton of lab work waiting for me and—"

"There'll be lots of sex, too."

Irene stopped, her hand on the doorknob. "Sex?"

"*Lots* of sex."

"Truly? Or is this some kind of Van Holtz torture?"

He stepped up behind her and she could feel his body heat, the touch of his hands on her shoulder, fingers sliding under the straps of her gown. "Oh, there'll be a little torture," he promised. "But only the good kind."

* * *

Van never realized until this moment how much of his childhood he'd taken for granted. Going to school, playing with the other pups in the Pack, dating human girls, and debating with his friends the best way to keep their fangs in during sex. Hell, even going hunting every Christmas in Connecticut with his parents and sister. Things he did for enjoyment, not because he'd been born into money, but because he hadn't been born any more or less special than any other shifter. He hadn't been any different from some pup from the Magnus Pack or the Smiths. All his parents ever asked of him was to not bare his fangs in public, not let his junior-high buddies pay to see his sister naked when she was getting out of the shower, and not to lick his balls when he thought the Pack wasn't looking . . . because they usually were.

He simply couldn't imagine people expecting any more from him than that at the age of five, ten, even twenty. But they'd expected it of Irene. At a charity event, he heard two older professors discussing how they once saw Irene give a speech at the United Nations nearly fifteen years ago. Why a ten-year-old needed to give a speech, in several languages no less, to U.N. delegates for any other reason than a dog and pony show, Van had no idea. Of course, it completely explained why she was the prickliest woman he'd ever known. How could she be anything but prickly and a tad uptight?

Yet as Irene stood in his kitchen, desperately trying to force herself to relax, he suddenly knew what he had to do. What he wanted to do. He wanted to show her what it was like to be brutally, painfully, wonderfully average. Not all the time— he knew she'd never allow that—but enough so she could learn to enjoy all the amazing things she could do. And so she wouldn't die of an ulcer and high blood pressure by the time she was forty-five.

First, though, he had to teach her basic relaxation skills. *Like taking a bath*, he thought as he tossed her naked body into his bathtub. She squealed like an actual girl until she hit the water and then she came up sputtering and pretty pissed off. But by then he was naked and in the water with her, so he easily grabbed her waist and dragged her back in before she could stomp off mad.

"You do things just to irritate me, don't you?"

Smiling, enjoying himself immensely, and determined to give her a wonderful and relaxing weekend, Van pushed Irene's wet hair from her face. "Don't be silly, doc." He kissed her lips, nuzzled her chin. "Of course I do things just to irritate you."

How annoying. She actually found him cute. And charming. When did that happen? She'd always thought of Van Holtz as a spoiled rich boy from a one-time barbarian Pack of ravening wolves. But, when so motivated, he could be cute and—*damn him*—charming. Even when tossing her into water. Something Irene had always hated. But she did like feeling him press his body against hers as the bath water lapped around them and the bubbles sneaked up her nose.

She also liked the way he looked at her. Most men looked right through her. Women, too. Everyone looked through her unless they wanted something from her. And what they usually wanted involved academia. At the moment, Van Holtz looked like he couldn't care less about her mind than those in the English department. Most women would be insulted. And, as a rather proud feminist, she would be too . . . if she actually wanted a discourse on the Chaos Theory. She didn't. She wanted him. She wanted to have sexual intercourse with him. Wait. That was wrong. No, she didn't. She had sexual intercourse with men like Bradley. She didn't want that with Van Holtz.

She wanted to fuck him. She wanted to be fucked by him. She wanted to get sweaty and transfer fluids and forget her name. She wanted everything that a night with Niles Van Holtz promised, but she refused to want more. She refused to get so caught up in her sexual urges that she would believe, for a second, that this thing they were indulging in would ever lead to anything more. When this was done—and it would be done sooner rather than later—she'd find another Bradley who'd make a great fourth at dinner with the dean.

Irene knew it was a very cold way of looking at relationships, even for her, but she had no delusions she'd ever get more. She was too strange, too off-key—and not in a cute, adorable way either—to ever hope someone could love her as she was, and she was smart enough to know she'd never change. Not inherently. Not where it counted. Even if she curbed her tongue and stopped scaring her students, she'd still be Irene Conridge, freak. Nothing she did would ever change that.

But she'd indulge herself this time. She deserved it. For at least twenty years she'd always done what people expected and wanted. Now she'd do what she wanted, even if it was only for the weekend. Only for this brief time in her life.

Big thumbs brushed her nipples and all Irene's important thoughts floated away, leaving nothing but deep-seated lust.

She wrapped her arms around Van Holtz's neck and her legs around his waist, pulling him close to her. She marveled at the heat of him. His body was always warm or sometimes, like now, hot. She wondered if that was normal for shifters. If their body temperatures were hotter than other, normal humans. She wondered if he'd let her take a sample of his blood. Then he lifted her up and laid her out on the tile floor and she quickly stopped caring about his DNA strain.

Before she realized what was happening, Van Holtz slid his tongue inside her and Irene gripped his wet hair, keeping his mouth against her. Her body rocked against his face, her hips and pelvis pushing into him. Leaving the warm water made her thoroughly aware of the chill in the air, her nipples hardening almost painfully, goosebumps racing across her skin. But the sudden cold also made her more thoroughly aware of Van Holtz's big hands tightly gripping her thighs, his mouth and tongue stroking her to orgasm as she shook and moaned beneath his mouth and hands.

Little else held her interest as he ate at her. Devoured her with a single-minded intensity that took her breath away.

Irene groaned as she came. She groaned and moaned and begged him not to stop. He didn't. He took her over again and again, until she lay exhausted on his tile floor, her breathing ragged, her body trembling.

He pulled her back into the warm water, the bubbles much less than when she'd first gotten in. He held her against his body, stroking her back and arms until her trembling stopped.

"Sorry about that," he ridiculously apologized. "But all I could think about was going down on you."

She rested her head in the crook of his neck and sighed. "Anytime. And no apology necessary."

He tried nothing else, even though she could feel his own unfulfilled lust resting hard and hot against her inner thigh.

Combing her fingers through his hair, she let out a satisfied sigh—and decided to have some fun of her own.

"You know, I read so many books," he heard her say softly in his ear. *Books?* She wanted to talk about books now? But he didn't have the heart to tell her to shut up. He quickly realized talking about books and what she knew gave her a sense of control she probably had in few other areas of her life.

"And," she went on, "I read this book once written by a young homosexual writer."

Van frowned, wondering where this particular conversation might be going. With Irene you really never knew.

"It was informational. About how to perform oral sex on men. You know, one man teaching another. It was really fascinating and I've always wondered about the techniques he discussed—ow. Ow! You're squeezing a little hard, Van Holtz."

Forcing himself to loosen the grip he had on her, Van leaned back a bit and looked at Irene. "Sorry."

"It's all right. Just remember I bruise easily. Now . . . where was I?"

"You always wondered about the techniques he discussed."

"Oh. Yes. That's right." She glanced at him under eyelashes he'd never noticed were ridiculously long. Dark brown and long, which contrasted with those ice-blue eyes of hers. But it was the look she gave him and Van knew, in that moment, she was teasing him. Not teasing him in the sense she'd leave him and his poor cock to fend for themselves, but playfully teasing him like a lover would. "Anyway, I found some of the techniques he suggested fascinating, but I didn't know if any of them could truly produce the response he promised."

Van gritted his teeth. "And?"

"Well, if you're willing to be my test subject—ack!"

He didn't mean to toss her out of the bathtub like that and when she went sliding across the tiles he'd made wet and slippery from tossing her in and out of the water in the first place, he did feel a twinge of guilt. But it didn't last as his cock took complete control of his brain. Slapping his hands against the edge of the tub, he gave one push and landed nearly five feet away. He grabbed a towel, wrapped it around Irene, and carried her to the bedroom.

He placed her carefully on the floor and walked away, giving them a little distance. He was terrified he'd pounce on her like some unsuspecting rabbit he'd found in his backyard.

Van closed the bedroom door—strictly because he needed something to do with his hands—and leaned against it. Letting out a breath, he looked at her. *Let her take the lead*, he warned himself.

"So . . . how do you want to do this?" he asked, and was damn proud of himself for managing that.

But Irene frowned in confusion.

"What? What's wrong?" Christ, how did he get it wrong so damn fast?

"Aren't you going to order me?"

"Huh?"

"You know. Tell me what you want."

Suddenly Van was confused. "I thought you hated it when I bossed you around?"

"I do. Normally. Out there." She pointed at the door he stood in front of. "But I've noticed that my sexual response is heightened when you order me around during intercourse."

Van stared at her. He didn't know what to say but he noticed she'd suddenly started to glow . . . *and are those angel wings?*

"Oh. Was that rude? I—"

"Quiet, Irene."

She immediately fell silent and Van had to lock his knees so they wouldn't buckle.

"Drop the towel."

She did, slowly letting it slip off her body.

"Come here."

She hesitated a moment, then slowly walked over to him.

He leaned over a bit, his nose nuzzling her chin and cheek. He breathed in the scent of her. *God, she smells good.* Irene responded to him, brushing her cheek against his. Her fingers, hesitant at first, slid up his biceps.

Van pressed his lips against her ear and softly ordered, "Now get on your knees, doc."

Hands on her shoulders, Van eased Irene to her knees. Her breathing increased as she kneeled in front of him, her hands sliding down his thighs.

Van Holtz braced his legs apart and waited. She had the feeling he was letting her make the first move, which she appreciated since she was still evaluating.

Irene stared intently at his penis, analyzing it. It was abnormally big, in her opinion. But not unmanageable. She simply needed to find the best approach.

"You're thinking too much, doc. You're not splitting the atom. It's just my cock."

"Yes. But even I will admit it's quite formidable. I only want to ensure the highest level of enjoyment."

He gave her a slow, easy grin and his eyes seemed to warm while he watched her. "The fact that you care enough to care at all ensures my highest level of enjoyment."

Irene smiled back, finding it easier to do each time she bothered, and then looked back at Van Holtz's ... well ... cock. Because, to be honest, "penis" simply wasn't doing it any justice.

Giving a mental shrug, Irene leaned forward, swiping her tongue across the head of his cock. His entire body jerked and

Irene gave a little hum of surprise. She didn't expect his response to be so . . . intense. Her confidence boosted a bit, Irene brought her hands up, smoothing them against the insides of his thighs, her fingers teasing the scar left behind from the knife she'd impaled him with, while she dragged her tongue from base to tip.

Van moaned, his eyes closed, and braced his feet farther apart. His fingers dug deep into her hair, silently urging her on. And, with another mental shrug, Irene wrapped her mouth around the tip and swallowed him whole.

She took him to the root on her first pass and Van let out a shuddering laugh. She pulled back, sucking hard while the tip of her tongue swirled around the head, before swallowing him again. Van let out another moan, this one loud and long. Talk about encouragement. Irene swallowed him again and she could feel him in the back of her throat.

"God, Irene," he gasped out. "You learned this from a book?"

Uh . . . actually, she hadn't really thought about the book since she'd started. She'd been too busy thinking about him. So, at the moment, she ran purely on instinct.

Which seemed to be quite effective.

Sliding her hands up his thighs, she took hold of his balls. She squeezed while she sucked and the hands in her hair gripped the strands tighter.

Irene continued to deep-throat him on every pass until Van tugged on her hair, forcing her to look up at him without releasing his cock.

"Stop, baby," he panted desperately. "I'm about to come."

Frowning, Irene debated whether to release him. For some ungodly reason, she wanted to see this through. *All* the way through.

"Irene?" One hand released her hair and touched her cheek. She pushed it away and deep-throated him again.

Van shook his head, staring at her in shock. "Jesus, Irene . . ."

She squeezed his balls again and sucked hard. He shouted a curse seconds before he exploded in her mouth. Irene swallowed, continuing to suck until he begged her to stop.

She did, pulling back slowly.

Van's head fell back against the door, appearing exhausted, and Irene looked up at him, curious. "Did that work for you?"

His eyes snapped open and he stared down at her, still panting. "Huh?"

"I asked if that—"

"Shut up, Irene." He closed his eyes and gave a short laugh. "Just . . . shut up."

Normally she'd be quite insulted someone had told her to shut up, but for some reason, she wasn't. Maybe because he looked so . . . satisfied.

"Fine. I'll assume from your abrupt response and the panting that it worked."

One eye opened and he glared down at her. When he growled, she tried to move away, but he grabbed her shoulders and dragged her to her feet. He kissed her hard, one hand gripping her breast while the other gripped her ass and pulled her tight against his body. She wrapped her arms around his neck and kissed him back. He didn't seem put off by tasting himself on her tongue, which was good because that *would* have insulted her.

Van walked her back until the backs of her knees hit the bed, then he tossed her onto the mattress. She bounced once before he crawled on top of her. Pushing his knee between her thighs, pinning her arms over her head with one hand and playing with her breast with the other, and the entire time he kept kissing her.

"You do know, Dr. Conridge, that you're not getting out of this bed anytime soon?"

"Oh. Well . . ."

"If you're going to drive a man crazy," he warned while alternately sucking on her breasts and sliding his fingers deep inside her, "you'll just have to pay for it."

And she had absolutely no argument for that.

Eight

Irene woke up and found Niles Van Holtz wrapped around her like a python. He had his head buried between her breasts, his arms around her waist, his legs entangled with hers. They rested on their sides, so she didn't have to take his full weight. Still, she had no idea what to do with the man. Did she grab his shoulders and shove? Hmmmm. That seemed a tad cold. And a bit reckless. With her luck he'd slam his head on something and die of an aneurysm. She could tap him lightly on the shoulder and tell him to move, but he didn't wake up easily. She'd probably be better off hitting him repeatedly. Wait. No. Hitting him would also be considered rude.

Sighing, she relaxed back against the pillows. Perhaps she should simply wait until he woke on his own. A man his size was most likely ruled by his hunger. He'd need to feed soon.

Irene glanced down at the pair of them and she realized her arms were flung out at her side. On a whim, she brought her arms up and folded them around Van Holtz. He growled in his sleep and she wondered if she should make a run for it. But before she could, soft lips brushed against her breast while big hands slid across her back.

Definitely not an unpleasant response. Wondering how far this sort of thing would go, Irene gently stroked her hands through Van Holtz's hair. He sighed in his sleep, his grip on her tightening, his mouth searching until it found a nipple and sucked.

She gasped in surprise and delight, enjoying the feel of his mouth on her body. He still slept on, his eyes tightly shut and the soft sleep-growl sounds he made while asleep coming from the back of his throat.

He pushed his leg between her thighs, his knee pressing hard against her groin, and his lips and tongue worked on her nipple. Before Irene knew it, an orgasm took hold of her and she cried out, her body writhing under his until the last shudder passed.

As she lay panting underneath him, he rested his head back between her breasts and commenced snoring. But five minutes later, his eyes opened and he glanced around, finally focusing on her. He smiled, a soft, sleepy smile, with his hair falling in front of his eyes. "Morning, doc."

"Morning."

"I'm hungry." She liked how he stated that so simply.

"Uh . . ."

"I'll make us some breakfast and then we'll go to the mall."

"Mall?"

"Don't worry. You'll enjoy it." He yawned and released her, rolling onto his back.

"I'm horny." He stated that like he'd stated, "I'm hungry."

"Uh . . ."

Van Holtz grabbed a condom off the nightstand. "You don't mind, do you? Before we get up?"

"Uh . . ."

"Good." Fingers gently probed, then he was inside her before she could even think what to say. As he thrust, and she arched to meet it, he let out a deep groan. "Christ, Irene. You're already so wet." Staring down at her, he gave her that smirk. "What *have* you been doing this morning?"

"Why are there so many people? Have they nothing better to do?"

"You keep asking me that and . . . goddamnit. Where did you go?"

She didn't say anything, but the bastard found her anyway. Damn canine senses.

"Have you no shame?"

Irene stepped out from behind the clothes rack where she'd been hiding. "I'm not good with crowds."

"It's a mall, doc. Nothing to be afraid of." He grabbed her hand and yanked her over to where he was. "There will be no more hiding. I swear, it's like dealing with a ten-year-old."

This time he kept a tight grip on her hand as he moved through the racks of the sporting goods store. "How do you go shopping during the holidays if you can't stand the mall?"

"I hand Jackie several hundred dollars and an itemized list."

"Oh, that's nice."

"She likes to shop. I, however, do not. If she wants to spend time fighting those holiday crowds, I'm more than happy to give her money to do it."

"Well, I'm telling you right now . . ." He held up a track suit in front of her, then shook his head. "Wrong color. Anyway, I expect you to buy my gifts yourself. Not send some lackey to do it."

When it came to one-on-one relationships with actual living and breathing human beings, Irene was the first to admit she wasn't the sharpest tool in the shed. But she'd noticed that as the day progressed, after what even the Marquis de Sade might consider a torrid night of sex, Van Holtz kept making statements that a more romantically inclined woman might believe suggested he wanted something much more permanent.

Good thing she knew better.

"The only thing I plan to get you is a restraining order."

"Ha ha." He held up another track suit. "This is it. The color's perfect with your eyes."

"My eyes?"

"Yeah. They're a gorgeous blue. You just need colors that will bring them out."

"I was told my eyes were freakish and disturbing. One of the professors in the theology department referred to them as unholy."

"I think they're hot." He held up the suit. "Wanna try this on?"

The expression on her face must have shown how she felt about that, because he shrugged and dragged her to the front counter. After a few more purchases they wandered through the mall debating about getting something to eat when Van Holtz suddenly pulled her into a comic book store.

"I need to check something out for my cousin."

"Exactly how many cousins do you have?"

"A lot. I told you that the Van Holtz men are breeders by nature. My dad quit after two, but my uncles—all eight of them—just kept going." He stopped and turned to face her. "How many children do you want?"

She shrugged. "I hadn't really thought ... wait. Why are you asking?"

He suddenly looked as uncomfortable as she felt. "No reason. Merely asking for politeness' sake."

"Okay."

Irene didn't say anything else and he began to skim through the racks. Five minutes later he suddenly said, "But you do want kids, right?"

"If artificial insemination is becoming as reliable as I've been reading lately ... perhaps."

"Artificial insemination?"

"Yes. That's when the egg—"

"I know what it is, Irene. I'm just wondering why that's your big breeding plan."

"Do you really think I'd allow the swapping of fluids between me and Bradley?"

Van Holtz's eyebrows lowered and she watched him go from relatively normal human to a male about to shift to his animal form.

"What? What did I say?"

"What does Bradley have to do with anything?"

"I didn't mean him specifically. I'm talking about the Bradleys of the world." She shuddered. "The thought makes my skin crawl. So, artificial insemination seems the safest and least repulsive route."

Van Holtz let out a sigh. "True, that's one option. Or you could simply have sex with someone you want to have sex with."

She shrugged and picked up a Superman comic. "True. But that happens so rarely. You're the first. Not my first sexual encounter, as I told you, but the first one where having sex wasn't a chore."

Laying the shopping bags he carried at his feet, Van Holtz ran his hands through his hair. "I swear, you are trying to drive me insane."

"Now what did I say?"

"Forget it. This discussion is over."

She shrugged. "Okay."

He went back to searching through the comics and Irene began to read one. To be honest, she found them hard to follow. Her eyes never knew which bubble to go to first.

"So," Van Holtz suddenly said, "whether it's artificial insemination or the good old-fashioned way . . . how many kids?"

Why he wouldn't let it go, she'd never know. But she didn't want to argue with him. She was actually having quite a nice time with the Neanderthal. "I was thinking a minimum of two. Jackie has siblings and seems to enjoy them. I had none and it would have been nice to have an older brother or even a sister as long as she wasn't as smart as me. Too competitive," she added when he glanced at her. "Yes. So at least two."

Van Holtz grunted. "Good."

"Why is that good?" But he ignored her and kept searching the stacks. "Van Holtz?"

"Uh . . . excuse me?"

Irene glanced over her shoulder at the three young boys

standing behind her. She'd place them at about thirteen or fourteen. She'd never been very good with guessing ages, though.

"Yes?"

The boys glanced at each other and then back at her. "Are you Dr. Irene Conridge?"

Irene's eyes narrowed the tiniest bit and one of the boys looked away from her.

"Yes. Why?"

The boys suddenly turned away and began whispering to each other, then they pushed one of them back over to the table they'd come from. Irene studied the table and saw maps, many-sided dice, books, and enough junk food to destroy an army. One of the books had a dragon on the cover in all his flamey glory. She stifled a smile. She recalled quite a few late nights as a powerful mage.

The one sent back to the table searched through his over-sized backpack and returned with a magazine. She immediately recognized her face on the cover and remembered that she'd written a piece on the Chaos Theory for a science magazine several months back. She'd forgotten all about it.

"Could you sign this for us?"

Irene took the magazine. "Of course." Before she could ask for a pen, Van Holtz pushed one into her hand. She didn't even bother to look at him to see his expression. She could imagine the smugness all on her own, thank you.

She got the boys' names and signed the magazine, not daring to ask them how they would share this particular item. While signing, she asked, "So what campaign are you gentlemen running?"

Their eyes widened in surprise. "You play D&D?" one of them asked in awe. He had an unfortunate case of acne she prayed he'd grow out of sooner rather than later.

"Played, actually. It's been a few years. Did you buy your models or make them yourselves?" Before she knew it, they'd dragged her over to the table and several other science and math geeks joined them. The discussion zigged between gaming to the Chaos Theory to science in general to math and back to gaming. She did her best to answer all their questions and glanced around several times, looking for Van Holtz. She didn't see him and she put the moment of cynicism out of her mind that he'd left her there in disgust. He could be an ass, but she didn't see him being that big an ass. So she continued answering questions and pretended not to worry.

Van sat on a bench outside the comic book store. He'd stopped by the local booksellers and picked up a book called *Science Made Easy*. One chapter in and he was already lost.

"Well, hello, Mr. Van Holtz."

Van immediately recognized that forced sultry voice and barely stopped his wince in time. He looked up and made himself smile. "Farica. Hi."

"What are you doing here?"

"Waiting for my date."

She blinked a few times before she caught herself, managing to keep that bright smile. "Date, eh? And who's the lucky girl?"

As if on cue, Irene walked out of the comic book store, her geeky fan club right behind her.

"Yes," she was saying. "I have the program every summer, open to students between thirteen and sixteen years old." The boys followed behind her and couldn't see as she desperately mouthed, "Help. Me."

Van grinned, feeling his heart squeezed from both sides by this incredibly odd woman. He'd fallen hard for her, and there was absolutely nothing he could do about it except go along for the ride.

"What about grades?" one of them asked Irene.

"It's more about potential."

She had the most adorable expression on her face. Like he'd trapped her in a room with rabid chipmunks. He could tell she wouldn't be able to keep the "nice" thing going for much longer, so Van decided to give her a reprieve from hero worship.

He didn't have to do much, just stand up. The boys stopped speaking and stared at him in mute horror while he towered over them.

"It's time to go," he stated simply, staring at the young men to make it clear that meant "go away." They did, but only after shaking Irene's hand more times than seemed necessary.

"You okay?" he asked when they'd finally walked away.

"I'm exhausted and now I'm starving."

"Then let's get you fed. Oh. Wait. I got you this." He reached into one of the bags and pulled out a T-shirt he'd picked up at a fun novelty shop a few doors down while she'd handled her fans.

Irene opened the shirt and read the words out loud, "I DOS, therefore I am."

"I thought that sounded appropriately nerdlike." He grinned, but Irene had such a strange expression on her face he became worried he'd made some sort of geek faux pas. "What's wrong? You don't like it?"

Irene swallowed and shook her head. "No. I . . ." She took a deep breath. "I love it. Thank you."

"You sure? I can take it back."

She held the shirt to her chest like he'd tried to rip it from her. "I said I love it," she practically snarled. His mother had sounded like that once when she thought a hyena came a little too close to her pups. "Back off, Van Holtz."

He lifted his hands up, palms showing. "Okay. Okay. Calm down."

"I'm hungry," she said while keeping a tight grip on her shirt.

"Now, Dr. Conridge, don't you think a *proper* thank-you is in order for my lovely gift?"

She stared at him for a moment before glancing around the mall, her face turning red. "Here?"

He closed his eyes and forced himself not to laugh. "Not that, doc. That's for later. When we're alone or we find a bathroom. A kiss will do."

"Oh!" Her face turned redder. "Oh." She went up on her

toes and kissed him on the lips. "Thank you," she whispered. "I really do love it."

"Good. Now let's feed."

Van grabbed the shopping bags and tried to lead her off, but she stared behind him. "What?" he asked.

"Um . . ." She nodded to a spot over his shoulder.

He turned around expecting to see some kind of trouble, but all he saw was the shocked and very red face of Farica Bader. "Oh. See ya, Farica. Tell your mom I said hi."

Van took Irene's hand and headed off to a restaurant he thought she might like. Of course, the fact that the woman mostly ate peanut butter and crackers suggested she wouldn't be too finicky about her meal.

Irene didn't know what shocked her more. The gift Van Holtz gave her—the most thoughtful gift she'd ever received from a man . . . *any* man? Or the way he ignored long-legged, man-eater Farica Bader? Hard to decide, since both were so exceptionally amazing.

Van Holtz took her to a restaurant inside the mall and they were quickly seated by a window. *Lovely, more mall visuals.*

"You know Farica Bader isn't going to be happy that you dismissed her so easily."

He glanced up from the menu. "Who?"

"Farica Bader. You were just talking to her two seconds ago."

"Oh. Her. Yeah. She'll get over it, I'm sure."

Irene stared at the lemonade put in front of her by the waiter. "She seems to like you."

"She likes the Van Holtz name more. The Baders are a small Pack. They'd love to be connected to us so they wouldn't have to lose any more territory to the Magnus or Smith Packs. Now what are you thinking about getting to eat?"

Irene realized she still had her wonderful T-shirt gripped in her hands, so she made herself put it down on the seat beside her. Then she worried she'd forget it, so she laid it on top of her leg, folding half of it under her thigh.

"What are you doing?"

Her head snapped up. "Nothing. I was thinking burger," she spit out in a rush.

"A burger works. But don't eat too much. I'm cooking us dinner tonight."

"Van Holtz, you don't have to—"

"Why don't you call me Van like everybody else?"

"You want me to call you 'of'?"

Van Holtz blinked. "What?"

"Van is Dutch for 'of.' So you're asking me to call you 'of,' which I have issues with. Although Holtz means timber or wood. So your name, literally translated, is 'of wood.'" She covered her mouth when she suddenly giggled, shocking them both. "Sorry." She coughed to stop the laughter. "Just, after last night, I find that name quite fitting."

"You know, Irene, you're the only person I know who can insult me and praise me all at the same time."

"It's a teacher thing." Her hand automatically reached for her T-shirt, stroking it lightly with her fingertips. "How about I call you Holtz? I'd much rather call you 'wood' than 'of.'"

"You'll be the only one." He put down his menu. "It'll be your own little pet name for me."

Irene cleared her throat. "I guess."

"I like you having your own name for me."

"I've always had pet names for you, but you always told me they were rude."

He laughed and shook his head. "Brat."

The waiter arrived and Irene ordered her food first. While Holtz ordered his, Irene looked out the window. After several seconds, she sighed. "He must be new."

"Who must be new?"

Irene motioned to the man on the other side of the mall floor. "Him. He must be new."

"New what?"

"Agent. An American, based on that tacky haircut. You know, hair gel is a privilege, not a right. Anyway, the good ones I don't spot for hours. I spotted his sophomoric butt about ten minutes after we left your apartment." The waiter returned with salads and Irene tore her eyes away from the bright red sweatshirt the man had the nerve to wear to eat Russian dressing–covered lettuce. That's when she realized Holtz was staring at her.

"What?"

"Why are agents following you?"

"There are always agents following me." She shrugged and sipped her drink. "When I was younger, about twelve, they actually took me into custody for my own safety." She snorted. "They really just wanted to keep me out of the hands of the Soviets. They brought teachers to the compound where they were keeping me. And I had to stay there all day with no friends, no family—not that they would have been much help, but still."

"What happened?"

"They let me go."

"Why would they do that?"

"I blew up half the compound and leveled a city street about thirty miles away. It was an accident. Sort of."

"You mean like you hitting me with a two-by-four and stabbing me in the leg?"

"Those *were* accidents. If I really wanted to stab you, I'd at least aim for the face."

"That's lovely, Irene."

"Sorry. Knowing they're still following me annoys me."

"They don't do it all the time?"

"No."

"Then why are they doing it now?"

Irene didn't answer him and Holtz leaned over the table a bit.

"What have you done?"

"What makes you think I did anything?"

"Because you're not looking me in the eye."

When she had to look at him to see his face, she knew she really hadn't been looking him in the eye.

"I won't discuss this with you."

"Why? Because I won't understand it or because you did something you know is wrong?"

"That's not fair." She lowered her voice to a whisper and leaned over the table so they couldn't be heard. "It's not like any of us go into this looking for something . . . troublesome. I had the best intentions."

"Then what happened?"

She sighed. "Side effects. Very bad side effects." Side effects screwed the best experiments.

"And these people want it for the bad side effects?"

"Most likely." She doubted they wanted it for its nature-nourishing powers.

"Then destroy it . . . or was that why you were out in the woods that night?"

"Yes. That's why I was out there. And I did destroy it . . . mostly."

"*Mostly?*"

"Don't snarl at me," she snarled back. "You have no concept of how many hours I put into that. All the work I did. You expect me to just toss it all away?"

Holtz took a deep breath. "First I need to ask you, is there any danger to the stuff you dumped out there?"

"No. Not at all. I give you my word."

"Good." Then he stared at her for the longest time before saying, "And second . . . don't you understand you have nothing to prove?"

Irene flinched. "What does that mean?"

"It means you don't have anything to prove to anyone but yourself."

"That's bullshit, Holtz. In this business, you're constantly proving yourself. Constantly striving for better. Otherwise—"

"Otherwise what? Otherwise you can enjoy a weekend out with your boyfriend? Otherwise the government stops following you around? Otherwise you can allow yourself to relax and simply enjoy your existence on this planet? Would that be such a bad thing?"

She specifically chose to ignore the boyfriend comment and

instead said, "When all you're recognized for is your vast intelligence, you're loath to lose it."

"You won't lose that. You've already made your mark, Irene. Now you can relax and do whatever the hell you want."

"No. I can't. Every day more come along wanting to unseat me from my hard-won throne. Wanting to take what is mine. Think of it in territorial terms, Holtz. Something you can understand. This is *my* domain. I have no intention of giving it up to anyone."

"So you risk yourself and others by keeping something you *know* is dangerous?"

Irene dropped back in her seat. She rested her elbows on the table, laced her fingers together, and rested her forehead against her knuckles. She absolutely detested the man for being right.

"Look, Irene, I'm not saying you need to take care of it this minute. I know you have it someplace safe. But think about it, baby. Remember how you felt over the hyena? Imagine that on a global scale."

Irene shut her eyes against the image but said, "I'll think about it."

"That's all I'm asking." He placed his napkin on the table. "Now if you'll excuse me, I'll be back in a minute." Then he was up and gone. She really hoped he would come back, because she had only five dollars in her pocket. Not enough to cover the bill. Of course, she could accost the agent outside. It wouldn't be the first time she'd used the fact that she'd spotted them to her advantage. She didn't necessarily think it was the right thing to do, but it was fun.

The food had arrived by the time Holtz slid back in the booth, and Irene had successfully wrangled her emotions so that she once again had herself in complete control.

Holtz took the ketchup from her and poured an obscene amount on his burger and over his fries.

"Everything okay?" she asked, picking up a fry and forcing herself to eat.

"It is now." He put the ketchup back in the middle of the

table and picked up his burger. "But, Irene, from now on you have to tell me this stuff." When her eyes narrowed, he shook his head. "No. Not about that. I mean about when you've got people following you."

"Why?"

His mouth full of burger, he mumbled, "How else can I ensure your safety if I don't know what's going on?"

"Ensure my safety? Why would you need to ensure my safety?"

"Don't piss me off, Irene. I'm already irritated because you didn't tell me about this before. Protection is not something the Van Holtzes play around with." He took another enormous bite and she realized he'd most likely devour that humongous burger in the next sixty seconds. "But you're covered. Starting Monday. Until then you're with me anyway."

Irene didn't like the sound of that. "Starting Monday what?"

"You'll have protection."

"Protection? I don't want protection."

"But you're getting it."

"But—"

"There's no arguing this, doc. If the government feels it's necessary to have you watched, then you need protection and I'll make sure you have it."

Irene dug her hands into her hair and stared at the Formica table. "I don't understand."

"What's there to understand?"

"Everything. I mean, why are you doing this? What do you care if I have protection or not?"

"Don't you know?"

"Do I *look* like I know?"

He grinned. "Nah. Ya look kind of pissed. You're cute when you get like that."

"Thank you," she said flatly. "So explain to me why you feel the need to protect me?"

His sigh was long and exasperated. "Because as my lifelong mate and eventual wife, I need to make sure you're protected."

"Your . . . your wife?"

"Of course. The Van Holtz wolves marry, baby. Unlike the Magnus and Smith wolves, *my* children will not be bastards."

"Children?"

"Yup. Remember? Two minimum. Although I'm leaning toward three or four total. But we can figure that out later."

Irene stared at Van Holtz with her mouth open and her mind suddenly, blissfully blank. Years later she'd call it that "brief catatonic thing I had in the eighties."

Holtz grinned at her, ketchup in the corner of his mouth, and glanced down at her food. "Hey, you gonna eat those fries, baby?"

Nine

"Explain to me how you get yourself into these situations."

"Don't start." Irene stopped in front of her office door, pulling her keys out and maneuvering her backpack so it didn't suddenly swing down and hit her in the face—as it had done many times before.

She'd finally finished her classes and, to quote one student, "Yay! She's released us from our bondage of despair!" Damn smartass physicists. She'd been worse than usual, she knew. But she blamed one man for her recent less-than-pleasant attitude.

"I just don't understand, Irene. Paul and I take off for three days to Mexico and we come back to you engaged."

"I am *not* engaged," she snarled. "The man is delusional."

Irene stormed into her office, Jackie right behind her. She dropped her backpack on the floor before moving over to her desk.

"I swear the man is on me like an isotope. I literally cannot remove him."

"I warned you about wolves." Jackie threw herself into the chair across from Irene's desk, planting her feet on the worn wood. "They're certifiable."

Irene practically fell into her desk chair. "He's driving me insane, Jackie. I mean . . . really. He suddenly decided that I'm . . . what are you staring at?"

"What's that behind your head? On your cork board?"

She didn't even have to turn around to look. Instead Irene simply sighed. "That's a picture of *him*, isn't it?"

"Paul and I were wondering why we found them all over the house."

"How does he keep getting into the house? And my office?"

"There's no self-respecting wolf who can't pick a lock."

Irene put her head on her desk. "I don't understand, Jackie. This wasn't supposed to happen. We were never . . . he and I . . . he can't seriously think we—"

"Oh, sweetie, he can. He does. I warned you, wolves aren't hit often but when they are . . . *bam!* Then they hold on for dear life. Especially the males."

"The worst part is, he's so damn nice. I mean"—Irene leaned up, resting her elbows and hands on her desk—"if he were a total butthead, I could rip him to shreds without even a thought. Slash, slash, slash and I'd leave him like so many men and students before him. But he's nice. Really nice. I've never had anyone be so nice to me."

"He's always liked you, Irene."

"Great. You're delusional too."

"He has. You've always been oblivious but I see all, sweets, and that doggie has had it bad for you from the beginning."

"I thought he only wanted sexual intercourse."

"Stop calling it that. And maybe that's all he wanted in the beginning. To start. But apparently that's changed. Personally, I knew it was a done deal soon as he got you to laugh."

With an annoyed growl, Irene laid her head back on the desk. As soon as she did, the phone rang. She didn't even have to answer it to know who was on the other end.

Snatching the phone off the receiver, she snapped, "Yes?"

"Hey, doc."

She viciously tamped down that burst of nervous excitement his voice elicited from her every damn time she heard it. "Van Holtz."

"I want to see you tonight."

"I've got work to do."

"How about seven? Meet me at the restaurant; we'll go from there."

"I've got work to do."

"Don't worry about dressing up. Just casual. Jeans, T-shirt."

"I've got work to do."

"See ya then."

"I've got work—" But he'd already hung up.

Irene returned the phone to the receiver. "I talk and talk and it's like I'm saying nothing."

"It's a wolf thing, sweetie."

"What is? Rudeness?"

"The ignoring. All canines do it. You say 'no, don't eat the food from the table,' and they go right on eating the food from the table, giving you that innocent look the whole time."

"So what do I do? Hit him with a rolled-up newspaper?"

"Well, that depends on you."

"How?"

"The question you need to ask yourself is whether you really want him to stop?"

"I don't under—"

"Do you love him, Irene?"

"What? No! Don't be ridiculous! Why are you even asking me? Shut up."

"Okay. I'll take that as a yes."

"Don't you dare. I don't love him. I don't love you, for that matter."

"Liar," Jackie mocked with a smile.

"I don't love anyone. I'm cold and calculating and a vicious, heartless bitch." She'd been repeating that to herself for three days. Even when he showed up on her doorstep every night and she let him in. Even when he took her to bed and made sure she didn't get a bit of sleep. Even as he fucked her so hard and long that she could barely remember her name, much less theorems and lab results. Even then, she kept reminding herself what a cold, calculating, vicious, heartless bitch she still was. "And when I see that rich idiot, that's *exactly* what I'm going to tell him."

"Uh-huh."

"You don't think I will?"

"I don't think you'll have the chance."

"I'll make the chance," Irene vowed.

"And these are my uncles Geert and Volker."

Even as Irene said her polite "hellos" and shook the hands of his many uncles, Van could hear those teeth grinding. He started wondering if dental work would be necessary at this rate.

"So, you've met everyone . . . who resides in North America."

"You can meet the rest of the brood at Christmas," his Uncle Ulbrecht promised, and Van saw Irene clench her fists even while she nodded. To his family Irene probably appeared the most polite woman any of them had ever brought home. But Van knew better. She wouldn't embarrass herself in front of them, but once he got her alone . . . eesh.

Irene looked at him over her shoulder and before she could speak he said, "Dinner's ready."

The family moved toward the dining room. He took Irene's hand and, to his surprise, she didn't pull it away. Instead, she turned and faced him. Leaning in close as if to whisper something to him, she grabbed his cock with her free hand and twisted.

Van grunted and closed his eyes. He wanted to do more than that, but Irene knew he wouldn't show the weakness to his family.

"What I'm currently doing, I can assure you, is *not* an accident," she spit out between clenched teeth and then tugged to make her point. "Understand?"

He nodded and she released him, heading off to the dining room.

Thankfully the dinner itself went quickly and as planned. Van could see Irene's years of experience coming to the fore as she deftly handled each of his uncles and aunts, never once betraying how angry she really was. Which, to be quite honest, he appreciated. He hadn't planned to ambush her like this but his father had put together this little event and made it clear he wanted Irene to attend. Since she'd kept Van at an emotional distance after he dropped her off at her house Monday morning—and told the wolves waiting for them to guard her like their lives depended on it—he knew she'd never willingly agree. So, yeah, he kidnapped her, in theory.

Sitting down next to her on one of the couches littering the family room while the rest of his cousins pulled out board games and cards, he whispered against her ear, "You still mad at me?"

She rewarded him with a slight shiver.

"Yes. I don't like to be blindsided."

"I know, but it was the only way to get you here."

"And I needed to be here why?"

"My father wanted to see us together."

"Next time tell him no."

"He's the Alpha Male, baby. I can't say no without a fight." Van shook his head. "Besides, the way he's been acting lately? No way. I'm trying to placate the old man. And come on, this hasn't been *that* bad, has it?"

She shrugged, her elbow resting on the couch arm, her chin resting on the palm of her hand. "The prime rib was quite satisfactory, I suppose."

He swallowed a chuckle. "Thanks. I made that."

"At least you have some talents besides being attractive and a pain in my ass."

Van took gentle hold of her free hand. The same hand that she'd twisted his cock with. He must love her . . . he hadn't killed her yet.

"Don't be mad at me, doc."

"This wasn't supposed to go this far," she whispered fiercely. "Sexual intercourse and nothing else."

"I never agreed to that."

"No. *You* said you just wanted to kiss me once and then you'd leave. Twenty seconds tops, I believe, was your statement." She looked at him and those eyes of hers still knocked the breath from his lungs. "Your twenty seconds are up, Van Holtz."

"Twenty seconds? Are you sure I didn't say twenty *years?*"

Growling, she tried to pull her hand away, "Don't even try it. I know *exactly* what was said."

"Maybe. Still, when one is lost in the arms of passion, maybe you misheard me."

She stopped struggling and looked at him. " 'Lost in the arms of passion'?"

"Yeah. What's wrong with that?"

She snorted a laugh and looked away from him. "Jack's right. You're all certifiable."

"This comment from jackals. And I've been meaning to ask, did her parents purposely name her Jackie the jackal?"

"Stop." Irene dropped her head, but he could see her struggling not to laugh. "You just stop right now."

"It's like the name of a cartoon character."

"She was named after her great-grandmother, and cut it out."

Van leaned in, nuzzling the nape of her neck. "Come on, doc. Let's go for a walk. I've missed you."

Irene swallowed and stared at him. He smiled and the way her body sort of melted in the seat told him he had her . . . until . . .

"Would you like to join us, my dear?"

Uncle Verner stared down at them with a damn annoying smirk on his face. *Christ, is that the look Irene always accuses me of having? No wonder she's so pissed off when I do it.*

"Join you?" Irene asked, pulling her hand away from Van's.

"In a friendly game of Risk." He motioned to the table two of his other uncles had set up.

Irene shook her head. "I don't think you want to do that, sir." It was the way she said it that had most of the family turning around to look at them.

"I don't?" Verner questioned, his smirk never leaving.

"You don't. Perhaps Monopoly or Life."

"Are you afraid?" Volker questioned while sitting at the table and getting comfortable.

"No. But I have incredible luck with dice and I am ruthless. You *will* lose, gentlemen. I will destroy your lands, take your women, ravish your men, and make your children my slave labor. I will own every castle, house, and farm that is within my reach. I won't be satisfied until I own all of it and you. I will destroy you all, gentlemen, and, to be quite blunt, I don't think you can handle it."

Van covered his mouth to keep from laughing out loud and he didn't dare look at his sister. Verner stepped back, motioning to the table. "Now I must insist."

"As you wish." Irene sighed and stood. She glanced at Van and gave him a quick wink before turning back to his uncle. "I do hope you're a 'sobber,' Mr. Van Holtz. Nothing I love more than the lamenting of the men I annihilate."

"I can't believe you made him cry."

"I did not. He just teared up a little."

"Yeah. I think it was when you told him, 'I now control your ports and own your manhood.'"

"His wife laughed."

Van pushed the bedroom door open and Irene stepped in. "This is nice."

"Yup. This is my room. Nice, *big* bed."

"Yes. It is a nice big bed. I'll enjoy experiencing it all by myself."

"Irene . . ."

"Don't whine, Holtz. It's not attractive."

"Okay, okay."

Holtz stood behind her and suddenly the gigantic room seemed so small.

"Irene, I did want to thank you."

She glanced up at him. "For what?"

"For playing along with whatever my crazy family is up to."

"Up to?"

"Yeah. They've all been acting weird lately. Especially my father. I don't know what's going on but I know I don't like it."

"Maybe he's afraid you're ready to step in as Alpha Male."

"I am. But I'm not going to fight my own father for it."

"But based on my readings—"

"Your readings?"

"Yes. I stopped by the library yesterday during lunch and read up on wolves and their social structure." Holtz grinned and she hoped he wasn't laughing at her. "Don't make fun of me."

"I'm not. Really. I think it's . . . adorable."

She rolled her eyes. "You do seem to like that word. Either that or your vocabulary is quite limited." She shook her head. "Anyway, based on how wolf culture is structured, you may have to fight your father for leadership."

He laughed. "If this were the 1200s, I'd agree with you, doc. But the Van Holtzes are civilized. I'm not about to maul my father to prove I'm ready to take over whenever he wants to hand me the leash. The old man will just have to suck it up."

Holtz let out a breath and his eyes focused on her lips. "Now that we've got that squared away . . ."

"Oh, no, you don't. Out." Irene pushed him—well, he let her push him, Irene guessed—to the door and out into the hallway.

"Come on, Irene." Resting his hands on the doorframe, Holtz leaned in. "Let me stay. I promise you won't regret it."

"Your mother and father are six doors down and have heightened senses. There is no *way* I'm letting you spend the night."

"You worried about the screaming thing you do?"

"Holtz—"

"If you ask me nice I can gag you."

Done with the conversation, Irene slammed the door in Holtz's face. "Go away. Do not return until breakfast is ready."

"Tease."

Van stared into the refrigerator and debated what he wanted to eat. True, he'd had a full meal with desserts, but he wanted more. Actually, he wanted Irene but, as usual, she'd decided to be difficult. Still, he finally had to admit, he liked being in love. He'd never thought he would. Always thought of it as another trap. But Irene wouldn't trap anyone. She really didn't want to be bothered. Actually, she looked as freaked out as he used to feel. He knew he'd convince her, though. Convince her that for some unknown reason, they were perfect for each other. Besides, he had to do something. He hated not having her in his bed. Only one night apart and he'd never been so lonely before in his life.

Van caught his father's scent behind him and didn't bother to turn around. "Hey, Dad." He grabbed an apple to control his hunger and thought about hunting something down. But before he could move, his father's growl had the hairs on the back of Van's neck snapping to attention.

Slowly, Van turned and faced the Alpha Male of the Van Holtz Pack. His father. Standing on the kitchen table, already shifted, Dieter Van Holtz stared coldly at his only son. He bared his fangs.

Still holding the apple, Van raised his hands, palms out. "Dad. Please. Don't do this." But he knew it was already too late. Knew what his father would do. Knew that the Pack stood outside the back door waiting for the old to challenge the new.

His father's paws slammed into him as he leaped from the table, knocking Van through the back door and out onto the porch. By the time Van hit the hard wood, he'd already shifted to wolf.

* * *

Irene sat in the big comfy chair in her room, her naked legs tucked up under her. She wore one of Van's T-shirts as a sleep shirt. Since she hadn't planned on spending the night, she hadn't brought any clothes.

She turned the page on the hardback potboiler she'd found on the room's bookshelf. This was the kind of book Irene rarely allowed herself the luxury of reading, but with nothing else to do and still too wound up to sleep, she felt no guilt for taking the time out now.

Nearly an hour before, she'd heard all sorts of snarling and growling coming from the back of the house. She'd ignored it even as she briefly worried what might be going on. They were probably taking down some poor deer and she'd rather not know about it. Kind of like how she didn't need to know where her beef came from.

The glass doors leading to her balcony opened.

"I thought we had this discussion, Holtz—"

Irene watched the dark brown wolf limp into her room. How he'd cleared the balcony, she had no idea. A rather disturbing amount of blood followed him in but she didn't know if that was his or another's.

"Holtz?"

He walked up to her and rested his head in her lap. By the time she stroked his hair, he'd turned back to human. He had bite and claw marks over most of his torso, but the bleeding wasn't as bad as she'd first thought.

His long arms wrapped around her and he held on. Carefully placing the book beside her chair, she used both hands to stroke his head and shoulders. "What happened?" she asked softly.

He let out a soul-deep sigh. "I just tore my father apart so I could be the next Alpha Male of the Van Holtz Pack. I left him bloody and lying there so I could take the Pack hunting in the woods."

"To prove what you'd done didn't bother you."

"Right." He burrowed his head deeper into her body, like

he wanted to crawl inside her. "To prove that I was stronger than any of them."

"He challenged you, didn't he?"

"You knew this was coming." It wasn't a question.

"Yes. I knew. Not when, but I guessed it would be soon. Your father watched you all night."

"If he wanted me to be Alpha Male now, he should have just handed it to me."

"That wouldn't have worked and you know it. We both know he had to do this or risk one of his brothers or their sons challenging you."

Holtz finally looked up, giving her a sad smile. "Is that also from your reading expedition yesterday?"

"Pretty much."

Holtz nodded and pulled his arms away from her body. "Well, thank you. There was absolutely no one else I could talk to about this."

"I'm glad . . ." Irene swallowed past her nervousness, knowing instinctually what the next step had to be. "I'm glad you came to me. But you're not done yet." She'd read about this in one of her books, knew what he had to do to secure his position of Alpha Male. Knew what *she* had to do.

Holtz turned serious amber eyes toward her. "What do you mean?"

"They insisted I be here for a reason, Holtz. And you know why. You have to finish it."

He stared at her in confusion for several seconds, then he shook his head. Adamant. "No. Absolutely not, Irene."

She pushed the chair back and stood, pulling the T-shirt up over her head and tossing it to the floor. "You need to finish this. Now." Finish it before she lost her nerve.

"No, Irene. I won't . . ." He cleared his throat. "What we have is ours. No one else's. I won't involve you just to . . . forget it."

Irene walked to the balcony doors and pushed them open all the way, then went to the top drawer of Holtz's chest of drawers and grabbed the box of condoms she'd found earlier when looking for something to wear to bed. She walked back to him and stared down into that handsome face. She had this weird feeling in her chest. For several moments she worried it was something that would need immediate medical attention. Then Van Holtz looked up at her and the feeling doubled, tripled.

She loved him.

And she'd protect what was hers.

Kneeling in front of him, Irene reached out and wrapped her hand around his cock. It had started to get erect as soon as she'd taken the T-shirt off. But once she put her hand on it, she suddenly held a steel pipe.

"God, Irene," he groaned. "Stop."

"There's no option here, Holtz. I'm not giving you one." To prove it, she leaned over and took the tip of his cock into her mouth. His breath hissed out and his hand slid into her hair, grasping the back of her head. Relaxing her throat, she swallowed all of him and sucked hard.

The hand massaging her scalp suddenly had claws, and Holtz pulled her off him. He gave her just enough time to put the condom on him before he slammed her flat on her back. He shoved his cock inside her before she could think of what to say.

Irene slapped her hands against his hips and gripped them tight, pulling him closer. Letting him know without words that she wanted this. Wanted him. And she didn't want him to hold back.

He stared down at her with the eyes of a wolf. But even through the cold eyes of a predator she saw more love and caring than she'd seen from any man.

Holtz placed his hands flat on the floor right above her shoulders, bracing his forearms against her body. They held her in place when he slammed into her that first time. And the next time. And the next.

And she didn't hold back how good it felt. So good she never wanted him to stop.

He powered into her again and again, never letting his eyes

stray from her face. Never letting her look anywhere else but at him. It should have hurt, the way he slammed into her. She should have begged him to stop. But instead she raised her knees up so he could get deeper inside her.

It didn't take long for that orgasm to rush up on her. To slam into her with such force that the scream he tore out of her was real and probably heard as far away as Löwe Pride territory.

She didn't know when the tears started, but she sobbed through that orgasm and right into the next. By the third, he ordered her to mark him. To make him her own. She found a spot already opened from his father's claw. Setting her teeth on the wound, she bit down hard.

His grunt told her it hurt him, but then his entire body went stiff and he was coming. The two of them joined in a way so primal they moved on instinct alone.

Holtz dropped on top of her, their sweat and all sorts of other juices commingling. And Irene simply didn't care. In fact, she'd at least admit to herself, she loved it.

"God, Irene. Are you okay?" His hands moved over her, soothing her.

She nodded, still unsure of her voice. And she really didn't want to start crying again.

He leaned back and stared at her. His eyes were human again, his incisors gone. "Are you sure? Did I hurt you?"

Irene reached up with one hand and ran her fingers down his cheek, across his lips. She stared hard at his face, taking a snapshot with her mind of every line, every scar.

"I love you."

She'd said it simply, plainly. The way she said most things. And like that Van's whole world changed. It became perfect.

He lay on his back, pulling her with him, not letting her go. His condom-covered cock still buried inside her, already itching to go again. "I love you, Irene. God, I love you so much."

She wrapped her arms around his neck and rested her head

against his shoulder. Nothing in his life had ever felt so right before.

Van gripped both sides of her face with his hands and forced her to look at him. He kissed her nose, her cheeks, her lips. He kissed her and loved her. "This time, Irene," he said softly while pushing her on her back once again. "This time is just for us."

He took her slow and easy after that, Irene's cheek braced against his chest, her arms holding him tight.

And when the Pack howled to them outside the window, his mother and father included, he felt her smile.

Ten

Van reached out for Irene but his hand touched an empty bed. Opening his eyes, he looked around the room and found Irene standing by the terrace doors, staring out at the nearby ocean. She had a sheet wrapped around her and her hair looked wild and completely untamed in the early morning light. She looked well-fucked and he wanted her to look like that as often as he could manage.

"What's wrong?"

She glanced at him over her shoulder. "What makes you think something's wrong?"

"You're not reading, complaining you have to get back to work, or working. You're just standing and staring, which means you're thinking . . . which means something's wrong."

"You figured me out rather quickly."

"Actually I've had seven years to figure you out. So what's wrong, doc?"

She leaned against the doorframe. "Thinking about last night."

"You regret it?"

"No." She turned those amazing blue eyes toward him. "But I'm hoping you don't."

"Why would I?"

"Because this isn't changing."

He didn't understand her. "What isn't?"

"Me. This is it. Based on genetics, the only changes I see happening are the widening of my butt and the occasional mole if I don't avoid the sun. My brain, especially, will not change barring Alzheimer's, dementia, or a tragic head injury."

Laughing, Van lay back in the bed. "Irene, what the hell are you talking about?"

"I'm never going to be suave or delicate or polite. I'll never look any better than I do at the moment and I'm severely average." She held up her hand before he could say anything. "I'm not blind and I'm always honest with myself. And it's never concerned me before. I'm very happy with who I am. I've got bigger issues on my mind than whether I'm wearing the latest Gucci outfit or if I look fat in photos."

"Okay."

"That being said, I am not going to spend my life worrying that I'm not pretty enough for you or disappointing you when we go out to some godawful dinner that I'd rather chew nails than go to. You wanted this and now you're stuck with it."

Van raised his eyebrows. "You done?"

"Yes. I've said all that needed to be said."

"Good. Now come here."

She turned from the door and walked back over to the bed. He lifted the comforter and she dropped the sheet and slid inside. He pulled her close, locking his hands behind her back and pushing his knee between her thighs. He rested his forehead against her shoulder.

He'd just begun to fall asleep when she tapped his arm.

"What?" he sighed.

"Don't you have anything to say?"

"No."

"Nothing at all?"

"Your concerns are groundless and you're looking for an excuse to run. I'm not giving it to you, nor am I going to bore *myself* with bullshit platitudes. If you wanted that you should have stuck with Bradley."

"You scared him away," she reminded him.

"And he ran like a girl. I didn't. So shut up and go to sleep."

"Well if you're going to be rude—"

"You know I'm cranky in the mornings."

"Currently you're downright satanic."

"Whine, whine, whine."

She punched his shoulder and he rolled her over to her back, using his body to hold her down.

"Clearly I need to teach you the proper way to respect the Alpha Male. Or, as you'll call me from now on, your lord and master."

Irene stared up at him, her face—as always during moments like these—expressionless.

"What? Would you prefer 'my savior'?"

For Irene, the strangest part of her recent life changes came when she finished her work. Normally, she didn't really finish her work until well into the next morning. Getting three or four hours of sleep pretty standard for her. But, for the first time in her steel-trap memory, Irene actually had a desire to leave at night. She had something to look forward to.

Van shared management of the main Van Holtz restaurant with his sister—requirements for all young Van Holtzes. The nights he worked late, so did Irene. The nights he didn't, she usually made it home no later than seven. He always had a meal waiting for her, constantly worrying she didn't get enough to eat. Or the proper things to eat. He flatly refused to buy her any peanut butter and crackers.

After she'd eaten and he chatted with her over his wine, he'd shift and go hunting with some of his Pack and Irene would grade papers or review lab work. They never spoke of her returning to her and Jackie's house and last Irene heard Paul had successfully moved in.

Strange how shifters did things. No big discussions or informing people of plans. One day you were living with a friend and enjoying your life as the town genius, the next thing you knew, you'd been moved into a mansion and were the average one among the populace.

A few times, due to her work, Irene did have to stay late and either Van or one of the wolves came to pick her up. Van hated her staying late, constantly concerned about her safety. But it couldn't be helped; she simply didn't have what she needed at the house.

Then, three days ago, she arrived home and as she opened the door to the room she and Van shared, she noticed a pile of boxes in front of the room across the hall. Because all boxes were addressed to her, Irene proceeded to cut open the first one. She couldn't hide her shock when she found a brand-new IBM PC AT Model 2 in one of the boxes. The rest were filled with the necessary wires and equipment, including a monitor with a color screen. He'd even gotten her an actual Trailblazer modem, which was so new she hadn't even gotten the dean to sign off on her request yet. She'd found a note between the boxes from Van. In his surprisingly clear handwriting—for a man—he stated, "Now you can get that cute ass home on time. You know I don't like to wait. Use this room as your office—it's so conveniently close to the bedroom—and be naked when I get home. Love you.—Van."

The overgrown baby had made it nearly impossible for her to stay at work when she wasn't actually teaching or focused on something specific. It used to be when she didn't have anything specific to do, she could find something. She'd come up with some of her most . . . uh . . . unstable but interesting ideas that way. Now she only wanted to finish up her day at the university, go home, work for a few hours there, and then spend the rest of the night rolling around her bed with Niles Van Holtz.

"How do normal people live like this?" she asked her computer, which suddenly didn't seem nearly as cool as the one she had at home.

Her phone rang and she stared at it. She knew it was him. The one she blamed for making her a slut. Or, at the very least, bringing out the latent sluttiness in her.

When the phone rang for the sixth time, she finally picked it up.

"Yes?"

"I knew you were there. How long were you going to make me wait?"

"Until the end of time," she sniped back.

"What's wrong?"

"I . . . it simply appalls me to say it, but I want to come home."

He didn't say anything at first, but she imagined she could actually *hear* his smile. "Then come home," he finally said.

"I was afraid this would happen."

"What?"

"You distracting me. I'll never get the Nobel Prize at this rate."

"Isn't that a peace prize? You won't get that because you're a—"

"Shut up."

He laughed. "Come home, doc. I want to see you. And my cock is dying to get in you."

"It was just in me last night. And this morning. And I thought you were at the restaurant tonight."

"That was the original plan but Carrie asked me to switch with her. She and the brain trust are going away for the weekend and she wanted Friday off."

"That was nice of you."

"I made her beg for it first. And then she had to promise to get me a Ferrari."

Irene sighed.

"What's the sigh for?"

"Nothing. It's too stupid to comment on."

"So you coming home soon?"

She glanced at the clock on her desk and noticed another framed picture of Holtz she'd never seen before sitting in front of it. With an annoyed growl, she moved it aside. Nearly nine o'clock and she'd gotten absolutely no work done. Now she'd go home and get no work done because Holtz would practically tackle her in the hallway . . . and she'd let him.

"Might as well, I guess."

"Man, could you sound more put-upon?"

"I could, actually."

"I'll come by to pick you up."

"Don't bother. Jackie will be here any minute and she'll drive me home."

"You sure?"

"Do I not sound sure?"

"You know if you're cranky when you get home, I'm going to have to fuck it out of you again."

She closed her eyes, her body heating at the memory of that.

"Irene?"

"Shut up," she snapped as Jackie walked through the door and then looked like she was ready to walk back out. Or run. Irene stopped Jackie's retreat with one raised finger. "Jack's here. I'm leaving now, you pompous, overbearing, self-obsessed, mentally challenged prick."

"Why don't you just admit it," he said on a sigh. "Admit you love me and my perfectly proportioned cock. And there's nothing you love more than its life-giving elixir."

Irene leaned back in her chair and stared at Jackie with her mouth open. "Life-giving elixir?"

"Well, what would you call it?"

"That over-salted fluid I can't get the taste of out of my mouth but that you keep insisting I swallow."

Jackie walked to the other side of Irene's tiny office and buried her face in the corner.

"Insist? We both know you beg for it." His voice lowered. "I want you home. Now. And naked within ten minutes of you entering the house. Am I clear?"

She stood. "We're leaving and the only thing you've been clear about is that you're clinically insane."

"This is true."

Irene hung up and grabbed her backpack. Turning her back on her friend, she opened one of her desk drawers and removed the small titanium case she had hidden in a secret compartment. Inside the case she had a syringe filled with the last two ounces of her creation. Every day that she held on to it, the more guilty she felt. Not only that, but she realized she truly didn't need it. Holtz, the smug bastard, had been quite right. She no longer had anything to prove to anyone but herself. Besides, anything this dangerous needed to go. And this time she'd make sure to avoid the Rubicon.

Slipping the case into her backpack, she zipped it up, and put it on her back, the straps over her shoulders.

She walked around the desk and Jackie frowned, stopping her in her tracks. If she found out Irene still had some of that stuff remaining, Jackie would nail her butt to the wall.

"What?" Irene asked, trying not to sound panicked.

"When did you start wearing jeans and T-shirts to work?"

Irene barely stopped herself from letting out that relieved sigh. "When I keep waking up too late to do more than shower and toss on these clothes. Funny, my students appear much less threatened by my attire, so I'm not sure how I feel about that."

Together, the females walked out of the building and down the steps while Jackie told Irene about how Paul had accidentally set the kitchen on fire.

"I swear, sometimes I don't know what he's thinking," Jackie said again.

"He's probably so wrapped up in your pussy, he can't think straight."

It took Irene a good minute to realize she walked alone.

Turning around, she found her friend sitting on the stairs. "What?"

"I was just wondering where my best friend went."

"I don't understand."

"Making jokes is one thing, but using the word 'pussy' is something else. For you, anyway."

"Oh. That. Well, 'vagina' seemed a tad clinical when discussing why your mate is currently so dysfunctional."

Shaking her head, Jackie deftly got to her feet. "I didn't see it coming."

"Didn't see what?"

Jackie walked down the remaining stairs. "I mean, I knew you'd fall for him. You two are so perfectly mismatched, how could you not fall for each other?" She stopped in front of Irene. "But I never thought he'd make you happy. Not like this anyway. And he does, doesn't he, Irene? Make you happy?"

Irene shrugged. "I hadn't really thought about it, but I guess he does. He isn't . . . uncomfortable with me. Even when he doesn't understand a word I may have said, he never looks uncomfortable." She gripped the straps to her backpack. "I have to say I'm enjoying that."

Jack linked her arm with Irene's. "Good. You deserve to be happy, sweetie. Now what about his Pack?"

"They look frightened and I have absolutely no idea why. I'm nothing but appropriately pleasant."

"Price you pay as the new Alpha Female."

"I understand all that, but running from the room every time I walk in seems a tad harsh, wouldn't you say?"

"You do have a point."

Irene spotted Jack's bright red Mercedes-Benz but held her friend back before she could head toward it, her eyes locking on the black four-door with dark windows parked right in front of it.

Jackie sniffed the air. "Irene, I smell ti—"

"Hi, Dr. Conridge."

Irene glanced over her shoulder and carefully pulled her arm from Jackie's. "Oh. Hello, Jenny." She turned to face the woman completely. "Do you need help with something?"

The corn-fed Iowan gave that bright smile Irene hated. "You know what I need, don't ya, professor?"

Irene nodded. "Of course, I do." She stepped toward the woman and let her take firm hold of her arm while three men, trained killers by the look of them, stepped out of the car and walked toward them. "I have to admit, though, I always thought it was Mark."

Jenny laughed. "Not nearly smart enough, that one. I've got her," Jenny said in Russian and motioned behind Irene with her head. "Kill her friend."

Reaching for his gun, one of the men turned but immediately froze. "Where is she?"

Irene didn't dare show any emotion. She simply stared straight ahead.

"Forget her." Jenny pushed Irene toward the car. "You're not going to give us any trouble, are you, Professor?"

Resting her hand against the car door, Irene turned back to Jenny Fairgrove, all-American girl. "Why would I do that?" she flatly asked. "We both know my only emotional investment is in my creations." She smirked. "For the right price, anyone can have me."

With a smile, Jenny followed Irene into the car. "Good to know, professor. Because I think you'll find our people quite accommodating."

Van went out on the back porch and stared out at the woods. He felt unsettled and had no idea why, but he did know he didn't like it. His fangs slid out of his gums and his vision changed from that of a human's to a wolf's. He watched restless wolves roam Van Holtz territory and he knew the rest of the Pack felt it too. Something wasn't right. In fact, something was horribly wrong. They just didn't know what yet.

His sister walked out on the porch and stood next to him.

"Any word from Irene?" he asked.

"Not yet."

"Jackie?"

"No."

Van stepped down the stairs, Carrie right beside him.

"What do you need us to do?"

He glanced down at her and said, "I need—"

The distinct, high-pitched howl stopped every wolf in a ten-mile vicinity. It wasn't a wolf howl. It was jackal.

He didn't even realize he'd shifted until he looked down and saw his four paws tearing through the darkness, heading for that howl, his Pack right behind him.

The large men in the car jumped and looked out the windows.

"What the hell was that?" one of them asked.

"Jackal," Irene stated quietly while watching city streets turn to suburb. They weren't taking her to a main airport but a small airstrip. One built exclusively for private planes.

"Did she just call us jackals?" one of them joked.

Irene grinned, which wiped the smile off the man's face. "No. I said the howl you heard was jackal." She looked at Jenny. "They'll be coming for you."

Jenny glanced at the men and back at her. She looked terribly concerned that she had a lunatic in the car with her. "The jackals will be coming for me?"

"No. The wolves."

Jenny sighed. "Why oh why do I always get the nutcases?"

"Oh!" Irene pointed excitedly. "See that spot up there?"

"What about it?"

"That's where it all started. Where I crossed the Rubicon."

Exasperated, Jenny snarled, "*What the fuck are you talking about?*"

"It's feeding time," Irene whispered.

"That's it." Jenny threw up her hands. "We're so medicating her."

Irene heard the high-pitched howl again and she moved, bringing her elbow back and into Jenny's nose. The crunch of cartilage had never sounded so beautiful before.

Jenny screamed and covered her face, blood flowing from between her fingers. Irene slammed her fist into the balls of the man sitting next to her. He grunted in pain but didn't pass out as she'd hoped. Instead, his hands cupped his groin but she used the opportunity to reach across the man and fling the door open.

The ground flew by and she quickly calculated the speed at which they were moving, the height of the car, her current weight, the weight of her backpack, and the potential car-to-ground impact.

Adjusting her body twenty-six-point-eight degrees, Irene took a deep breath, hoped for the best, and threw herself out of a moving vehicle.

Eleven

Irene's body flipped forward several times before landing against the unforgiving road. Gasping, her entire body aching, she lifted her head. It took her a second to realize the fingers of her right hand were numb. Okay, so her calculations were off a smidge. Good thing she was left-handed.

The sound of squealing brakes forced Irene to turn her head. The car had spun around and she knew it would be heading back toward her at any second.

Forcing herself to her feet, Irene stumbled into the woods. She ignored the blistering pain emanating from her wrist and the sticky feel of blood sliding down her face. What concerned her more was the way her vision seemed to be dimming. The last thing she needed now was to black out.

Shaking her head and pushing herself to take each step, Irene kept going, knowing exactly where she needed to be. Exactly where she needed to lead them. It was her only chance and might get her killed in the process. Better to die in her own country, though, than someplace she'd never been before.

They were behind her, closing in fast, although she could hear one of the men telling them not to follow. Irene still had the backpack on and it had become a dead weight. But to take it off now would lose her even more time, so she kept pushing forward.

Her memory steered her, told her where to go. A gift and a curse, her memory. Without it right now, she'd be dead. With it, she might end up slave labor in the Soviet Union. Nice choices.

Irene saw the clearing through the trees and focused her will on making it through those trees to the clearing. She had to.

Big hands grabbed her hair and backpack, yanking her back. Irene swung her arms and slammed her foot into his instep, causing a healthy grunt of pain before he threw her face-first into a tree.

Stunned, Irene used the tree for leverage and maneuvered around it. She stumbled forward, tripped, and hit the ground. But she'd made it to the clearing. She'd crossed the Rubicon.

"You fucking bitch!" Jenny Fairgrove spit at her as she dragged Irene up by her hair. "Where were you running, Professor? Where did you think you'd go? You'll never get away from us."

Male hands yanked her from Jenny and Irene waited for it. A slap, a punch. The reminder that they controlled the situation, not her.

Unable to put up much more of a fight, Irene waited. But she knew that if they didn't knock her out, she'd still fight. She'd fight until they killed her.

Unfortunately that was in her nature too.

Yet the big hands in her hair were the only thing keeping her from falling to the ground.

She looked at the other angry male striding toward her, spitting curses at her in Russian. He was only about five feet from her when they all heard that laugh and he stopped.

Irene grinned. "Welcome to *my* country, comrade."

Quickly wiping the blood from her eyes, Irene watched the agent turn toward the sound as one of the Dupris Clan slammed into him, jaws wrapping around his head.

The big Russian screamed, going for his weapon, but he never counted on how large the Dupris family and its Clan were. "They breed like rabbits," Van would always complain. And she'd never been so grateful.

They grabbed hold of parts of that agent he probably didn't even know he had, and an ugly tug-of-war started. The whole time, as they ripped the flesh from his bones and the limbs from his torso, they laughed—the sound they made when excited.

Clearly they were quite excited.

The other agent raised his gun and tried to pull Irene back into the woods even as he watched the carnage in front of him. But by then the wolves were there, tackling him from behind.

Pushed by the momentum and the fact that he still had her hair, she went with them all, right into the middle of the battlefield. He got off a shot, but a giant gold paw slammed the man's hand down, crushing it under its weight. The agent's high-pitched scream so loud it could be heard above the growls, roars, and howling.

Irene untangled the man's fingers from her hair and pulled herself away. But before she could make a run for it, the barrel of a gun pressed hard against her throat.

"Get up."

She almost groaned. The third male agent. The driver. She'd forgotten all about him. He dragged her to her feet, spun her around, and wrapped his hand around her throat.

He snarled, his fingers tightening against her neck, his gold eyes reflecting in the dark. "I should kill you now." And she thought he just might, but he stopped when that angry male face leaned up close to his and growled low and long.

The agent looked over at a very naked Niles Van Holtz. But it was most likely not the nudity that concerned him, but those fangs.

Van didn't even have to tell the motherfucker to let his female go, he simply knew it was the smart thing to do. Irene stumbled back and Van focused all his attention on the male who didn't belong in his territory.

"And what are you going to do about it, little doggie?" the male sneered.

Christ, he *hated* Siberian tigers. Always had. They could be worse than the lions.

But he didn't have to make the first move. His sister did. Carrie used to date a tiger and she still hated the bastards. She slammed into the back of him as he shifted from human to tiger and Van followed them down. A few more of the Pack joined in. The big bastard had to be topping at least seven hundred pounds and ten feet long once shifted. But then two of the Löwe breeding males grabbed hold.

The fight didn't last long once the hyena pulled one of the tiger's legs off. But Van heard the slide of a gun yanked back. He turned and saw the barrel of a .45 aiming right for him, held by a blond piece of ass with what looked to be a shattered nose.

He bared his fangs, ready to go for her throat, but then there was Irene, who he'd ridiculously believed had run home like a frightened girl. Instead, she came up behind the blonde and wrapped her right arm around the woman's neck, her forearm hard against that slim throat. Her left arm slipped under the blonde's, lifting it and the gun up while she raised her left hand, showing the other woman the syringe Irene held.

"You want to know what I'm working on, Jenny?" Irene demanded. "Well, here it is!" She slammed the needle into the woman's jugular and compressed the plunger with a vicious growl worthy of any She-wolf.

Gasping for breath, Irene stumbled back and the blond female dropped to her knees. She yanked the needle out of her neck and stared at it. But within seconds, whatever Irene had used on her went to work, eating through the blonde's neck and ravaging her face.

The woman's screams became choked sobs, her skin festering and dissolving right in front of them. Blood no longer kept in by human flesh poured to the ground. And by the time Jenny's rotting bones hit the dirt . . . she was long gone.

"What . . . what did you do?"

Irene opened her eyes. She didn't know she'd closed them until she opened them. That's when she realized they were all staring at her.

"Don't worry," she said to one of the Pride females. "That was the last of it." Irene didn't bother to mention she could easily make it again with a few basic household products and a wad of gum. Nope. Not a good idea to mention that.

Holtz walked up to her, his sister and Jackie right behind him. He stared at her face. "What is it?" he asked softly.

"Broken wrist, I think."

He winced for her and motioned to a few of the Pack who charged off into the woods. "We're going to have to take you to the hospital, baby. Our doctor can't fix this here."

Irene shrugged, then wished she hadn't. She again closed her eyes until the nausea brought on by pain passed. "That's fine."

"And what about her remains?" Another Pride female demanded. "Our children play here. We hunt here and—"

"What remains?" Irene asked.

She watched them all stare at the spot where Jenny Fairgrove had died such an agonizing death. Not a piece of bone or speck of blood remained.

Which was exactly the reason the Russians wanted it. A nice, clean, efficient way to kill.

"Don't worry. It leaves no residue, nothing unsafe. Tomorrow there will be flowers on that spot."

Van grinned as he pushed stray sweaty hairs off her face. "Flowers?"

"Don't judge."

"I'm not. It just seems such an 'Irene' kind of thing to do."

Irene glanced at her arm. "I really think I should get this taken care of. The pain is becoming quite unbearable."

"You're in unbearable pain right now?" one of the She-wolves asked. Irene hadn't bothered to learn the Pack members' names yet.

"Yes," Irene answered simply. "I'm just not much of a screamer . . . shut up, Holtz."

"I didn't say a thing," he laughed.

Holtz took hold of her uninjured hand. "Come on, baby. Let's get you to the hospital." He easily lifted her into his arms, careful not to jostle her wounded limb.

Never before had Irene felt so safe or cared for. And his body heat soothed her like nothing ever had. . . .

"Irene!"

Irene opened her eyes. "What?"

"Don't pass out on me, baby. I need you to stay awake."

Irene didn't know what he meant until she looked around and realized they were almost back to the house.

"Sorry."

"Don't apologize. Just keep those pretty blue eyes open."

She chuckled. "You are the only person I've ever met who likes my eyes."

"I think they're gorgeous. And what I say is all that matters. Haven't you learned that yet?"

"Yes, I have. I've also caught you chasing your own tail, so excuse me if I'm not ready to sign you up for a think tank just yet."

He growled when a few of the wolves looked back at them and started laughing. "Is nothing sacred between us?" he demanded. Then he added against her ear, "Besides, it was harassing me again."

She laughed and felt his smile against her cheek. Yeah, that was definitely one of the things she loved about Holtz . . . that, in his own way, he was as weird as she was.

Of course, that also meant their children would be absolute freaks.

Van paced the hospital hallway while the doctors worked on her. Since the hospital had a Van Holtz pediatric wing, he had no doubt they'd give Irene only the best care. Still, he wouldn't feel settled until he saw her. Until he knew she was okay.

"You're making me nauseous."

Van ignored his sister and walked back toward the double doors leading to the emergency room.

"Niles Van Holtz, don't you dare."

Swinging around, Van stalked back over to his sister.

Irene had passed out on the ride over. Nothing he did could wake her, which really worried him. He knew he couldn't lose her now. She meant everything to him. Absolutely everything.

Which was why he'd never wanted to fall in love in the first place! And, to be quite honest, he blamed *her* for his current bout of unhappiness. How dare she make him fall in love with her! How dare she be so damn cute and adorable and absolutely clueless about anything remotely normal and human so that he had no option *but* to fall in love with her.

"Stop panting or I'm getting you a dog bowl," his sister snarled.

The doctors walked out into the hallway and if his sister hadn't gotten to the men first, he would have tackled the first one he could get his hands on.

"How is she, Dr. Bennet?" she asked while holding Van off.

"She's actually doing quite well. She informed us of the proper way to put on a cast and we had a nice long debate about whether medication of any kind was necessary for her particular problem."

At that point, Van stopped fighting his sister and stared at the doctor. "She didn't."

"Oh, but she did."

"So I can assume she'll be just fine?"

"Oh, that you can. We've checked her from top to bottom and performed an MRI."

"An MRI? Why?"

"Because she had concerns about blood clots."

"Does she have a blood clot?"

"No."

"Then why—"

The doctor held his hand up while his colleagues kept their heads down and their laughter in. "Please, Mr. Van Holtz. I believe I've had all the questions and unasked-for information that any man can tolerate. We're going to keep her overnight for observation. Strictly a precaution. Tomorrow . . . preferably in the morning . . . you can take her home. Or simply far, far away."

There were more snorts from aborted laughter as the other doctors began to move away and Van nodded his head. "I understand."

"Good. Now give them a few minutes to get her into a room and then you can see her. Now if you'll excuse me, *I* need to go far, far away."

The doctor walked off and Van looked down at his sister. She gave him what he now knew to be the Van Holtz smirk. "And you were worried."

Irene stared down at her cast. Thankfully a clean break—the doctor only had to set her arm and put a cast on. No surgery necessary. Although she did debate with the man whether that was the correct way to go. Her past research had shown . . . *ahhhh, morphine. What a lovely drug.*

Smiling for absolutely no reason, Irene let her eyelids droop down. She was tired and she wanted to go home.

Home. Her home. With Van.

But the doctors were making her stay the night. With her insurance, they usually kicked her out within hours but apparently she was a Van Holtz now. And that meant a single room and the utmost care. Oh, yes, she could easily get used to this kind of treatment.

The hospital room door opened and Irene didn't bother opening her eyes. Another nurse or doctor to hover. They all hovered, it seemed.

"How are you feeling, Professor?"

Irene frowned. She knew that voice. Opening her eyes, she looked up into the face of her teaching assistant.

"Mark? What are you doing here?" She looked him over. He wore hospital scrubs. Why?

"I wanted to check up on you. You need to know I tried my best to protect you from her, Professor Conridge. I really did."

Irene didn't wait for him to say anything else; she simply swung her broken arm at his face, hoping the cast would smash his nose. At the same time, she tried screaming but Mark's hand slapped over her mouth and the needle he shoved into her arm turned everything black.

Half-dozen roses in hand, Van pushed open the hospital door. He frowned when he saw the room empty.

"Irene?" He checked out the bathroom but found that empty, too. He walked out of the room and crashed into his sister.

"What's wrong?"

"She's not in there."

Van walked over to the nurses' station. "I'm looking for Irene Conridge."

The nurse frowned. "She isn't in her room?"

"Would I be here if she were?"

"Calm down, Mr. Van Holtz. I'm sure she's around somewhere." She stood and leaned over the counter, focusing on a nurse walking out of one of the other rooms. "Josie, did you check on Conridge?"

The nurse nodded. "They took her down to X-ray."

Van felt the growl in the back of his throat. "Why? She's already had X-rays."

His sister put a hand on his arm. "Who took her to X-ray?"

The nurse shrugged, not seeming remotely concerned. "Must be a new orderly. I've never seen him before."

The only thing that kept Van from going for both nurses' throats was his sister's hand on his shoulder, her cool voice in his ear.

"Not here. Not now."

Van turned on his heel and stalked out. As soon as he made

it outside, the flowers he'd bought for Irene were slammed against the wall.

"I shouldn't have left her."

"You went to get flowers," his sister argued. "How long were we gone? Ten minutes?"

"I shouldn't have left her," he said again. "We have to find her."

"You don't think they'll try and take her out of the country again, do you?"

"That's it." Van walked over to a pay phone outside the hospital. "I'm sick of this shit."

"Wait. What are you doing?"

"We're Van Holtzes, goddamnit," he snarled, shoving coins into the pay phone. "Grandfather always said we stick together in the worst of times. Even when we despise each other."

His sister's eyes grew wide. "You can't be calling *him*? Have you lost your mind? Dad will skin you alive."

"Dad's still licking his wounds. This is *my* mate we're talking about. We both know I'll do whatever I have to to get her back . . . and I *will* get her back."

Twelve

Irene stared up at the ceiling. She'd spotted the vent as soon as they dragged her into this room, kicking and screaming. But with her arm in a cast—and itching like Satan—she'd never be able to get up and out of it. So she'd had to come up with other options. And she had.

They'd brought her to a top-secret Air Force base. Somewhere in Texas.

She would say that they'd treated her well. Good food, wine, TV with cable and some ridiculous amount of channels. Perhaps twenty? Who in their right mind would spend time flipping through twenty channels?

But with all the good food and everything else came questions. Lots of questions. They wanted to know what the Soviets wanted, and whatever it was they wanted it for themselves. As if she would ever trust human males with anything so dangerous. Oppenheimer never got over what he unleashed on the world; she wouldn't go down the same road.

Not only that . . . but she missed Van. To her horror. She missed another human being. What next? She'd start crying over cat commercials and buying cookies from those little fascists, Girl Scouts? Whom, to this day, she never forgave for not letting her into the local troop. Bitches.

Even worse, she wondered if Van missed her. No one ever had before. Irene was not the kind of woman people missed when she wasn't around. Instead they mostly felt relief. Her students this semester must have been in absolute heaven with all the times she'd been out of the office the past few weeks.

Well, no bother. Everything was set. And they'd regret the day they ever set eyes on her.

Agent Harris walked into the room with two cans of ice-cold soda and smiled at her. She hated that smile. She hadn't seen anything that fake since Jackie and Paul had talked her into going to dinner with them at the Playboy Club.

"Here you go, Professor Conridge." He placed the can in front of her.

"Thank you."

"You know, Niles Van Holtz is quite determined."

"Yes. I've learned that."

"He's actually contacted the president about you."

Irene snorted. "Reagan? He won't help. He still hasn't gotten over me doing a comparison between him and Hitler that time I was invited to the White House."

Harris cleared his throat and sat down catty-corner from her. "Why don't we talk a little about Jenny Fairgrove?"

"Jenny Fairgrove?" Irene blinked. "Oh, yes. She wants to be my teaching assistant. Although I doubt I'd give her the honor."

"And why's that?"

"She's perky. For that alone I won't give her the job."

"That seems pretty harsh."

"Albert Einstein could apply to be my TA, and if he were perky . . . I wouldn't give him the job either. Of course after finding out that Mark worked for you the entire time, I'm not sure I'd trust anyone. And how is his face doing?"

Harris' jaw clenched. "You fractured his right cheekbone with your cast."

Irene stared at Harris but didn't respond. Finally, the agent snapped, "Well? How do you feel about that?"

Blinking slowly five times, she flatly replied, "I feel nothing." She shrugged. "It's a gift and a curse."

Irene glanced at the never-speaking agent, Marshal. "Do you think you could get me something for a headache? Aspirin is all that I require."

The stalwart agent glanced at Harris, who gave him an affirming nod. He walked out, closing the door behind him, and Irene returned her attention to Harris, Mark's shattered face already forgotten.

"So why are you asking me about Jenny Fairgrove?"

"We have intel she's not quite who she says she is."

Irene stared at Harris until he shifted uncomfortably in his chair.

"Something wrong, Professor?"

"You're of Scandinavian descent."

"Uh . . . yes. I am."

"Yes. I can tell from your bone structure." Then she slammed her cast against his nose, angling it so she knocked him out but didn't kill him.

Irene knelt beside his prone body and dug into his pants until she found his set of keys.

"Gotcha."

"He said you were determined."

With a sigh, Irene gripped the keys in her hand and glanced over her shoulder.

She didn't know who this man was, but he didn't seem friendly.

"Dr. Conridge?" he asked.

"Yes."

He motioned to her. "Come on." He held his hands out to her. "Let's get you up."

Really big hands took surprisingly gentle hold of her arms and pulled her to her feet.

"And you are?"

"All you need to know is I'm family." He patted her on the head and she had the overwhelming desire to punch him in the testes. Which meant only one thing . . .

"You *must* be a Van Holtz."

He grinned. "You can call me Uncle Edgar." He pushed her toward the door. "I'm sorry I didn't get here sooner. I was in Bogotá."

"Why?"

"Aren't you cute" seemed to be his only answer. "Now, let's get you back before that nephew of mine turns the whole Pack and the United States government against him."

Irene sighed. "I really wish I'd known you were coming."

Uncle Edgar, who was an inhumanly large man, stared down at her, his eyes narrowing. *He looks* exactly *like Holtz.* "Why?" Although he looked like he didn't want to know the answer.

Unfortunately he received that answer anyway thirty seconds later, when the east side of the base blew.

Before he could say anything, Irene explained, "Don't worry. I took out the part of the base they'd closed down. But it'll still wipe out the"—the lights flickered and went off, leaving them in complete darkness—"electricity."

"Good thing I can see in the dark then, huh?" He took hold of her arm. "Let's go."

"What about Harris?"

"Don't worry about him. He won't be bothering you again."

"Oh?" She didn't need light to make herself crystal clear.

"No. No. I won't kill him. Although I could. And your mate probably wants me to." He led her into the pitch-black hall, and she let him because she really had no choice.

"You're CIA, aren't you?"

"Aren't you cute," he said again.

"Yes. I'm painfully adorable." He led her outside, the airmen scrambling to put out the strategic fire she'd planned. "Is there ever a time that the Van Holtz men don't sound pompous?" she asked, unable to stop herself from smiling.

"Not since before Christ."

* * *

Van stormed into the Van Holtz house and he watched every Pack member but his parents disappear. Even his sister grabbed her mate's arm and pulled him from the room.

"Well?" he snarled. "Any word from Edgar?"

"Nope," his father replied calmly, turning the page of his *Wall Street Journal.* The old man's wounds had completely healed, a six-month trip around Europe for him and his mate booked, and the disturbing noises coming from behind their bedroom door suggested Old Man Holtz was thoroughly enjoying his retirement.

"Then I'm done waiting."

"And what will you do, my son?" his mother asked as she worked on her needlepoint.

"Something!" he roared. "Which is more than any of you are doing. My mate is gone and no one cares!"

"Of course we care," his mother chastised gently.

Afraid he'd say something that would irrevocably damage his loving relationship with his parents, Van turned and walked up the stairs toward his room. Throwing open his door, he tore off his jacket and tossed it across the room, moving over to the phone. He picked up the receiver but stopped when he heard sounds he found annoying and exhilarating all at the same time.

Tapping and beeping.

Dropping the phone back in its cradle, Van walked out of his room and across the hall. He pushed the door open, ignoring how it snagged on the multitude of wires and cords.

And there she sat. At her computer, plugging away at something he never would or wanted to understand.

He heard her give a little curse, annoyed that the fingers of her right hand weren't moving as fast as she'd like them to. And he sensed that they hurt a bit too, since she kept bending them and wincing.

Van gave himself a moment to enjoy seeing her there . . . safe. And where she belonged.

She cursed again and turned sideways in her chair, bending her fingers and frowning down at her defenseless cast.

"Don't even think about taking that cast off, doc."

Irene's head snapped up and she gave a relieved smile ... seconds before she jumped out of the chair and charged into his arms.

Van held Irene tight against him, his relief at having her back in his arms nearly dropping him to his knees.

"I didn't think you'd ever get home," she said into his neck.

"Me?" he laughed. "You had me worried sick."

"Blame the government. They wanted my formula."

"Did they break you?"

Her sniff was arrogance personified. "Not in this lifetime. Although ..."

"Although?"

"I wish I'd known your uncle was coming. They were really quite upset about the damage."

Unwilling to release her, Van pulled back enough to see her face. "Damage?"

"From the explosion," she answered simply.

"I don't want to hear this, do I?"

"Probably not. Besides, your uncle said he'd take care of it."

"Good enough." Van lifted her and carried her back into their bedroom, slamming the door with his foot.

He laid her on the bed, stretching out beside her. "I missed you, doc."

"I missed you, too."

They stared at each other for several seconds, then they both sighed sadly.

"What have we done to ourselves?" Van asked.

"I don't know. I was so happy not caring about anyone. Now I have all these ... these ... *emotions*. And it's all your fault!"

"My fault?" Van began pulling off her clothes. "I'm Alpha Male of the Van Holtz Pack. That's a female magnet, doc. I should be knee-deep in pussy. Instead I'm madly in love with you. Can't imagine my life without you."

"What about me?" she demanded, leaning up to let him get her T-shirt off her before she took hold of his sweatshirt and lifted it up. "My life was organized and controlled. *I* was controlled. Now all I can think about is having sex with you. The most irritating human being I've ever known."

"Like you're a ray of frickin' sunshine? Uncle Verner is still trying to recover from that game of Risk."

"If you can't handle world domination, don't pick up the die."

Van stood at the end of the bed and dragged her jeans off. "Oh, that's a very nice way of talking about your own family."

"Family? When did they become family?"

"As soon as you agreed to marry me."

"I never agreed to marry you."

"Yes, you did. You just don't remember."

Irene got on her knees and undid his jeans. "Holtz, I have a memory computers dream about."

"Don't brag, baby. It's tacky." The fingers on her right hand wouldn't cooperate, so he helped her get his jeans unzipped and pushed them down, kicking them, his shoes, and socks away. He shoved her back on the bed, pushing her into the mattress with his weight. "We're getting married. Just deal with it."

"Fine. But I'm not changing my name."

"That's fine. But we're having a wedding."

She made a clear sound of disgust.

"I don't want to hear it, doc. I've got a lot of family. We're having the wedding. A year from now, I've decided."

"Well, I don't have time to sit around worrying about napkins with our names on them and flowers or whatever."

"I'll handle all that."

"Yes. You will." She lifted her right arm with its cast above her head and wrapped her left around his neck. "Now. I've gone without sexual intercourse—"

"Fucking."

"... *fucking*, for four days. Get to work. You have much to make up for."

* * *

Since she'd had the printer going nonstop for forty minutes, she never heard a thing. Then Jackie slapped her shoulder.

Startled, she spun around in the chair. "What?" She stared thoughtfully at her friend. "What's with the dress?"

Jackie looked at the white dress she held in her hand and back at Irene. "It's for you."

"Forget it. I'm not going to any dinners tonight." She faced her computer. "Holtz will understand."

"Not this time, he won't."

"Besides," Irene added, "I would never wear white to a charity dinner."

"Irene Danielle Conridge!"

Glancing over her shoulder, "What? What did I do?"

"Apparently you forgot your wedding."

Irene rolled her eyes. "No way. That's not for a year."

"It has been a year."

"Don't even try it. The wedding isn't until October."

"It is October."

"October 1985."

"It *is* 1985."

Irene's fingers froze over the keyboard. "Not the 19th, though."

"Yes, Irene. It's Saturday, October 19th, 1985."

"But it's not eight o'clock."

"No. It's not."

Irene let out a breath.

"It's seven-forty-five . . . p.m."

"Damn!" Irene stood up, rounding on her friend. "*Why didn't anyone tell me?*"

"We've been telling you. Didn't you notice the decorations, the people coming in and out . . . the dress fittings? Or how about when I walked in an hour ago and told you that you needed to get dressed for the wedding?"

She shrugged. "Not really."

Jackie's eyes closed. "Tell me you at least showered."

"Uh . . . yesterday."

"Oh!" Jackie stormed out into the hallway. "I need She-wolves! We have an emergency."

"Aren't you blowing this out of—"

"Shut up!"

She glanced at Jackie's already protruding stomach and groused, "I'm so glad you and Paul decided to breed."

"Don't make me kill you. Because I *will* kill you."

For the next thirty minutes, the She-wolves and one jackal subjected Irene to a litany of physical abuse including a shower, forcing her unruly hair into a lethally tight bun, slapping what she considered useless makeup on her face, and forcing her into a white sheath dress she'd never buy for herself.

Standing outside the closed doors leading to the ballroom and the waiting groom and guests, Irene glanced down at the bracelet Carrie placed on her wrist while Jackie put a matching necklace around her neck.

"This is nice."

"Van got this for you," Carrie stated on an exasperated sigh. "Don't you remember?"

"Was that the day he got me the Zenith Z-171 PC?"

Jackie laughed and said, "You owe me twenty bucks, Van Holtz. I told you she liked that computer more than the forty thousand dollar's worth of jewelry your brother got her."

"What can jewelry do? Do you realize that PC is portable? And it's battery powered with backlighting!"

"I don't know why he bothers," Carrie muttered before stepping away and looking Irene over. She shrugged. "I guess it's the best we can do."

"Gee, thanks."

"Don't listen to her." Jackie slapped a small bouquet of red roses and baby's breath in her hands. "You look wonderful."

A string quartet began to play and the She-wolves started walking into the ballroom single file.

"This is such a waste of time."

"Irene, suck it up."

"I have things to do!"

"What? And I don't? Now stop whining and in ten seconds follow me down that aisle or so help me God, I will kick your lily-white ass!"

Jackie turned around and the pair paused, realizing they had the attention of all the guests.

Forcing a smile, Jackie whispered, "I'm so getting you for this later."

Then she was off, slowly walking down the aisle, while Irene impatiently and quickly counted to ten. She followed after her friend and several times almost passed her. The third time, Jackie slammed her elbow into her gut, which effectively slowed Irene down.

When she finally reached Holtz's side, he had tears streaming down his face, but she knew it wasn't from the beauty of the moment.

"Stop laughing at me," she whispered.

"Could you look more annoyed?" He laughed, keeping his head down while the priest or reverend or whatever droned about why the hell they were there.

"There are a myriad of things I could be doing at this moment. Useful, life-changing things. This is a waste of time."

"Excuse me?" The priest/reverend/whatever snapped. "Do you mind?"

"Sorry," Irene said and then added, "But feel free to pick up the pace."

Which got a snort out of Holtz.

She lasted a good five minutes before her foot started tapping.

"Cut it out," Holtz growled, although she had the feeling he was still laughing.

"I'm bored," she whispered back. "Too much longer and I'm going to start taking things apart. And you know how you hate when I do that."

"Speaking of which, what happened to my Mercedes?"

"What are you talking about?"

"I came home yesterday and it was nothing but burnt metal."

"Oh. That. Yes, I wanted to see how engines worked. I walked away for a few minutes to get a glass of orange juice and when I came back . . . boom."

"*Boom?*"

The priest/reverend/whatever cleared his throat.

"Sorry," Holtz mumbled.

A few more lines about commitment and love and Holtz snarled under his breath, "What do you mean 'boom'?"

"I was merely trying to see if I could get more speed out of it."

"How much speed?"

She shrugged. "I don't know. I've been toying with this idea of being able to travel from one country to the next in a car. I figure if you make it fast enough, it might hydroplane."

"All right, that's it. Stay away from my cars."

"But you have so many."

"*That's not the point!*"

"Excuse me!" the priest/reverend/whatever snapped. "This is a sacred and time-honored ceremony, so do you think you two could act like it and shut the holy hell up?"

Annoyed, Irene tapped at the spot on her wrist where her watch would be if those vicious She-wolves hadn't taken it off her. "Or you could speed it up. I've got things to do and your rambling is boring me!"

"Fine!" the priest/reverend/whatever yelled. "Do you?" he asked Holtz.

"Yup!"

"And you?"

"Yes, yes."

"Ring?"

"Here." Holtz placed the white-gold band next to the sizable diamond he'd insisted on getting her.

"Good. You're married."

"See?" Irene asked sweetly, just to annoy. "That wasn't so hard, now was it?"

For a second there, she really thought the man might hit her.

* * *

Van watched Irene work the room. For someone enormously bad with normal human relations, she really amazed him when it came to trying to get donations for the university.

He didn't want her to work, but he knew he had to do something. During the toast portion of the evening, he realized she'd taken his watch off and had the back pried off. *A twenty thousand–dollar watch and she takes it apart.*

Well, at least giving her a task had calmed her down. And she looked absolutely beautiful. Especially once she took her hair out of that bun. Stray hairs kept slipping out and she finally went to the bathroom and tore out all the pins. But he made a good choice with the dress since she couldn't be bothered choosing her own beyond stating, "Nothing puffy like Princess Di wore."

He should be annoyed. But he wasn't. He loved that Irene couldn't give a shit about their wedding. Because in the end it didn't matter. With or without some piece of paper, they were together for life. No one else was as perfect for him as this one blindingly brilliant woman.

Irene walked back over to him but before she could drop into one of the chairs, he pulled her into his lap.

"You doing okay?"

"Yes. Mikolev Thornapple—an actual name, mind you— just promised ten thousand to the science department." She looked down at him. "Are we going on a honeymoon?"

"Yep. Right after we're done here."

"Where?"

"Aruba."

He had to bite his tongue when she frowned.

"Because my pasty butt does so well in the sun?"

Laughing, Van nipped her shoulder. "Switzerland, Germany, Norway, Scotland. We'll be staying at lovely castles and B&Bs . . . all of them near very old, very *interesting* libraries."

"You don't mind me spending tons of time in stuffy old libraries?"

"Not if you promise to tell me anything interesting you learn . . . and you give me regular sex."

"That is a promise I can commit to."

"Figured."

Suddenly Irene gently clasped his face between both her hands and kissed him. "As you may or may not know," she said against his lips, "nearly 41 percent of all marriages end in divorce in this country. But I feel we'll beat those odds simply because we're so freakishly unusual and unstable enough to make this work. Especially with your unique DNA strain and my less-than-enthusiastic interest in legal actions of any kind."

"Irene, you sweet talker, is that your way of saying we're perfect for each other?"

"Yes. Wasn't I clear? Also, we love each other and that's most important. Because, really what *is* perfect? What does that—"

And Van kissed her before she could head down that long-winded road, happily wondering to himself how he *ever* got so lucky.

Epilogue

Twenty years later . . .

Irene waved and forced a smile until the last SUV disappeared down the road. Then she stormed into her house, slamming the door behind her.

Holtz reached for her. "Doc—"

"Not a word!" she snarled before heading up the stairs and going straight to her daughter's room. She practically kicked the door open and the little viper didn't even look away from her PC. No, that wasn't right. Her *Apple* computer. Oh, the shame!

"How dare you!"

Finally startled away from whatever she was working on, Ulva Van Holtz turned in her chair to face her mother. "How dare I what?"

"Why did you tell her she was pregnant?"

Ulva blinked in confusion. "Because she *is* pregnant."

"That's not the point."

"I'm not sure what the issue is."

"You simply can't say whatever comes to your mind. And *stop* telling my students you found flaws in their thesis."

"But you say whatever comes to your mind."

"That's not the point."

"Then I believe I am unclear on what your point is. And I did find flaws. In fact, she should rethink those last ten chapters altogether."

Irene stepped closer to her daughter, with the possible intent of wringing her neck, but the two females stopped arguing when the Van Holtz men stumbled into view. Holtz held both his sons in his arms—upside-down.

"What are you three doing?"

"Nothing," they replied in unison, which meant "something."

"Papa says we can go over to Aunt Jack and Uncle Paul's." This said with her son's sweetest smile. Not even twelve and already a heartbreaker.

"Oh, he did, did he?"

"I've already called," Holtz admitted. "They said they'd love to have them over."

"Well, with their other ten thousand children, what's three more?"

"I'm not going," Ulva said with a haughtiness that annoyed Irene no end.

"Yes. You will. Or you won't play Warcraft again until the second coming. Do you understand?"

"Fine. I prefer Aunt Jackie's company to anything I find around here anyway." And then Ulva turned back to her computer, effectively dismissing her.

Irene went to choke her, but Holtz grabbed her hands and dragged her out of the room.

"Pack your backpacks for a couple of days. The driver will be waiting in ten minutes."

"That girl is driving me insane!" Irene snarled after slamming the bedroom door.

"She didn't mean to make things difficult for your student."

Irene gave a dismissive wave and began pulling out the laundry. "I mean, did you see that poor boy? He's like nine feet tall, two thousand pounds, and he looked absolutely terrified."

Holtz stretched out on the bed. "He wasn't terrified. He just knew it would be a painfully long drive home."

"You can get that smirk off your face, Van Holtz." She dropped the laundry basket by the bed and crouched next to it to retrieve his socks. "I saw the looks passing between you two. And how do you get your socks so far under here?" She knelt down and reached under the bed.

"Sorry, baby."

"You're so anal retentive about the mess in your precious kitchen, but you and your damn socks . . ."

"I know. It's so sloppy. I don't know what I'm thinking."

Socks in hand, Irene sat up, blinking when she came face to face with Holtz. "What are you doing?"

"Nothing."

"I still think you put these socks under here just so you can stare at my butt."

"Dr. Conridge! What a horrible thing to say." Then he gave her that grin. The same grin that, even after all these years, still knocked her on her proverbial ass.

Of course, the fact that he still wanted to watch her butt amazed her like the discovery of uranium. And it was one of the reasons she didn't let the cleaning staff touch their laundry.

"And stop telling people I set your car on fire and stabbed you. Did you see that poor boy's face?"

"But you did do those things."

"*They were accidents*," she growled.

"So you say. And Conall Víga-Feilan is not a boy. Although why he'd involve himself with a midget, I'll never know."

"Miki Kendrick is not a midget. And he's with her because she's brilliant and dangerously unstable."

"Like you?"

"I am not dangerously unstable. Those tests proved it," she groused.

Laughing, Van grabbed Irene's arm and dragged her onto

the bed. He pinned her to the mattress, arms above her head. "I've got an idea, doc."

"What?"

"That once we get the kids off, we spend the next forty-eight hours completely naked."

"You act like only the kids live in this house."

"Trust me. The Pack will find other places on the territory to stay this weekend."

"Ogre."

"When it comes to this pussy, you're damn right."

She sighed thoughtfully. "It amazes me how that kind of talk sexually arouses me."

Holtz leaned down and nipped her breasts. "It amazes me that I find you saying that so goddamn hot."

Irene's back arched as he sucked on a nipple through her T-shirt and the lace of her bra.

"Perhaps you're delusional," she groaned.

"No. I just love knowing this pussy belongs to me and no one else. Doesn't it, doc?"

"It seems to. I find all other men repulsive."

"And it better stay that way," he teased, grinning up at her, his chin resting against her breastbone. "I don't share what's mine."

Digging her hands into his hair, Irene pulled him up until they were face to face. "Wolves." And she gave him that smile no one ever saw but him. "So damn demanding."

"Geniuses," he sighed back. "So damn hot."

WICKED WAYS

Cynthia Eden

*For Megan and Laura—thanks, ladies,
for all that you do.*

One

Miranda Shaw had understood that she was on the date from hell ever since the appetizers were served at the too-expensive restaurant and she'd caught sight of the tiny bugs crawling over her cocktail shrimp. But she didn't truly realize just how bad the situation was until her date took her home and then attempted to bite her with two-inch-long fangs.

"Oh, my *God!*" She caught sight of the teeth just in time. She'd thought Paul Roberts was just in macho-aggressive mode. Moving in for a lick on her neck. Miranda had fully intended to jerk away from the guy before he made contact—

Then she saw his teeth.

Oh, hell, no.

The scream that burst from her throat should have deafened him. Or at least broken one of the lovely glass picture windows that lined the front of her house.

But it did neither.

When she tried to run, Paul grabbed her arms, holding her tight. "Don't make me hurt you," he growled, and Miranda wondered if she were in the middle of some kind of really, really vivid nightmare, because there was no way that her boring, all-I-can-do-is-talk-about-myself date had just sprouted those deadly fangs.

Things like this so didn't happen in nice, normally quiet Cherryville, Florida.

She twisted her body, trying to break free, but the guy's grip was too damn strong. *Shit.* "What are you—*Ow!*"

His teeth had pierced her neck. Torn the skin. She shoved at him again, harder, and those teeth of his just seemed to cut deeper into her flesh.

Then she heard the muted sound of him swallowing.

He's drinking my blood. The freak is actually drinking my blood.

Weakness began to trickle through her body. His hold was too powerful. Fear made her dizzy. *This shouldn't be happening.* She'd done everything right. Talked to the guy over the Internet for a good two months before she'd met him in person.

He wasn't supposed to be some kind of blood-drinking psychotic!

He was grunting now and making little moaning sounds, and she was pretty certain that she was going to pass out. At any moment.

Then the weirdo would probably kill her.

Not the way she'd been hoping her night would end.

I'm not going out like this. Her neck was on fire. Her body quivered. But her Grandma Belle hadn't raised a quitter.

Miranda managed to lift her knee and ram it as hard as she could into the jerk's balls.

He stiffened against her, lifted those terrible teeth for just a moment—

And Miranda twisted like a snake, managed to break free of him, and then lunged for the door.

Just a few more feet . . .

If she could get outside, she might be able to get help. Or maybe her new neighbor, the *only* neighbor she had in the boondocks, would be able to help her and—

Paul grabbed her by the hair and hauled her back. She shrieked as he pulled her, reaching up with her hands and clawing his wrist.

"You're going to be so damned sorry, you bi—" His snarled

words ended in a gasp when her front door was literally kicked open.

Miranda blinked, stunned and damn grateful to see her neighbor of five days, Cain Lawson, standing in the doorway. Over six feet three inches of pissed-off male. Tousled coal-black hair. Handsome face etched into lines of fury.

He glanced first at her, then at the psycho still holding onto her hair with a death grip. Miranda was on her knees, scratching and clawing, and she didn't think it was necessary, but she still screamed, "Help me!"

Then the really, truly unthinkable happened. Cain's lips pulled back from his perfect white teeth and damned if those teeth didn't look far too long and way too sharp for a human's.

"Get the hell away from her, vampire!"

Vampire? No, that wasn't right. Vampires weren't real and—

And blood was still dripping from the wounds in her neck.

She chilled as goosebumps rose on her flesh.

Date. From. Hell.

Paul laughed, a high, grating sound, and his hold tightened.

She'd be lucky to come out of this situation with her life, not to mention her hair.

"*You* get the hell out of here, before I decide to kill you, too," Paul snarled.

Then his hands were on her throat. Only his fingernails felt too sharp. Like knives. Miranda stopped breathing, afraid that if she so much as moved, he'd slit her throat right open.

So much for trying to date one of the good guys.

If she made it through this mess, she'd go back to finding the normal asshole biker guys who were nice and safe. The ones who occasionally drove up from Miami looking for a fresh start, only to get burned out by the smalltown life less than a month later.

Cain lifted his hands and his nails started to grow. Lengthened. Sharpened.

Miranda blinked. *No way was this happening.*

"Come and try, vampire," Cain's voice rumbled, dark and dangerous. "*Come and try.*" A muscle flexed along the strong width of Cain's square jaw. His face was a tense mask, and his high cheekbones gave him a harsh, predatory appearance. His golden eyes were blazing. So bright. So fierce. So . . .

Glowing?

He growled, then leaped across the room in one fast move. A snap sounded right next to her ear and when Paul screamed, she realized the sharp noise had been the cracking of his wrist.

Then she was free. Cain jerked her forward, tossed her toward the couch, and the air she'd been holding escaped in a *whoosh.*

Miranda scrambled around the cushions, turned back just in time to see the men crash to the floor in a heap of limbs and muscles. Snarls and growls escaped them, making the two seem more like animals fighting than humans.

She put her hand to her neck, wincing at the sting and the sticky feel of her blood.

She really hoped that Cain kicked Paul's ass.

Fumbling, she managed to grab the phone on the end table beside her. Her fingers trembled as she dialed 911 and kept a wary eye on the men.

"911 operator. What's your emergency?"

Paul kicked Cain off him, sending the taller man hurling back about five feet.

"I—I was attacked." *Bitten by a freak.* Cain lunged for Paul. Swiped out with his hand and caught the other man along the face. Deep bloody grooves—Jesus, but what looked like *claw marks*—immediately appeared on Paul's previously perfect right cheek.

Paul's teeth snapped together. *"Shifter."*

What?

They were getting too close to her. Miranda jumped over the couch, keeping her fingers clenched around the phone.

The emergency operator was asking frantic questions in her ear, but Miranda couldn't break her focus from the two vicious fighters long enough to answer her.

They were circling each other now. Cain bared his teeth. "She's not for you, asshole."

Paul laughed at that.

"101 Lakeview Street," Miranda finally whispered to the operator and let the phone drop from her hand.

Paul was just a few feet away. The men were both pretty much ignoring her now, and if Paul kept his advance going, he'd be in front of her in seconds.

"Do you think she's going to be yours?" Paul asked, voice that of the dull, annoying gentleman she'd had dinner with that evening. "Women like her don't go for animals."

Cain flexed his hands. "Yeah, well, they don't tend to go for sadistic parasites, either."

Miranda had no clue what they were talking about. Parasites? Animals? *What?* Keeping her gaze darting between her would-be rescuer and the biter, she began to edge to the left. Toward the very, very big crystal vase that Grandma Belle, rest her sweet soul, had given her when she'd first moved into the house five years ago.

Her fingers wrapped around the crystal. Tested its cold weight.

"I can have any woman," Paul boasted. "They all beg for my bite."

Now Miranda was the one choking back a growl. The bastard was almost in range. She lifted the vase, heaving it over her head.

He took another step forward.

Then he spun toward her with his face twisted in fury.

She didn't hesitate. Miranda hurled the vase at Paul, slamming the crystal right at him.

The vase shattered with a crash. Shards of crystal littered the ground. Blood covered Paul's face, trickling down his already-battered cheeks and his chin.

But the man didn't fall. Didn't so much as stumble.

He smiled at her. "I knew you'd be special."

Special? She'd just tried to brain the guy!

His hands lifted toward her and her stomach tightened.

Then Cain was there, clenching his hands around Paul's

shoulders and throwing the bloody bastard against the wall. The impact seemed to shake her small house.

And Paul didn't get up.

Cain stared at her. Those mysterious golden eyes of his gleamed with a feverish intensity. "You all right?"

Not really. She suspected she might be minutes away from a breakdown and—

"Why the hell are you dating a vampire?"

Uh, no, she wasn't. Because vampires weren't real and—

And her date had just tried to bite her and drain her blood. Like a vampire.

Vampire.

Her knees buckled. Miranda hit the floor, almost as hard as Paul had just hit the wall.

Cain leapt over the couch. "Miranda?" His gravelly voice was tinged with a faint drawl. One that had made her think of cowboys the first time she'd heard that deep rumble.

"I—I just need . . . a minute." Or maybe an hour.

He reached for her, pulling her into his arms and pressing her against the soft front of his T-shirt and that rock-hard chest of his.

"It's okay. You're safe now—"

Yeah, well, she wasn't exactly ready to believe that one yet.

"He didn't drain you. And he didn't give you an exchange, right?"

She blinked up at him. "An exchange of what?" She hadn't even kissed the guy, so it sure as hell wasn't like they'd exchanged anything—

"Shit." Cain stiffened against her. "The cops are here."

No, they weren't, but the local deputies would probably be on their way soon, provided the dispatch caller had managed to get someone at the sheriff's office and—

The shrill cry of a siren reached her ears.

"They aren't equipped to handle him."

She pushed away from Cain. Painful that, because the man sure felt good. Her gaze darted back to Paul. He was still unconscious. Should be easy enough for Sam Michaels and the other deputies to handle.

Paul's eyes snapped open. Only they weren't the light blue eyes he'd had before. They were pitch black. Blazing with fury.

The guy seemed to fly to his feet.

Cain shoved her back.

But Paul didn't come for her. He ran for the broken door. Dripping blood. Swearing.

Cain followed right on his heels.

So did she.

Just as she reached the edge of her porch, two patrol cars roared up the gravel drive and braked in a cloud of dust and rocks. Paul ran straight toward them, then *over* them as he jumped onto the hood of one car and then appeared to soar over the other.

Cain rushed after him, only to be brought up short when Sam brandished his gun and yelled, "Freeze, asshole!" Then he turned to the group of deputies, muttering, "Dammit, where the hell did that other bastard go?"

But it was too late. Paul had run straight into the woods. His abandoned SUV waited near the side of her house.

"Go after him, now!"

Two men scrambled to obey.

Cain stood before her, hands up. "Uh, Miranda, tell him I'm not the bad guy here."

For an instant, she remembered the brutal look on his face when he'd knocked in her door.

He'd sure looked pretty bad then. And he'd more than left his mark on Paul.

"Miranda . . ."

But he'd saved her ass. "Th—the other one, Sam. He's the one who—who"—*bit*—"attacked me."

Sam swore and lowered his gun.

"You're not gonna catch him," Cain muttered, dropping his hands. "The bastard will be long gone before your men can even catch his trail."

Now Sam's already tense face hardened even more. "Oh, yeah, and just how do you know that, buddy?"

"Because scum like that is used to running and hiding. You won't find him." He glared at the dark woods. "But I will, and that asshole can count on it."

The pretty schoolteacher looked pale. Too pale.

Miranda Shaw sat huddled on her porch steps. Her small shoulders were slumped. Her dark hair was a tangle around her heart-shaped face. She kept glancing at him with those big, blue bedroom eyes of hers. She'd look at him, then when he caught her staring, that gaze would dart away.

The lady was afraid of him. Figured.

But *he* hadn't been the man trying to kill her. Shit. He'd saved her life. Didn't he at least merit some kind of hot-and-heavy thank-you kiss for that?

Ah, *Miranda Shaw.* The sexy lady next door who'd brought him a dozen cookies when he'd moved in beside her. The computer teacher at the local high school. The teacher with the long, slender legs. With the softly curving breasts and the mouth that he ached to taste.

He'd dreamed about the woman for the past four nights. Hot, wild dreams that left him aching and pissed when he awoke alone.

Cain had wanted Miranda from the first moment he'd seen her. Wanted her naked and moaning his name.

He'd thought he'd play the gentleman. Get her used to him. Then take her.

Idiot. He'd wasted time playing the good guy when the woman was hanging out with the undead.

He wouldn't make the same mistake again.

If Miranda wanted to take a walk on the wild side, she could damn well walk with him.

It wasn't like she could find a guy much wilder, anyway. He could get downright primal and knew that with her, he probably would.

"Uh, Miranda? You gonna be all right tonight?" The question came from the uniformed deputy with the buzz-cut red hair, a fellow who apparently thought he was in charge. Miranda had called him Sam. Cain had no idea what the guy's last name was.

Her head lifted, and he caught sight of the bruises, scratches, and *bite* marks on her neck. His hand clenched. Oh, yeah, he'd be finding that vamp. Very, very soon.

"You didn't catch him," she said, and sounded both alarmed and disgusted by that fact.

Of course they hadn't. Humans weren't equipped to track vampires. Not like he was. Cain knew he should have run full force into those woods after him, and if the deputies hadn't trained their guns on him, he would have.

Then Miranda wouldn't be sitting there looking furious and afraid.

But neither he nor Miranda had confided to the deputies about her date's true nature. Cain hadn't spoken up because he knew the uniformed men wouldn't believe him.

Was Miranda keeping silent for the same reason? Or was something else holding her tongue?

Sam crossed to her side and put a hand on her shoulder.

Cain frowned at the man.

"I can keep a patrol car in the area. We've got an all-points bulletin out for him—"

Like that would do anything.

"We've fixed your door—"

Okay. His fault. Cain winced at the reminder. But when he'd heard Miranda's scream and caught the scent of her blood on the wind, he'd been frantic to get to her side.

He barely remembered kicking open the door.

"You didn't fix it," she muttered. "You pretty much just nailed the thing shut."

A cough from Sam. "Well, you can go in the back, can't you?"

Miranda sighed and shrugged off his hand. Then she rose, holding tight to the railing.

"He's not going to come back, Miranda. He'd be an absolute fool to head this way again."

Unfortunately, most of the vamps Cain had met were fools. Or sadistic killers.

"I—It's all right," Miranda said. "I'll put on the alarm and—"

Oh, hell, no. Cain marched toward her. Breathed in the sweet honeysuckle scent the woman carried, caught the richer smell of her blood. "You're not staying alone." Not until he'd caught that vampire.

A frown appeared between her brows. There was only a little moonlight trickling down on them, but her porch light shone brightly on the small area.

Yet even if it had been pitch black, he would have been able to see her almost perfectly. One of his kind's little gifts.

He caught her hand. Became aware of just how small and delicate she was. He could crush her bones with a careless touch.

But he'd never be careless with a human female.

And certainly not with *her*.

She licked her lips and the sensual swipe of her pink tongue had his cock swelling. "Wh—what are you proposing?"

The deputy glared at him.

"My place." His bed, but they'd get to that later. "You can have the guest room, and you won't have to worry about that vam—ah, jerk coming back."

She blinked at him. Damn, but he loved that woman's eyes. "That's very kind of you—"

Kind. He snorted. If the woman knew just how many hot and heavy fantasies he'd been having about her, the last word she'd use to describe him would be *kind.* "Baby, I want you safe. I don't care what Sam here says"—he jerked his thumb toward the glowering human—"but that creep could be back." And he didn't want to take any chances with Miranda's life.

Damn. Why had the woman been with that guy?

"There's no reason for him to come—" Sam began.

"Miranda's the reason." The perfect temptation. Sensual woman. Sweet blood. How could the vampire resist?

How could he? Especially once he got lovely Miranda locked inside his house?

The beast within began to growl.

He could easily hear the sound of her indrawn breath. Even over the dizzying call of the insects. The mutters of the men. The racing of his own heart.

Then she was pulling her hand away. Easing down the steps.

Running?

Forcing his gaze to break its lock on her, Cain surveyed the area. A large lake separated his place from Miranda's. The woods surrounded their homes, effectively cutting them off from the rest of the town.

To the right, the way the vampire had fled, waited swamps. Alligators. Snakes.

If he was lucky, maybe one of them would attack the parasite.

Maybe.

"Miranda, if you want to stay with someone, you can stay with me," Sam said, raising his voice and catching Cain's attention.

Oh, hell, no. Not one of his options. Bad enough he had to compete with a bloodsucker to get the lady's attention. He didn't want to go against some kind of hick deputy.

"I don't need to stay with you, Sam." Her voice was clear.

"Then I'll send the patrol and—"

She met Cain's stare. "My neighbor has room for me. I'll be staying with him."

His blood seemed to heat. Miranda in his house. Perfect.

"Ah, hell," Sam muttered. "Cuz, you know what you're doing? You just had one guy who hurt you—"

Her chin lifted, but her gaze never wavered. "And one guy who saved me. Yeah, I know what I'm doing."

Cuz. Cousin. Cain relaxed muscles he hadn't even realized that he'd tensed.

"I'm still sending out my patrol."

Cain gave a slight nod. "Good. And make damn sure that the men you send out are well-armed." Not that a normal bullet would be able to do much damage to one of the undead but—

It would sure sting like a bitch.

"And you come in to the station first thing tomorrow, Miranda, you got me? You come in, finish this report, and then we'll get Stan to come out here and put up a new door *and* a damn sight better security system."

"No arguments there," she said, and again lifted her hand to press lightly against her throat. When she winced, Cain ground his back teeth.

"You need to go to the hospital." Sam was tapping his foot against the stone steps as he made this decree.

"I've told you five times already, I'm *not* going. I let that crime scene guy photograph me, but that is it! I've got a few scratches, I don't need to drive forty minutes to get to Springs Memorial to have a doctor tell me I'm fine," she snapped.

Cain blinked. Oh, but the lady had a nice temper on her. He liked that—a lot.

"Okay, calm down." Sam motioned to the other deputies.

"I am calm!" she yelled. "I've just had one hell of a night and I really, really just want to get in bed now and try to pretend that all of this crap never happened!"

That's what the humans usually did. Made excuses for the things they saw. Tried to act like reality wasn't some screwed-up mix of heaven and hell.

Sometimes those lies worked.

Sometimes they didn't.

Sam hugged Miranda. "Fine, but I'll be close. Call if you need me."

She brushed his shoulder a bit awkwardly. "Okay, uh, thanks."

He turned his attention to Cain. "Watch her, and you damn well don't even *think* of taking advantage."

Well, other than his plans to rip apart the vampire, taking advantage of Miranda was the only other thing occupying his mind. Not that he was going to confide that little tidbit to the uniform, but—

"All right, guys, let's pack it up and get out of here. I want to search Smith Swamp and get the status on the men in the woods," Sam said, snapping out orders as he walked away.

A few minutes later, the cars disappeared in a swirl of blue and white lights.

Cain was left alone with Miranda.

Finally.

Two

She had to be crazy. Miranda paced the length of Cain's living room, spared a brief glance for the unpacked boxes lined neatly along the left wall, and tried very hard to make her hands stop shaking.

Alone with Cain Lawson. Jeez. Had she taken leave of all her sanity? She should have gone with Sam or locked her house up tight and—

"You're safe with me, Miranda. Relax." His voice sounded from right behind her and Miranda spun around, surprised to find that Cain had crept silently from the kitchen.

He held up two glasses, each filled with a dark, amber liquid. "Here, drink some. It'll make you feel better."

Well, since she doubted that she could feel any worse . . . Miranda took the offered drink and downed the fiery contents in two deep gulps.

When she handed him the glass back, her hands weren't shaking any longer, but her gut seemed to be on fire.

He smiled at her and damn if the man didn't have the sexiest dimple she'd ever seen along his right cheek.

Get a grip. You're running on adrenaline and fumes right now. Stop lusting after the man next door.

Cain set the glasses down with a soft clink on a nearby table.

Miranda exhaled slowly. "I, um, didn't get a chance to thank you before." When Sam had appeared with his sirens wailing, there'd been no time at all to speak privately with Cain. It had been a mad rush of explanations, searches, and general chaos.

No, there'd been no time to thank Cain for saving her life. And there'd been no time to ask if he truly thought Paul Roberts was a vampire.

And what about Cain? For a while there, he'd been sporting teeth a hell of a lot sharper than the ones he showed now.

Hadn't he? She rubbed her brow, suddenly confused.

"You don't have to thank me." A deep rumble of sound, almost like a growl.

The man had the deepest, roughest voice she'd ever heard. One that made her toes curl and her thighs quiver.

Down, girl.

Her hormones were going crazy and her mind was turning into mush. Had to be the excitement of the night.

"I did what any man would have done."

She shook her head at that. "Uh, no." Miranda could still see the men locked in brutal combat. "I don't know many guys who would have kicked down a door to save me."

He caught her hand. Brought her fingers to his lips and pressed a kiss to the knuckles. "Then you don't know the right kind of men."

Oh, damn. Now her knees were shaking. And was he staring at her with hunger in those golden eyes?

He kissed her hand again, and for a second, she felt the warm brush of his tongue against her fingers. Miranda tensed. "I—I should be going to bed." *Alone.* Because while her hormones might be jumping on the adrenaline party, she wasn't about to go falling into bed with her neighbor. Even if he had quite probably saved her life.

And even if he was sexy as all hell.

And even if just the sight of him did have her whole body tightening with arousal.

She pulled her hand away from Cain's warm grasp and stepped toward the guest bedroom he'd shown her earlier.

"If that's what you want . . ." The words were soft.

For an instant, she imagined him following her into that dark room and stripping.

Miranda swallowed, felt the faint sting along her throat. "Thank you, Cain. Really." Her fingers wrapped around the doorframe.

He gave a faint nod.

Miranda turned away from him, stepping over the threshold.

"Just got one quick question for you, baby," he murmured, and the floor squeaked beneath his feet.

Glancing back over her shoulder, she waited.

His dark brows pulled down low over his eyes. "Why the hell were you out with a vampire?"

Her jaw dropped open. *Again with the vampire talk.*

"Those bastards are sick. You can't trust them, not one damn bit. Parasites. And they all fucking smell like the grave."

Her head shook, although she wasn't sure if she was denying his words or her own fears. "Paul isn't a—a vampire." There had to be another explanation for what happened. Because vampires weren't real. They were on TV. In the movies. In books. But they weren't real.

Some sicko with a blood fetish had attacked her. Simple as that. No vampire. No monster. No—

"Bullshit. That jerkoff was undead, and if I hadn't gotten to you, he would have drained you dry in less than five minutes."

Not a good image.

"Y—you're wrong—"

"Oh, he would have. I've seen the bodies his kind leave behind."

He was just trying to scare her.

And it's working. "Vampires don't exist." Said with more

certainty than she currently felt. The wounds on her neck seemed to burn.

Cain stared at her, then slowly shook his head. "Baby, just what do you think happened tonight?"

"I was attacked." Her shoulders straightened. "By someone very, very sick." She didn't want to think about the rest just then. Didn't want to think about the white flash of Cain's teeth or that terrible moment when she could have sworn that his nails lengthened into claws.

Because that couldn't have happened. *Could. Not.* She'd been stressed. Things had been moving fast. She'd been confused and—

And she didn't know what the hell was going on, but Miranda knew she was scared.

Maybe staying with Cain hadn't been the best idea.

Sanity had decided to raise its annoying head too late.

Cain growled. Stepped toward her. "That's the way you're gonna play it, huh?"

"I'm not *playing* anything." The words sounded false. Miranda had the sudden, stark feeling that she was standing on a precipice. And if she moved, if she stepped forward and saw what waited over that deadly edge, she'd fall and her life would change. Forever.

Cain's eyes were on her. Seeing far too much. "There's something I need to show you." Then he grabbed her hands and all but jerked her back into the bedroom.

"What are you doing?" She tried to dig in her heels but the man was strong. Crazy strong. Miranda remembered the almost effortless way he'd tossed Paul across the room. *Uh-oh.* Okay, so she hadn't imagined that part of the night.

He shoved open a white door. Stepped inside a bathroom. He freed her hands and hit the light switch, then he pushed her in front of the mirror. Cain caught her hair and pulled it back, exposing the savaged column of her throat. "Take a long, hard look."

She did. Scratches. Mottled skin.

And two tiny puncture wounds.

Her hands flattened against the sink and she rocked forward, straining to get a better view. She'd expected to see the imprint of a man's teeth. This was—

Oh, God, what the hell was this?

Two puncture wounds. Deep. Spaced about an inch and a half apart.

Just like a vampire bite in the movies.

He'd had fangs. Two-inch-long fangs.

She closed her eyes a moment. Saw that damn precipice again. Then felt her body being shoved right over the edge.

"Still think vampires don't exist?" Cain asked, his breath feathering over her right ear. Her eyes opened and met his in the mirror.

"They aren't supposed to be real," she whispered and felt a desperate pounding in her temples. Would this night never end? Cain's scent—man, slightly woodsy—wrapped around her. For a moment, she was tempted to lean back against him. To let her body melt into his.

Then he spoke. "Yeah, well, I've got a news flash for you. Vampires aren't the only creatures running around on this earth that 'aren't supposed to be real.'"

"I—I can't deal with this." She needed to think. *A vampire. A real blood-sucking, creature-of-the-night vampire.* And she'd picked him off the Internet for a date.

Her luck just *sucked.* Strike three for her in the romance department.

Miranda turned and stared up at Cain's hard features.

Good-looking, yes. Undeniably so. Sexy. With those gleaming eyes and that sinful mouth. But there was power there, too. In the lines of his face. In the strong brow, the square jaw.

His head lowered toward hers.

Her lips parted.

"You didn't know what he was, did you?"

"No." A whisper.

"A lamb to the slaughter," he muttered and his mouth tightened.

"What?"

His hands wrapped around her upper arms. She was pinned between him and the bathroom counter. He stepped closer, bringing his body flush against hers.

His *aroused* body. Miranda sucked in a sharp breath when she felt the heat of his erection pressing against her.

"You have to be more careful." His body felt good against hers. Right. His voice was soft when he said, "You never know what's out there, just waiting to take a bite out of you." His gaze dropped to her lips. "And you are so damn tempting."

"Cain—"

His lips took hers. The kiss was hot, wild. His tongue pushed past the entrance of her mouth, thrust against hers. She responded instantly, heat flaring through her body as her tongue met his.

He lifted her, settling her along the edge of the countertop, then his hands were on her thighs.

And still he kissed her. Tasted her.

His fingers curled around her thighs. Her sex began to quiver and her mouth became more demanding against his.

He spread her legs with his grip. Settled his hips in the cradle of her body, and Miranda arched toward him, feeling the hard length of his jeans-covered cock against her sex.

Talk about a temptation.

She wondered what it would be like to strip those jeans off him. To yank off her own pants and underwear. Flesh to flesh. Sex to sex.

Her fingers dug into his shoulders.

Cain ripped his mouth from hers. Stared down at her with blazing eyes. "I can smell your desire."

What? Was he—

"Your scent is fucking driving me wild. . . ." He kissed her again. Harder. With need and with a stark possession.

Her breasts pushed against his chest. The nipples were tight, pebble-hard. She wanted his hands on them. His mouth.

God, when was the last time she'd been this turned on by a kiss?

Certainly not with either of her two ex-fiancés. Or the handful of men she'd dated in the past year.

She was literally panting now. Squirming against him, her sex creaming.

And all the guy had done was kiss her.

But he was making her need so much. Building a fierce, wild lust within her.

His hands drifted up her thighs. Squeezed the flesh. Caressed. So close to the center of her need. So close. Just a few inches more—

Cain pulled away from her and Miranda could have snarled in frustration.

"You—shit, you don't want this now."

Her body did.

"You've been through hell tonight." His hands clenched, and Miranda noticed that his face looked a little different. Tighter. Sharper.

"I shouldn't have kissed you, not now."

But she'd wanted him to, and she was woman enough to admit it. "You—you don't have to apologize." She'd wanted his mouth on her, still did. But with his withdrawal, that damn sanity—and its friend control—were coming back.

His gaze bored into hers. "There's something here, between us. Make no mistake about it."

A nod was her only reply because Miranda didn't trust herself to speak just then.

"Things aren't ending here. They're just starting." Those golden eyes raked down her body and she saw the lust that flared in his gaze. "And you should know that I always finish what I start."

Good to know. Her heart was drumming too hard and way too fast against her chest. Her fingers clamped over the edge of the countertop. The urge to reach out to him was strong, but now wasn't the time.

Not yet.

"Get some sleep." He turned toward the door, hesitated. "If you need me—"

Oh, but she did.

"—for anything, I'm just down the hallway."

He'd be waiting in bed.

She exhaled heavily.

Then he was gone and Miranda was left alone with the hunger he'd stirred within her.

He smelled her as he slept. The sweet, tantalizing scent of female flesh. The rich temptation of her sex's cream.

He'd had her within his grasp. Moaning. Twisting against him. Breasts close enough to kiss. Sex close enough to touch.

And he'd let her go.

With his eyes still closed, Cain reached out and caught the sheets in his hands. A faint ripping filled the air and he swore, knowing that his claws had slashed the fabric.

But his control was weak. Because *she* was so close. And because despite the performance he'd given earlier, he sure wasn't a gentleman.

He was much more of a taker and he definitely wanted to take Miranda.

The perfume of honeysuckle and woman grew stronger in the air. Cain tensed.

Then he heard the soft creak of the wooden floor.

His cock, already half-erect, begin to swell in anticipation.

She was coming to him.

He'd tossed and turned for hours thinking of her, caught in a world of fantasies and feverish dreams and *she was coming to him.*

His eyes opened. He could see her perfectly even in the darkness of the room. She stood silhouetted in the doorway, clad in one of his oversized white T-shirts. Her legs were bare.

That would make things infinitely easier.

"Cain . . ." A whisper, the sound hesitant and . . . afraid?

He sat up slowly, drawing in more of her scent with a deep breath.

"I have to . . ." A step closer. "I have to know . . ." More slow movements across the floor.

The bedsheets were around his hips. Hiding his arousal, for the moment.

Cain reached over, flipped on the bedside light. For her benefit, not his.

She blinked, hesitated a moment at the flood of light. Then she inched toward him, stopping at the side of the bed. Her wide eyes gazed down at him. "When you first came into my house, you—you looked different."

Hell. He'd known this would come, sooner or later. Cain had just been hoping for much, much later because when she learned the full truth about him, his fantasies would die a quick death.

An animal. *Women like her don't go for animals.* The vampire had been right about that one.

"I didn't imagine it, did I?" Not as much hesitation now, more determination. "Your eyes—they glowed. Your teeth were sharper." She reached for his hand, fumbled a bit, then caught his fingers. "And you—you had claws."

The shock had worn off. While he'd been lusting, she'd obviously been in there replaying the whole night and coming to the conclusion that he—

She released his hand. "You're not a human, are you, Cain Lawson?"

No sense in lying. He stared up at her and let the beast glow from his eyes. "No, baby, I'm not."

Three

"Miranda, honey, there's, uh, something you need to know." Sam Michaels stared at her with a worried, slightly hangdog look on his face that immediately had her shifting uncomfortably in the worn leather chair.

It was just past eight a.m. on Saturday, and she was truly not in the mood to go around and start learning more things that she *needed* to know. After last night, she'd learned more than enough about the world.

Once Cain had made his confession, and his eyes had started to *glow*, for God's sake, she'd turned carefully on her heel and walked from his room. Her knees had trembled like crazy and she'd sworn that she'd tasted sawdust on her tongue.

But maybe that had just been fear.

She'd locked her bedroom door. Then lodged the desk chair under the doorknob.

Cain hadn't so much as tried to follow her.

And when she'd woken up and her gaze had fallen on that chair, she'd felt a flash of shame.

The man had saved her life. He deserved better than for her to run from him and hide.

"Uh, Miranda? You listening to me?"

She shook her head because, no, she had no idea what Sam

had just been muttering about. Cain was in the lobby of the sheriff's station, pacing like a caged animal, and she wanted to go to him.

And apologize.

So the guy wasn't human. She wasn't perfect, either. And—

"Paul Roberts is dead."

Now she was listening to him. "What? What happened? Did one of the deputies—"

A long, hard sigh. "He died five years ago. Killed in some kind of animal attack." He leaned forward in his desk chair.

"That's not possible, he's—" *A vampire.* Wait. Vampires were dead. No, undead. Cain had said that. He'd said—

"Good thing the bastard's dead, too," Sam continued, scratching the top of his head. "The guy had a rap sheet a mile long and a serious appetite for hurting women." His brows beetled. "He liked to cut 'em."

She could certainly pick winners.

"I don't know who that guy really was last night, but he was *not* Paul Roberts."

Was that supposed to make her feel better? Miranda's feet dug into the worn carpet. "So Paul Roberts, he's in the system?" The database, whatever the hell the cops and deputies called the computer link that showed all the criminals and their records.

A nod.

"With a picture?" She pressed.

His hands skated across the desk. "I've got a picture right here."

"I want to see it."

Sam pursed his lips but opened the file and pushed the photo across his desk.

Miranda looked down and saw the face of the man who'd bitten her the night before. Blue eyes. Long, straight nose. High cheekbones. Chin that was a little weak. Dark hair a bit longer than it was now, but—

Definitely the same man. "Could you, um, could you call Cain in here, please?"

"Ah, sure." He pressed a button on the phone and asked the clerk out front to show Cain inside.

They were sitting in the sheriff's office. Sheriff McMillan was out of town. He'd gone fishing in Biloxi, and since Sam was the undersheriff, the second-highest officer in Melvin County, he was holding down the fort.

Less than a minute later, Cain marched inside. Miranda felt the lancing heat of his stare. She looked up and met his look directly. "Paul Roberts is dead."

He didn't look particularly surprised.

"According to Sam, he's been in the grave the past five years."

Again, no surprise. Not so much as a flicker of an eyelash.

Sam said, "Miranda's told me she met this guy on the Internet—"

Now one black eyebrow did lift.

"—she never saw his ID, so it's safe to say the guy gave her a false name. And the SUV we towed from her place, well, it had been stolen two days before, so we got no help on ID from that end."

She lifted up the photo. "Want to see the real Paul Roberts?" Her fingers shook just a bit.

He took the photo. Scanned it. Glanced back at her. Waited.

"Interesting, huh?" she whispered.

"Very." He dropped the photo onto the desk.

Sam cleared his throat. "I actually think that Miranda got very, very lucky last night."

Her focus jumped to him. "What do you mean?" Yeah, she felt damn lucky the bastard hadn't drained her dry but—

"Three women in Florida have been murdered over the last three months. All with their throats slit." A pause and his expression tensed. "And all the women told their friends they'd recently met a 'Paul' online."

Chill bumps rose on Miranda's arms. "Are you telling me the guy I was out with last night is some kind of-of—"

He held up his hands. Glanced from her to a silent Cain. "All I'm saying is the situation fits the MO. I'm gonna be calling the FBI later today, briefing them on what happened. But, to me, well, like I said, I feel like you got damn lucky."

The phone on the desk rang with a shrill cry. Sam frowned and picked it up. "Michaels. What? Hell. Yeah, yeah, I'll be right there." He slammed down the receiver. "Jack Thompson pulled another all-night drinking binge and just tried to break into his ex-wife's house. He's pissed and disorderly as hell. I got to help the boys process 'im."

Miranda nodded, feeling more than a little numb.

"I'll be right back." He stalked from the room.

She rose to her feet, lifted her chin, and walked closer to Cain. "About last night—"

"Forget it," he snapped, and a muscle flexed along his jaw. "We've got more important matters to deal with now. So you think I'm some kind of freak—"

She caught his hand. "I—I don't."

His nostrils flared and she saw his pupils dilate. "I wouldn't do that if I were you. When you touch me, it makes the thing inside me hungry."

He was trying to scare her. But from the sound of things, she'd almost been prey to a vampire serial killer, and Cain was probably the only reason she'd escaped.

Her fingers tightened around him. "I shouldn't have left you last night."

"If you hadn't, I'd have taken you." Stark. Predatory.

Her heart did a hard thud against her chest.

"I want you, Miranda Shaw, and I'm not one of your human men. Don't make the mistake of thinking I am. I don't play by their rules, and when I want something, I reach out"— his left hand lifted, caught her chin—"and I take it."

He wasn't dealing with the same woman he'd faced last night. She'd been at the end of her rope then. So his words now didn't scare her.

But they did turn her on.

"I didn't know how you felt." He'd given no indication of his attraction before. She hadn't even realized he'd wanted her until his lips had been on hers and she'd felt the heavy length of his erection pressing against her.

Hard to mistake those signs.

"Now you do."

Yes. "Cain, I—"

He exhaled and stepped away from her, muttering, "Damn but you smell too sweet."

That was good, right? Or was it—

She wanted to catch his hand again. To touch him. But time was running out, and though she wanted to make amends to him, now, well, *now* she needed his help.

Before Sam returned.

"The man last night," she began.

"The *vampire*," he corrected, voice sardonic.

"Fine. Whatever. That guy, he's a killer."

His head moved in the faintest of agreements.

"Sam isn't going to believe me if I tell him the truth about what happened."

"Humans rarely understand just what the word 'truth' means."

Not the most helpful of answers. She sighed. Miranda knew she couldn't just walk away from this case now. And she knew that he was the one with the creature-feature knowledge. "What do we do?"

Three women. Three months. She would have been victim number four. And she didn't believe for a moment that Paul Roberts was just going to walk off into the sunset and never kill again.

Last night the devil had been in his eyes, and evil that strong didn't just stop its blood quest.

She couldn't stand by and wait while another woman was killed. "We can't let this guy get away," she said, when he didn't speak. "There has to be a way to stop him."

He laughed, the sound too hard. "Ah, baby, let me clue you in to a few facts."

She bit back the sharp retort that sprang to her lips.

Cain jerked his head toward the closed door. "I'd say, in less than five minutes, a team of suits will be arriving at the station. Your Sam won't have to contact the FBI, they'll have monitored the call systems for this station—they do that for all the offices—and they'll know what happened."

Her palms were sweating. "They'll go after Paul?"

"They go after killers like him every day." A shrug. "Sometimes they catch them—well, they catch the human psychos—and sometimes, when the killer is . . . different, like your friend Paul, well, then they are pretty much just shit out of luck."

"So you're telling me this jerk is going to get away?" And get to keep killing?

He shook his head. "I'm telling you, the boys and girls in the suits are going to lock you up for the next few weeks—"

"*What?*" She was the victim, not—

"Sam isn't as clueless as he appears. I think he was right about the killings, and the FBI will, too. Hell, there have probably been more murders, scattered around the country. No way has our vamp been playing nice the last few years. The agents, they'll want to keep you safe until they're sure Paul isn't coming after you again."

Now that gave her pause. "Will he?"

He didn't answer, but Miranda supposed his silence actually *was* an answer. Oh, damn.

"Go with them. They'll keep you safe, and Paul—"

"Will what? Move on to another victim?" She'd be all safe and protected by the Bureau while some other poor woman had her throat ripped open by razor-sharp fangs. No, that didn't sound fair. Not at all.

Her chin lifted. "Why can't they catch him?"

"Because vampires are damn strong, far stronger than humans. And bullets, well, they can wound vamps—not kill 'em—and usually they only serve to piss off his kind."

Cain sure seemed to know what he was talking about. Both with the vampire and with the FBI.

"I can't let him hurt anyone else," she whispered.

His eyes narrowed. "You might not have a choice on that, baby."

"There's always a choice."

"Don't be too—Shit." He stiffened. "They're here."

How did he know? What was—

His lips hitched into a half-smile. "Stop applying human rules to me, Miranda. I heard 'em when they entered the building."

Superhearing, check. She'd have to remember that little perk.

And she'd have to find out just what, exactly, Cain was. Not a vampire, there was too much hate in his voice when he talked about the undead.

Cain didn't particularly seem the self-hating type.

"They'll take care of you," he said, "just—"

"I'm not going with them." No way was she going to disappear with a bunch of strangers. Her summer vacation had just started last week, and she wasn't about to lose her carefully ordered life because of one nightmarish evening.

"Choices, remember?" she said softly. She was about to make hers, but she needed him. "Help me, Cain. I know you can. You know about vampires. How they're strong, how they're weak." They had to have some kind of weakness, right? "We can do something, I don't know, go after him. Stop that bastard from hurting anyone else."

His eyes narrowed. "You'd risk yourself?"

"I—"

The door was pushed open.

"Look, dammit, I said you can't go in there! I don't care who you are—" Sam's voice blared angrily.

Two men in immaculate black suits stepped over the threshold. One was darkly tanned, short, and stocky, with a long scar bisecting his left eyebrow and sliding down his cheek. The other guy was about average height, pale, with a thin, slightly haggard face.

When he caught sight of Cain, the scarred fellow seemed to

stiffen. But his partner directed all of his attention to Miranda, saying, "Ms. Shaw, I'm Donovan Delaney from the Federal Bureau of Investigation. It's come to our attention that you've been the victim of—"

"Cut it, Donovan Delaney," Cain said, rolling his shoulders. "She's not in the mood to hide."

The scarred guy cursed softly. "One of yours, is she, Lawson?"

This guy knew Cain?

That same twisted smile was on his lips as he glanced her way and said, "Miranda, baby, did I happen to mention that I just recently, ah, retired from the good old FBI?"

Uh, no, he'd forgotten that lovely little tidbit. "You retired? What are you, thirty-five?"

Cain's lips twisted in a brief glimmer of amusement. "Just about, and it wasn't your typical retirement." His stare returned to the men and the amusement vanished. "And yeah, for the record, she's most definitely *mine*. She's not your bait. Not your hostage. If we work this case, we work with *my* rules, and we make Miranda's life the priority."

Okay. So he was talking like he was the boss and damn if the scarred agent wasn't nodding his head in *agreement* while Sam stared at Cain with widening eyes.

"We're gonna have to get the okay from above," the shorter guy stopped nodding long enough to say. "It's gonna be shit with paperwork because you pulled out already—"

"Make the calls, Santiago. This case is *mine*."

Delaney swallowed a few times, glanced back and forth between the guy identified as Santiago and Cain, then muttered, "Look, buddy, you might have worked the crimes before but—"

"You're not point on this one," Santiago said softly. "And trust me, kid, you're playing out of your league if Lawson's already involved."

Delaney flushed.

"You'll be backup here," Santiago told the guy. "Cain and I will be lead."

Ah, so he was the senior agent. Miranda was trying to follow things but she still felt like she'd stepped into the Twilight Zone.

"You're not going to get approval for—"

"I'll get approval." Santiago's lips thinned. "Wish I wouldn't, but I will."

Cain grunted and shrugged his powerful shoulders. "All right, now that we all know it's a new game, this is how it's going to work." He crossed his arms over his chest. "The rules are simple, really. I hunt, *my* way. And I won't stop until this bastard is brought down."

"You back with us 100 percent, Lawson?" Santiago asked.

"No." A pause. "I'm with her."

And he was going to fight a vampire for her, again.

Talk about knowing how to sweep a girl off her feet.

"Miranda knows this guy," Cain continued. "She lured him out once, and I'd bet a week of your pay, Delaney, that she can lure him again."

Santiago rubbed the bridge of his nose. "Okay, then it's your game, *gato grande*."

Miranda blinked. Her Spanish was way rusty, but she was pretty sure the agent had just called Cain a big cat.

Cain smiled. "Then let's start the hunt."

Four

She was lying in her bed. The front door had been fully repaired. An FBI agent was sitting in his car outside, and Cain was asleep on her couch.

It was after midnight. Miranda *should* have been asleep hours ago. But her mind wouldn't shut down.

Cain was too close.

Her body felt too tight, too hot. She kept thinking about the feel of his lips on hers. The touch of his hands.

Cain was too close.

And not nearly close enough.

Miranda shoved off the covers. Threw her legs over the side of the bed. Enough of this crap. Time to settle things between the two of them.

She turned on her bedside lamp and the glow of the light spilled into the room.

Miranda thought she was being pretty quiet. The thick carpet muffled her steps as she crept down the hallway. She turned the corner and—

"You know, these late-night visits are starting to become a habit for you," he said from the darkness, his voice a deep growl of sound.

Miranda hesitated. She couldn't see him. Could barely see

anything. She inched forward, found a small lamp, turned it on with a snap.

Cain was on the couch. Hair disheveled, as if he'd run his fingers through the dark locks. Eyes gleaming. Muscled chest bare. There was no sheet over his body as there had been last night. Instead, he wore a pair of black boxers and nothing else.

Miranda gulped. The man looked *good*. "We, ah, need to talk." Her sex quivered a bit as she stared at him. *Damn good.*

One black brow rose. "Is that really why you walked so softly all the way in here? To talk?"

"You could hear me?" He'd said he had good hearing, but she'd tried to be so careful and quiet.

A slow nod. "Yeah, but more than that..." His nostrils flared just a bit. "I could smell you." He smiled at her, showing a lot of teeth. "And like I said before, baby, you sure you came here to talk?"

I could smell you. Understanding dawned. Cain knew she was aroused. Her cheeks burned, but she didn't flinch. "I wanted to thank you."

If possible, the smile widened even more, revealing the curve of his dimple. "Ah, my thank-you kiss. And here I was thinking I wouldn't be getting another one from you." His voice flattened as he said, "What with my being a monster and you being such a good little human."

Okay, he was still pissed. "I shouldn't have left last night."

A shrug. And for a second, a flash of—hurt? pain?—appeared in his eyes but vanished when he slowly blinked. "Hey, I'm the big, bad bogeyman. You were smart to run from me."

No, she hadn't been. "Shifter." She said the word softly, testing it.

His smile vanished.

"That's what the vampire called you." And just what the hell was a shifter?

"Yeah, well, I guess your date had come up against my kind before." He held up his hands, and claws, fiercely sharp and long, had replaced his fingernails. "These are usually a pretty good giveaway, as are the teeth." His lips pulled back to show just a glimpse of fang.

He was trying to scare her. Miranda kept her chin up and took a step forward.

Cain dropped his hands. "Demons can sprout claws, too, but your vamp must have known that—"

"Uh, demons?" Just how many supernatural creatures were there?

"Yeah, demons." He whistled softly. "Lots of 'em walking the streets. Using glamour to blend in with the humans. And those bastards can get pretty strong, especially the level tens." A pause. "Not all of the demons are real threats, though. The weak ones, level ones or twos, hell, they can't cause much damage at all."

Right. Good to know.

Demons. He'd just told her that demons were real. She shook her head, tried to focus. "How many . . ." She licked her lips, swallowed, and asked, "How many of your kind are out there?" Another tentative step forward. His nostrils widened.

"There are hundreds of thousands of shifters. Men and women who can change into animals. Small. Big. Deadly. Course, then there are the charmers, the djinn, the—"

Her hand lifted. "Charmers?"

"The ones who talk to animals."

She blinked. "The djinn? Would that be like—what? Genies?"

"Something like that. But it sure takes a hell of a lot more than some old dusty bottle to contain their power."

Okay, too much information. Her head was seriously starting to spin. "How can they all be real?" Hushed words. It was too wild, too—

"I'm real." A shrug. "They're real, too. And the ones I've told you about, well, that's just the tip of the supernatural iceberg."

And she was the *Titanic*, going down, fast. Miranda took a deep breath. She needed to focus. At that moment, she didn't want to find out about every supernatural creature that was strolling around the earth.

She wanted to know about Cain. "A shifter," she repeated quietly, turning the topic back to him. She'd already seen his face change a bit. "What kind of animal do you become?" When he'd attacked the vampire, he'd looked positively predatory. His cheekbones had sharpened. Eyes glowed. "A wolf?" Jesus, like a werewolf?

He threw back his head and laughed at that. "Ah, baby, relax. I'm not one of those psychotics."

So the wolves were psychotic. Nice mental note for her. She took another step toward him. Her body hovered over the couch now. Just a foot or two away from him. Cain was close enough to touch.

And she did want to touch.

Her gaze swept down his body. Over the sculpted muscles of his chest. Down the rock-hard abs. Over the material of his boxers, material that was stretched tight to accommodate his thick arousal.

Her nipples tightened as a wave of yearning swept through her. She'd felt that arousal last night, but the barrier of the clothes had been between them, as it was now.

Miranda didn't want anything between them.

"You looking to walk on the wild side tonight?" His voice snapped like a whip.

Her stare jerked back to his. Found him glaring at her. "Cain . . ."

"You come out here, wearing a shirt that's so thin it shows your nipples, your sex smelling so good that it makes me ache, and then you look at me like you could eat me alive."

Because she could. Or she wanted to try.

Hell, she was scared. Not of him, but of the world she was suddenly discovering around her.

Yet more than her fear, she *needed*.

Yearned. For him.

Shifter.

"Go back to your room," he ordered, and she saw his fingers dig into the cushions of the couch. "It's not time to play with the animals."

Okay, now he was pissing her off. She reached out, touched that golden skin, and trailed her fingers down his chest. "I don't see an animal. Just a man." The sexiest man she'd ever come across. A man who had her aching inside.

"I'm both, Miranda. Don't ever make the mistake of thinking I'm not."

A warning, clear and simple. One that she was going to ignore.

She lowered her body over his, placing her thighs on either side of his legs so that she could straddle him. The position put her face close to his and had her sex brushing against the hard cradle of his erection.

She curled both of her hands over his shoulders. Jeez, the man was warm. "I've been in my room, thinking about you." But he knew that. He knew she wanted him. Miranda brushed her lips over his. "Have you been thinking about me?"

He moved in a blur. Cain lifted her, spun around, and before Miranda could even gasp out a breath, she found herself flat on the cushions of the couch. Cain leaned over her, his face hard and lust shining in his eyes. "Don't fucking tease me. If you yank a cat's tail, you will get bitten." His teeth came together with a snap.

"I've already been bitten once," she said, rising up on her elbows. "Wasn't to my liking."

"You weren't bitten by *me*." Then his mouth was on hers. Tongue thrusting. Lips pressing. Taking. Devouring.

And the lust she'd felt all night went from a flame to a blaze.

She met the kiss full force, loving the slightly wild taste of the man. Her mouth was frantic on his, demanding—a perfect match for his kiss.

When his head lifted, when his eyes gazed down at her with that soft shine, she knew what was coming even before he spoke.

"Your choice."

She'd made her choice.

"You can run back to your room, lock the door again, and forget about tangling with someone like me." His head lowered toward the crook of her neck and he inhaled deeply, drawing in a long gulp of air as he caught her scent. "Or you can stay, and I'll take you, and show you just how powerful sex with a shifter can be."

Like she was going to be able to walk away from that offer.

Grandma Belle hadn't raised a fool.

Her fingers trailed over his chest. Paused over his heart, feeling the hard and fast rhythm beneath her hand. "I'm not running anywhere, not tonight." She was exactly where she wanted to be.

Tonight she was with the right man. Her body knew it. It was responding completely to him. Softening, moistening. Her breasts aching. Hips arching. Readying.

For him.

Only him.

The smile that twisted his lips could only be called feral. "You were warned, baby." Then he lifted his hand, eased it between their bodies, and with one swipe of his fingertip—no, *his claw*—he cut the T-shirt she'd been wearing in half. The edges slid open, and her breasts tightened at the sudden rush of air.

"So damn pretty. Pink and round, just waiting for my mouth." His breath feathered over her sensitive flesh seconds before his lips closed over her right nipple. His mouth was warm, wet, and he knew just how to stroke her with his lips and his tongue. Soft caresses. Hard licks. A suckle that had her back arching and her breath hissing out.

"Taste so sweet. Just like you smell. Honeysuckle." His mouth locked on her other breast. Showed it the same sensual care. Licks. Kisses. The faintest sting of a bite.

You weren't bitten by me.

Now she had been. Oh, God, she had been.

He eased down her body, making a trail with his mouth and tongue. His sensual caresses made her ache with need.

Her sex was wet, and Miranda was so eager that her body trembled.

Her drawstring shorts were shoved out of the way. By her, by him, she couldn't really tell for certain. Then he was touching the crotch of her panties. Feeling the warm cream that coated the fabric.

Then he ripped the panties away.

His fingers closed over her thighs, a move reminiscent of the night before. She parted her legs quickly for him, wanting to feel that hard ridge of flesh against her sex again. But he needed to ditch his boxers. She wanted to feel him, skin to skin and—

He touched the hungry flesh between her legs. Not with his cock, but with his fingers. He parted her folds. Strummed his fingers over her clit. "Miranda . . ." His voice was a velvet growl in the darkness. "Your scent is *driving me crazy.*"

Then he was on the floor. Crouching on his knees. One hand wrapped tight around her thigh. The other explored the secrets of her sex. His head hovered over her stomach. The dark locks of his hair were close enough to touch and—

His mouth brushed against her sex. His tongue laved her, licking away the cream that coated her flesh, then driving deep inside her in one hard plunge.

Her fingers sank into his hair and her hips slammed up to meet his hot kiss. Moans rose in her throat, because what he was doing, *it felt so good.* His tongue retreated. Teased. Drove inside.

Her sex tightened. Her orgasm threatened. So close. The promise of pleasure was just a few seconds away.

Damn but the man was one good lover. Certainly the best at—

Another lick from that skilled tongue. A caress of his hands, fingers harder now, more demanding as her body struggled for her peak.

It had been so long for her. Over six months since she'd kicked Peter out—

Cain's tongue drove deep and Miranda shattered, seemed to literally fall apart, as a blast of pleasure rocked through her.

The tremors still shook her sex when he rose above her. Cain was on his knees and he jerked her body to the end of the couch. He fumbled, reaching for the jeans that were on the floor. A sharp *rip* of sound filled the air. Then he was moving again, and pressing the tip of that thick cock between her legs.

"Hold on," he ordered, voice barely recognizable as a man's.

The beast had to be close.

No fear. Not now.

Only hot pleasure.

Her legs wrapped around his hips.

His cock slammed deep, a driving thrust that intensified the soft aftershocks of release vibrating through her. His fingers clenched around her hips and he lifted her up, plunging deep again and again in a rhythm that became increasingly wild.

And she loved it. Every frantic second. His jaw was clenched. Those eyes of his shining bright with that powerful inner light. She caught a glimpse of his fangs, but instead of frightening her, the sight caused a lick of heat to burst inside of her.

More than a man. So much more.

Cain angled her body so that with every thrust of his cock, he brushed over the tight nub of her desire. The pleasure built again. The need grew just as desperate as before and suddenly she was the one clawing at his arms. Moaning. Thrashing beneath him.

He made a low sound in his throat, one that she couldn't quite discern. His head dropped to her chest and he licked her breasts. Rough flicks of his tongue that made her nipples tingle with arousal.

His tongue. Wet. Strong.

Damn good.

His mouth trailed up to her shoulder.

And Cain pressed his teeth against her flesh. Not too hard, oh, God, no, not like the vampire, but *just right*.

Her body buckled as she came beneath him.

The light in his eyes burned brighter. His cheeks hollowed and she felt the faint scrape of his claws against her hips.

His hips jerked as her sex milked his thick flesh with the contractions of her climax. Then he was coming, holding her with a grip of steel and driving straight to her womb. Cain shuddered against her, threw back his head, and managed to grit out her name.

The release held them in a tight grip. Time passed. She didn't know how long she lay half on that couch, body replete, mouth dry, legs limp.

Cain looked down at her and she could see the glow of his beast begin to slowly fade. He smiled at her, then lowered his head toward her. His mouth hesitated over hers, and he licked her lips, a heated caress that took her by surprise. Then he dropped his head toward the side of her neck, and he nuzzled her lightly.

Her arms, which had fallen from his body, now rose again and she looped them around his back, liking this moment. The warmth. The touches.

His breath feathered over her skin. "Tell me . . ." A soft press of his lips against her neck, almost as if he were kissing her tender wounds. "Why in the hell is a woman like you looking for men on the Internet?"

The question, coming right after the truly fabulous sex, threw her off.

He pushed up, bracing on his palms. "Are the men in this city just shit crazy? You're the sexiest thing I've ever seen in my life."

Her lips parted in surprise. Okay. The man was going to get serious points for post-sex flattery. "Meeting men isn't, ah, really the problem." Cherryville wasn't exactly overflowing with studs, but she could find dates. The problem was . . . "I was hoping to meet someone, um, different."

That black brow of his rose. "Baby, you did that." His hips pressed down against her in a soft thrust. "And if you wanted different, well, I was right next door."

But she'd already agreed to the date with Paul before she'd met Cain. She'd thought about canceling with him once she started fantasizing about her neighbor, and now she sure wished she'd gone with that impulse.

His lips brushed over hers, then he eased away from her, pulling his still-firm flesh from her body.

Dammit.

"I'll be right back." He tossed her a hard look over his shoulder. "And then you'll finish telling me why you were surfing the Web and wound up with the vamp." He headed toward the guest bath, and Miranda took a deep breath, inhaling the scent of sex in the air.

Damn, but that had been good. Better than good. Her body ached, but it was a fine, satisfied feeling like—

"So finish talking, Miranda."

She jerked at his voice. Too close. Jeez, the man moved fast. Her eyes narrowed as she stared up at him. The guy was sure soft on those big feet of his. "I—ah—" She caught sight of his perfect abs and, momentarily lost her train of thought.

"Miranda?"

"Tired of jerks," she muttered, dragging her gaze away from the tempting abs. "My fiancés were—"

He froze in front of her.

"Uh, Cain?"

Slowly, he held up a hand and wound up looking like some kind of sexy naked statue. "Hold that. Did you just say 'fiancés'?"

"Um." But Ryan and Peter really weren't important. No, the important thing was to get Cain closer so that they could go a second round.

The statue came back to full life as he snagged her hand and crowded her back against the couch. "Just how many fiancés have you had?" There were sparks in his eyes.

"Two." The sparks burned a little brighter. Miranda shook her head. "Look, Ryan and I got together right after college. Honestly, I think I liked the guy's bike more than I liked him."

He'd driven one prime Harley. "The engagement ended almost as soon as it started."

"And the other guy?" His voice was expressionless, but that fire still simmered in his gaze.

"Peter." She said his name on a sigh. "Big mistake." She'd let him move in with her. "Peter didn't want a fiancée so much as he wanted a free ride through life, and let's just say that I got tired of paying." Two losers, but there had been more.

"Do you still love him?"

"Oh, God, no!" The words burst from her. Miranda shook her head. "I don't even try to think about the guy if I can help it." A close escape, that's what she'd had. "I was online because I wanted to find someone different. And it's not like I'm the only one out there looking for—for—" Miranda cleared her throat. "Well, you know." Actually, her partner teacher, Sally Jennings, had been the one to encourage her to create a profile.

Sally had met her husband, Ted, online just over a year ago. Not a vampire. Ted was a perfectly normal, handsome accountant.

Some women just had good luck.

And some women just got dates with devils.

"You're not going to be looking for 'you know' anymore." Cain's voice was firm. The drawl she liked so much trickled through his words.

A smile curved her lips. Okay. Maybe she wasn't quite as unlucky as she'd thought before. "No, I'm not." Miranda pressed her finger lightly against the middle of Cain's chest. "I've got what I need."

His jaw tightened. "I mean it, Miranda. I'm not the sharing type."

"Neither am I." Best to get things clear from the start. "When I'm with a man, I don't cheat, and I expect the same promise from my lover." Not that she'd had a ton of lovers, but she wasn't exactly Snow White, either.

"I don't want anyone else." Stark. "Just you." Said with more than a hint of possession.

Miranda swallowed and held his bright stare. No one had ever looked at her quite that way before. With such demanding need. A stark hunger.

Her heart did a fast kick and started drumming in a double-time rhythm. "And I want you." Her finger trailed down his chest, headed for those absolutely perfect abs—

A gunshot rang out, the loud blast piercing the quiet of the moment and sending a spike of adrenaline through her blood.

In the next second, Miranda was on the floor, and Cain's naked body was covering hers. He waited a beat, two, then slowly lifted his head. All signs of the replete lover had vanished. Now, a hunter looked out from those golden eyes.

"Cain . . ." Her thoughts were flying. The FBI agent. He must have fired. Oh, God, was he okay?

"Stay inside *and away from the windows.*" A growl. An order.

She'd never really been the order-taking type, but when gunshots were involved, that changed things for her.

Cain headed for the door.

Her jaw dropped. *What the hell?* He was running outside without even taking a weapon? The guy was ex-Bureau; he should know well enough to take a weapon with him into a gunfight! And the man was naked!

Miranda slithered across the room, making damn sure she didn't present a target. She jerked on her shorts. Realized her shirt was damaged beyond repair. "Shit." She crawled five feet, snagged her jacket from the back of a chair, managed to zip it up, fast. "Dammit, give me a minute—"

Too late.

Cain jerked open the door and disappeared into the night.

The coppery scent of blood filled his nostrils. It was a smell he'd become intimately familiar with over the years, and one that had the beast inside yanking against his leash.

Cain launched off the porch steps, feeling the beast rage inside his body. That blood wasn't a human's. It had a slightly stale scent. Cloying.

Vampire.

He knew who his enemy was, and he knew he couldn't go against the bastard in human form.

Running low to the ground, he headed for the cover of the nearby woods. Then he let the beast free.

The power of the change swept through him, the burn sending him falling onto all fours.

Bones snapped. Twisted. Fur burst through his skin. His vision sharpened. His mouth burned as his teeth lengthened. Hands became paws. Fingernails razor-sharp claws.

The man disappeared in a frenzy of teeth and growls, and the black beast took his place, tail snapping in the air, paws digging into the dirt.

Cain had a moment to hope that Miranda heeded his order and stayed inside the house. He didn't want her out in the open, not with the vampire around. And he didn't want her to see him in his animal form. Not yet.

He'd reached paradise with her moments before, and he wasn't ready to give that up because she had to face the reality of his existence.

His hind legs pushed back against the ground, and he sprang forward, following that heavy scent deeper into the woods. He bounded easily over the earth, strength pulsing through him. Every smell was ten times stronger and every sound from the woods was heightened. He could hear the croak of the frogs. The whistle of leaves. The soft crunch of the earth beneath Agent Santiago's feet.

Cain jumped, caught the lower limbs of a tree, and climbed up easily, his thick claws digging into the wood. He could see the agent from his perch. His gun was up, aimed at the darkness beyond.

The agent's heart was racing too fast, the telling thud reached his ears, and Cain could smell Santiago's sweat.

The agent was hunting. Just as he was.

He eased farther along the limb. Jumped agilely to the next tree. His tail thumped against the branch.

A swift pounding had his head jerking to the left. Footsteps. Fleeing. His nostrils widened, drawing in all the scents of the woods. *The blood path was that way.*

The vampire was on the run.

Santiago had succeeded in wounding him, but at the rate he was going, he'd never be able to bring the guy down.

Even a wounded vampire was a damn fast vampire.

And a very, very dangerous prey to stalk.

Time to take over.

He leapt from the tree, landing lightly on his feet. He'd worked with Santiago more than a few times in the past, and the other man knew his secret. A select few in the Bureau did, and those men had sworn to carry the truth of his nature to the grave.

They'd used him on cases. Ruthlessly. Sometimes it took the devil to bring down the killers. Especially when those killers couldn't be stopped by normal means.

But they'd given their word to keep the truth of his nature quiet, and they all knew if they betrayed him, well, they'd have to face the beast.

He advanced quickly on Santiago, covering the ground easily. The guy had never been too fast on the trigger in the past, but Cain didn't want to take any chances. He growled low, then let out the series of grunts he knew the human would recognize.

Santiago had whirled at the first growl, but Cain saw his shoulders relax the faintest bit. Then the agent nodded and lowered his weapon.

Cain sprang past him, the thrill of the hunt making him salivate at the prospect of catching the vamp's throat between his teeth.

The ground disappeared beneath his feet in a blur. The blood tickled his nose, the scent growing stronger, and his whiskers twitched.

The land here wasn't suited to man. The thick brush of the woods would soon give way to the swamp and marsh. The vampire would have a hell of a time finding his way out of the swamp, even with his enhanced vision and smell.

There was a shift in the wind then. The faintest of moves in the distance that had Cain freezing in mid-crouch.

The vampire was turning. Cain waited a moment, understanding. The bastard was circling back, probably realizing his mistake in fleeing toward the swamp.

Oh, but he would catch him. Cain knew his black fur was perfectly camouflaged by the night. His movements were so careful that the vampire wouldn't be able to hear him until it was too late.

Such was the fate of all his prey.

The vampire would regret coming back for another attack.

He crept forward, head low, back arching. *There.* To the left, in that thicket, he knew the bastard was waiting.

His muscles tensed. There was damn good reason the Indians had once given his kind a name that meant "the killer that takes its prey in a single bound." Most never even had the chance to scream before he took them down.

Cain launched forward, claws out, jaw open.

And found the vampire waiting with a gun.

Dammit. Apparently, the bastard was smarter than most of his brethren. And prepared for him.

The vamp fired just as Cain jerked away. The bullet blasted across his side, leaving a trail of fire burning into his flesh.

Not silver, thank God. Though the myths said silver only worked on the wolves, the true fact was that silver could poison most shifters.

A fact the vampire bastard apparently didn't know.

Cain bounded across the bushes, hurrying for cover. The blazing pain combined with his rage, and a snarl burst from his mouth before he could control it.

The vampire fired his weapon. Once. Twice. Again. Again. Cain dove into a large bush just as one of the bullets grazed his shoulder.

Heavy footfalls. The vampire running again. Fast.

Cain threw back his head. His mouth opened wide as he let out the rumbling roar of his kind.

No mercy.

His wounds would heal fast. No bullets had lodged in him. The skin and muscles would mend.

And the vampire would pay.

Cain sucked in a deep breath, trying to shake off the pain that weighed him down. There was no time for weakness. The asshole was heading back toward the two houses.

Going back toward Miranda.

Fuck.

He snarled. Launched forward. The vampire didn't get it. He was a damn jaguar shifter, and there were few things on this earth faster than he was.

He'd take the vamp down, and a few bullets sure as hell wouldn't stop him.

Five

She heard the sharp retort of gunfire, seeming to echo in the distance. "Oh, shit." Her heart was jackhammering in her chest. Where was Cain? He'd better not be hurt. If he was, she'd kick the guy's ass.

Another shot.

Screw this. She wasn't going to keep hiding inside while all hell broke loose outside and two men risked their lives for her. She'd find Santiago or Cain, and do whatever she could to help them.

Miranda's fingers tightened around the steak knife she'd grabbed moments before. Not much of a weapon, sure as hell not something that could stop a bullet, but better than nothing, which was what Cain currently had.

Carefully she eased open the door. Her gaze swept over the porch. The winding drive. Santiago's car was to the left. She could just make out the edge of his trunk.

That was where she needed to go. One step at a time. Check the car. Find the men. Simple enough plan.

She used the house for cover as long as she could. Miranda had never had any experience trying to sneak up on a killer, but she'd watched enough spy shows to know to keep her head down and stay to the shadows as much as possible. She bit her lip as she moved, not wanting to make any unnecessary sounds. The hilt of the knife was slick with her sweat, but she tightened her hold.

Just a few more steps.

She caught sight of a man. Crouching. Moving alongside the car.

Santiago.

She breathed his name.

His head jerked toward her. His fingers lifted to his lips and she instantly got the message, choking back any additional sound.

His fingers were wrapped tightly around his gun. He crept forward and—

Paul charged from the darkness. He grabbed Santiago by the shoulders, wrenched him around. "If you wanted to find me, all you had to do was bleed, like this . . ."

Miranda screamed and lurched forward as his fangs shot toward Santiago's exposed throat.

Too far. Not enough time.

The vampire had knocked Santiago's gun out of the agent's hands and his fangs were sinking into the man's flesh, too deep, too—

A snarl of fury had the hair rising on her arms. Not a human sound. Far too savage.

A black shape charged from the darkness. For an instant, all Miranda could see were gleaming white teeth, a mouthful of razor-sharp teeth that put the vampire's to shame, and then the animal sprang forward from the shadows.

Jaguar. One huge, freaking scary wildcat. She'd seen one of them before, on one of those Discovery Channel shows, but, oh, God, the thing was big. Muscled. With claws that looked far more dangerous than the blade of her knife.

Then the animal's body was flexing, moving, attacking in a lethal glide of muscles and power. The jaguar slammed into the vampire. Paul shrieked, dropping his prey. Miranda grabbed Santiago's arm and jerked him toward her, even as she swung out with her knife, catching the vampire along the right side.

She felt the jaguar's hot breath on her skin, and Miranda stumbled back. Santiago was moving now, cursing and wrapping his arms around her and yanking *her* away from the fray.

The battle was brutal. The jaguar fought in a blur of movement. Claws. Teeth. Blood.

The vampire was attacking just as fiercely. Swiping with claws of his own, snapping those fangs at the beast. Grabbing the large cat and tossing the beast onto the roof of the car.

But the jaguar stood quickly. Launched off the car and caught the vamp in the chest with its front paws.

The cat's body vibrated with a fury she'd never seen before. The cat was incredible. Easily over seven feet in length and solid muscle. Its black head was broad, its nose twitching, its ears flat against its head. The jaguar's powerful jaws were open, dripping with saliva. And its eyes . . .

Glowing, golden eyes. Eyes that she knew well.

Her lover's eyes.

Not an *it,* she realized, her mouth drying. *He. Cain.*

Shifter.

A shifter fighting, spilling his blood, to protect her.

"Don't get near him," Santiago muttered, holding on to her with one hand and using the other to press against the wound on his throat. "He's in a frenzy, and he might take you down just as easy as the vamp."

But he—

A swirl of sirens. Screaming in the night. Coming closer. Closer.

The jaguar hesitated. Turned his fierce head toward her.

He doesn't want the others to know.

The vampire slashed out at him, sending the cat jumping back. Then Paul turned and pulled out a gun from the back of his jeans.

"Cain!" She screamed the warning.

But the vampire wasn't trying to shoot her lover.

He aimed the gun straight at her.

Smiled his fanged smile.

And fired.

Santiago shoved her to the ground, two seconds too late.

Her breath gasped out at the burning pain in her shoulder. Realization dawned as tears trickled from the corners of her eyes. *Holy shit, that bastard bit me, and he's shot me, too!*

Snarls. A roar. The sound of claws scraping over metal. Then the jaguar was there, crouching over her, its warm body pressing against her side.

"Easy." The word came from Santiago.

Miranda was still struggling to catch her breath. Speech was sure as hell beyond her.

He'd shot her.

A low mewling vibrated up from the big cat's throat. She blinked, stared up at him, and became trapped in his heated gaze.

He could kill her with one bite. Rip her throat right out. Or use those claws to cut her open.

But he just lowered his head. Pushed his nose against her throat.

"She's gonna be all right." Santiago's voice was gruff.

The sirens were close now. The sound grated on her ears.

And the vampire? Where the hell was he? Miranda tried to get up—

The cat snarled.

"Stay down!" Santiago snapped.

"P—Paul . . ." She was shaking now. And her shoulder was pulsating with pain.

"Bastard's gone." Santiago's hands were on her shoulder, and he was clamping down, hard. "Shot you because he knew Lawson would get distracted. Made a break for it the second you hit the ground."

Dammit.

More sirens. The swirl of lights above her head.

"Get the hell out of here, Lawson. You know they can't see you."

But the jaguar wasn't moving. Miranda lifted her right hand. The fingers were trembling as she reached for him. Her hand brushed over his fur. So soft. And wet. Her hand lifted.

Blood.

The jaguar was hurt too. And judging by that fight, probably even worse than she was.

Santiago grabbed her hand, swearing. "Dammit, be careful! A few swipes of that cat's tongue could peel the flesh right off your hand."

Miranda swallowed. Found she couldn't look away from those golden eyes.

Santiago was still muttering, telling her to stay on guard, but she just wasn't afraid of the jaguar. Of Cain.

Because in those eyes, she didn't see an animal. She only saw Cain.

But the cops were so close. If they saw him—"Go!" The word was ripped from her throat. "Dammit, don't w-worry . . . about m-me." Patrol cars roared onto the graveled drive. "R-run!"

His body was tense.

"R-run," she whispered now.

His gaze held hers.

Then he turned and ran away, heading toward the woods.

Her eyes closed. A tear trickled down her cheek.

Fucking shot. What a damn bad night.

"Shit! Miranda! God, cuz, what have you done to yourself?"

To *herself?* Hell! At the clearly insane question, her lashes lifted and she glared up at Sam's frowning face.

Damn. Damn. *Damn.* Cain bounded through Miranda's house, once more in human form. Maintaining the male body was hard, though, with the rage spewing from his every pore.

The bastard had shot her.

To vamps, even the normally vicious degenerates, blood was life. Precious. To be taken with teeth and mouth and tongue.

It was never wasted. Not human blood, anyway.

But Paul hadn't cared about spilling Miranda's blood. He'd been intent only on causing pain. To her.

To Cain.

And his plan had worked perfectly.

Cain grabbed his pair of jeans, jerked them on, and shoved on his shoes. Screw a shirt, he didn't have time to waste finding one somewhere in the couch cushions.

He rushed toward the door, aware of the pounding in his temples from the shrieking sirens.

She's all right. The wound had been shallow. The vampire had wanted to kill her, but he'd missed her heart. Caught only the edge of her shoulder. Thanks to Santiago. Now he'd owe the human a new debt.

Her blood had been on the ground. Her face had been too pale, but *she was all right.*

Cain's hand slapped against the screen door, sending it flying back as he ran outside. He'd had to trek back around the house, shift in the woods, then run, naked, into the rear entrance of her house to avoid detection when the cruisers had blared onto the scene.

The humans were everywhere. Searching with flashlights. Guns drawn. Voices muttering.

He'd barely escaped being caught in his animal form.

And as for the vampire, well, it had sure as hell been his lucky night.

But his luck wouldn't last forever.

His gaze scanned the yard, looking for the one human who mattered.

He found her almost instantly. Miranda had been strapped to a stretcher.

"This is crazy!" she was saying, voice furious, but a little weak. "It's a scratch, okay? I don't need to go to the hospital for some—"

He pushed through the gathered deputies and EMTs. Caught her hand. *So soft.* "You're going." A white bandage covered her shoulder. It was soaked red with her blood.

"Bullet's out, but it cut her up like hell," Santiago told him.

Cain shot him a fast glance. Saw that someone had already

bandaged his throat. Cain's fingers tightened around hers. "You're *definitely* going."

Her head shook frantically, the inky black strands of hair fluttering around her face. "N-no, I-I can't leave. Paul—"

"Is gone for tonight." And now that the vampire knew they were hunting him, it was doubtful he'd be back.

They'd have to try a new plan.

Her eyes were so wide. "Y-you were hurt." Voice softer now. An attendant began pushing her toward the back of the open ambulance.

His wounds were nearly closed now. Shifters healed *very* quickly as a rule, but when they transformed, the healing process sped up about five times the normal rate. "Don't worry about me."

Dammit, her blood was everywhere. He was going to make the vamp pay. Blood for blood.

Cain stepped back when the attendant loaded her into the ambulance.

Time to go. Santiago could handle the scene while he—

A hand landed hard on his shoulder. "Just what the hell is going on here, Lawson?" Sam's furious voice. "Why the hell was my cousin attacked? Why'd I get a dozen reports of gunshots tonight?" The questions fired one after the other. "And just why the hell are the Bureau folks acting like you're the man in charge of this mess?"

Glancing back over his shoulder at the other man, Cain bared his teeth in the semblance of a smile. "Because I am." The attendant was trying to close the doors of the ambulance.

Cain's hand flew out, catching the edge of the metal. "I'm coming." He wasn't about to take a chance that Paul would get another shot at her.

"No, Lawson, you're staying right here and—"

He shrugged, breaking the deputy's hold. "Straighten him out," he ordered a watchful Santiago and saw the man's nearly imperceptible nod. Cain jumped into the ambulance, and the young blond woman checking Miranda's pulse looked up. Her gaze dropped momentarily to his bare chest.

The driver started the engine. The lights began to flash. Right before the doors closed, Cain told Sam, "This isn't your game anymore, Deputy. So stay out of my way, and let me track Roberts on my own."

Sam's mouth dropped open. "Paul Roberts is dead!"

Cain threw a hard glance to Santiago. "Straighten him out," he repeated, just before another attendant slammed the doors.

At the hospital, a too-friendly doctor—Dr. Ben Abrams—stitched up the jagged wound on her shoulder, after ruling it as nothing more than a flesh wound. Then the doc discovered she had a mild concussion—courtesy of Santiago's nice hurling of her to the ground—so Dr. Abrams sent Miranda to a sterile white room with not-so-friendly instructions to stay overnight.

Dammit.

When she went to sleep, Cain was sitting in the chair beside her.

And when Miranda woke the next day, Cain was still there, but now he was wearing a shirt. One of the scrub tops that the doctors wore. Dark green. And he was sleeping.

She stared at him, noting the shadows beneath his eyes. The tension that still lined his mouth.

So much more than a man.

Shifter.

Power. Strength. He was—

His lashes lifted. When he caught her stare, a little of that tension disappeared from his mouth as he smiled and said, "Hello, gorgeous."

She snorted. "Yeah, right." Oh, jeez, but she sounded like some poor frog that had nearly been choked to death. What the hell was the deal with that? The paltry dose of pain meds? She cleared her throat and tried again, "I-I probably look like hell." Better. Not perfectly normal yet, but a definite improvement.

She'd been bitten, mauled, shot—no way was she going to win any beauty prizes.

"You look beautiful."

For a creature with supposedly superior senses, he seemed to be missing a few things.

Miranda tried to sit up and winced at the sting in her arm. Glancing down, she saw the thick bandage that circled her shoulder. "How bad is it?" It hurt, ached more than anything, but she really hoped Paul hadn't screwed up her arm permanently.

The smile stretched a bit more. "Don't worry, in a few days, you'll be as good as new." A pause. "You just bleed like crazy, baby. You had everyone on the scene worried."

And Paul had probably been in the woods somewhere, salivating.

"The doctor was in here earlier. He gave orders that you're to do no major lifting or"—now his eyes heated—"any other too strenuous activity."

Oh, damn.

He leaned forward and brushed a strand of hair away from her eyes. "So I guess we'll just have to make certain I do all the work, you know, so things don't get too strenuous for you."

Now, she sure liked the sound of that.

"But first, we need to get you the hell out of here."

Her breath caught. "Can we?" She hated hospitals. Hated. Them. Had ever since she'd been a kid and her mom had been brought in to St. Vincent's. Her mom had been sick, much sicker than a child could ever understand, and once she'd been wheeled past the sliding doors of the hospital, she hadn't come back out alive.

And Miranda's life with Grandma Belle had begun.

Her lips pressed together. Shit. She didn't need to be thinking about that time now. There was more than enough crap to deal with at the moment without—

Cain's fingers wrapped around her chin and she realized that she'd turned her face away from him.

To better hide the memories.

"Miranda?" Worry. For her.

She licked her lips. "I'd really like to get . . . out of here."

The smile she sent him felt terrible on her mouth. "I'm not much for hospitals."

He just stared at her, waited. "Why?"

"The smells." Bleach and death. God, but she hated that stench. "I just—I don't like 'em."

A calm stare that waited, so patiently.

Ah, damn. "My-my mom had cancer. I was ten when she was brought to St. Vincent's. I didn't know what was happening. She went from being this warm, laughing woman to this person who was so pale and thin that-that"—and this was one of the parts that pained her the most—"I was afraid to touch her, afraid that I would hurt her even more than she was already hurting." And her mom had been hurting, so very badly.

She could still remember when Dr. Bradley had come to tell her that her mother had passed away. His face had been blank, his eyes watchful. He hadn't softened the words, just said, "Your mother passed, Miranda. Someone will be coming to pick you up soon."

And she hadn't understood. Not a word he'd said. Where had she passed to? Why hadn't her mother taken Miranda with her?

She'd begged to see her mother, but Dr. Bradley had refused.

Since then, well, she'd pretty much hated hospitals, and she hadn't exactly been filled with wild love for the doctors.

"She died?"

His rough voice pulled her back to the present, partially. "Yeah."

"I'm sorry." And he sounded like he truly meant those words.

"Thanks." Her fingers were toying with the sheet. Pulling out a piece of thread. "I just . . . don't like these places much, okay?" Intellectually, she knew the hospital hadn't caused her mother's death. She knew hospitals saved thousands of lives every day.

But they smelled of death.

And she wanted *out of there*.

"Did your father raise you, then?"

Her gaze jerked to his face, and for a moment, she almost forgot about hating the hospital. "What? Are you kidding me? He ran off when he found out that my mom was pregnant." She shook her head. "No, I've never met the guy and probably never will." She was fine with that. Had been for years.

"Then who—"

"Grandma Belle." Not her real grandmother. "My foster mom. The sweetest lady in the county. She took me in, me and Sam. Raised us both." And gave them a good home when they so desperately needed one.

Sam. The first time she'd seen him, he'd been a thin boy with bruises all over him. She'd never asked about the bruises and he'd never talked about them. But he'd become close to her. So close.

Even though he often annoyed the hell out of her.

Yeah, they were just like a real family.

She exhaled heavily. "So, now you know all about me. My weird fears, my past—"

"And you learned more last night than you probably ever hoped to know about me." His hand fell away.

No. Her fingers reached out, caught his.

Cain stilled. "I didn't want you to see me like that."

But he'd been beautiful. Ferocious. Strong. Deadly.

Absolutely terrifying.

But the most amazing creature she'd ever seen. "I wanted to see. *All* of you." She wasn't going to turn away from him because of what she'd seen. He needed to know that.

She'd made love with Cain because she wanted him. Every bit of him. Good and bad.

"Miranda . . ."

The door flew open and Sam sauntered in, pushing a wheelchair. "All right, cuz, I know you've got to be going nuts in here, so it's time you got sprung—" He caught sight of Cain and his brows jerked up. "Hell. Are you *still* here?"

Cain's face tightened and he stood. "I'm here for Miranda. Got a problem with that?"

"Look, Lawson, this shit with the killer might be all fun and games to you FBI guys—"

"I'm *ex*-FBI."

"Bull. You're running the case; that means you're active. And this blood-and-guts crap is all in a day's work to you, but it is *not* Miranda's life." He moved to the bed, standing protectively over her. "Is it, cuz?"

Cuz. He'd started calling her that on her thirteenth birthday. Told her then it connected them. Made them a real family.

Their last names were different, so folks knew they weren't real brother and sister. So they'd pretended to be cousins. Pretended to be family, and, well, they'd become family.

"I checked up on you," Sam said, directing his words to Cain before Miranda could answer him.

"Good." Cain didn't budge from his position beside her bed. The men were less than two feet apart.

"Called Atlanta. Wanted to talk to some folks other than those Bureau assholes."

Sam had always had a thing against the suits, as he called them. She didn't really know why. He'd just told her, after working a few cases with them, that the Bureau boys "didn't like to get their hands dirty."

"Um." Cain didn't seem particularly concerned with Sam's dislike of the FBI. "And did Santiago tell you to call the Atlanta PD?"

"Yeah, he told me you walked the beat there when you were first in uniform. Got your street cred before you joined the FBI."

A slow nod.

Sam's lips pursed, then he admitted. "I talked to Captain Danny McNeal."

Cain raised a brow. "And what did McNeal have to say?"

"That you were a tough bastard who wouldn't stop until you brought your man down."

Yes, that sounded about right.

"I don't." Simple. Direct.

"Miranda's not like that," Sam growled. "She's not used to this crap, she—"

"—is right here," Miranda snapped, glaring up at him. She appreciated that he was worried about her. She knew he was scared, she could see the fear in his eyes. Sam might not be perfect, often he was *far*, far from perfect, but he cared about her. She'd always known that, so she refrained from screaming at him. Instead she said, "I'm right here, Sam, and I know exactly what I'm doing."

"Getting shot. Getting assaulted. That's what you're doing!"

Okay. He had a point there, but—"I'm going to help Cain. I will find Paul, because if I don't, if we don't, the guy will just keep killing."

"Look, Miranda, I get that the guy faked his death and he's been preying on women—"

Ah, so that was the story he'd been told while she'd been stuck in the hospital.

"—but you can just leave this alone. This isn't a job for you. You work with kids, for God's sake. You don't chase criminals."

She hadn't, not until this criminal had literally walked right through her living room door and come after her. "This time I do."

Cain watched the exchange between them, eyes intense.

"Let the Bureau gang handle it. They can afford a little spilled blood. *You* can't."

Well, not much more, anyway. She opened her mouth to reply—

But Cain beat her to the punch, saying, "*You're* looking for him, Deputy Michaels. You started searching after the first attack, and you've been working nonstop to find Roberts."

Her eyes widened at Cain's statement, but she wasn't particularly surprised. Beneath his I-don't-give-a-damn persona, she'd found the real man sometimes cared too much. "Sam?"

He was a good deputy, a little too lax with the pretty women, a little too slow to break up the occasional bar fight at Pete's, but he didn't let abusers walk. Killers he took down, and men who hurt women and children, well, he'd always seemed to make a special point of putting them away. For as long as he could.

His gaze didn't meet hers. "I don't want you gettin' hurt, Miranda."

The bastard. Her lips parted in surprise. He'd been deliberately downplaying his concern, telling her she had nothing to worry about, when he'd been out there tracking the vampire.

Of course, he didn't *know* Paul was a vampire, but . . .

"Those deputies sure got to the scene fast last night," Cain murmured.

Her eyes narrowed. Yeah, they had.

A small shrug from Sam. "Some of 'em might have been stationed in the area." To keep an eye on her. His gaze lifted, finally held hers. "But even with my men and the Bureau boys and girls, you weren't safe. This is way out of your league, and you need to pull out of this mess before you wind up with something one hell of a lot more serious than just a flesh wound."

"I know you're worried"—her voice was calm, a serious effort that—"but I'm not just going to back off this thing and go hide—"

"You're a damn computer teacher, not—"

"I'm one of the women he chose. He came looking for *me*, tried to kill *me*. And he'll do the same to others." She shook her head. "I'm not going to stick my head in the sand and pretend I'm not involved. I *will* help Cain stop him."

She saw the fury that hardened Sam's expression. He jabbed his index finger into Cain's chest. "Then you damn well need to keep a better watch on her, 'cause if she gets hurt again, I'm coming after your ass."

Cain didn't look particularly worried. One black brow rose.

Sam grunted. "Now let's get the hell out of here—"

"Because we've got a killer to catch," Cain finished softly.

* * *

They'd just left the hospital when Cain got the call from Santiago. Apparently, Paul Roberts hadn't just snuck off into the night to lick his wounds.

He'd stopped at Pete's, the busiest of the local bars, picked up a visiting co-ed named Christie, and killed her in the back alley.

Sonofabitch. The news of the woman's death hit Cain like a punch in the gut.

His fault.

He should have known. The vampire had lost a lot of blood the night before. He would have needed to restock, and a psychotic like Paul wouldn't be satisfied with a stop by the hospital and a few bags from the blood bank. No, he'd like his food fresh.

And fighting.

Dammit.

If he hadn't been so worried about Miranda, he might have been able to think straight. To realize that Paul was like any wounded animal, a shitload more dangerous when he was hurt.

"We're on our way," Cain muttered, then snapped the cell phone shut. Miranda sat beside him in the car, now clad in a pair of jeans and a loose button-up shirt. She was still too pale, and the bruises on her throat were too dark. He should stop by the station, let her out, and—

"He killed another woman, didn't he?"

He jerked his head in agreement and heard the soft sigh that passed her lips.

"Did he hurt her very much?"

Probably. The bastard sure seemed to enjoy hurting women. "Santiago says he drained her nearly dry. Then cut her throat." Vamps usually did that, to throw the humans off track.

"I-I thought he hunted women over the Internet, picked out his prey."

His fingers tightened around the wheel. "He was desperate last night. He'd lost too much blood, had gotten too weak—"

"So he fed on the first poor woman he found." He could hear the painful sound of her swallow.

He caught her hand in his. Tightened his fingers around hers. "We're gonna get him." He didn't tell her that there were dozens, hundreds, more twisted vampires out there like Roberts.

She'd figure that out on her own, later.

Right now, he was focused on taking care of the monster who'd made the mistake of stumbling into his backyard and threatening the woman he was coming to need.

Besides, the world would be a damn sight better once Roberts was eliminated from it.

Then he could always start hunting the next supernatural who crossed the line.

There were always others waiting. He'd learned that lesson early in his FBI career.

And the true monsters, well, they weren't always *Other*.

Six

A week later, Miranda sat at the computer in Sam's temporary office. The sheriff was still fishing, somewhere in Louisiana now, so Sam continued to run the show in Cherryville. She typed quickly on the machine, vaguely aware of the hum of activity just beyond the door. The stitches were gone now, but every few moments, her arm would ache as she punched on the keyboard. Other than those mild twinges, she was doing pretty well.

Okay, except for the nightmares she'd been having. Those were a bit of a bitch.

There had been no sign of Paul Roberts for the past seven days *or* nights. The man had gone underground, perhaps literally.

So it was time for her to take some action.

Cain was out with Santiago, interviewing some of the folks who had been at Pete's the night Christie Hill was murdered. God, that poor woman's funeral had been hell. Her mother had just stood there, shaking and weeping, while Christie's younger sister, a kid who'd just graduated and had been one of Miranda's best students at Cherryville High, had stared at the coffin with dry but desperate eyes.

Yes, definitely time for stage two.

And she wasn't going to wait for Cain and his FBI buddies to give her permission.

A woman from the FBI had confiscated Miranda's computer three days ago, and the systems at the school were locked up for the summer, but, luckily, good old Sam never secured his temporary office.

Her fingers tapped faster and faster as she created her profile. No, not her profile. *The* perfect profile to catch Paul's interest. Because she knew he was out there, just looking for the right woman.

She'd been that woman once, and she'd be the unlucky one again.

Miranda was back on the site where she'd originally met Paul, but this time, she was a brunette named Angie Phillips. A woman who lived about forty minutes away, right near the beach. A woman who was thirty-three. Divorced. No children. An artist. And a serious lover of antiques.

Paul had talked about his antiques on their date. Damn, but he'd talked about them *a lot*. Particularly, his collection of ancient knives. He'd been collecting them all his life. He had knives dating back to ancient Egypt. Knives from the Middle Ages. The Victorian era. The Civil War.

Since he loved to cut his prey, the fascination made a sick sense to Miranda.

Now she just had to set a nice lure in her trap and wait for the knife-freak to show.

"What are you doing?"

Cain's voice. She jerked, startled. Jesus, but the man moved like some kind of, um, cat.

He closed the door behind him. Lowered the blinds. Then turned the lock with a soft *click*.

His predatory gaze narrowed as he stalked toward her. "Miranda? Why do I have the feeling you aren't just checking Sam's e-mail?"

Her fingers stilled above the keyboard. "Because I'm not." No sense denying it. Her chin lifted. "I'm doing a bit of hunting on my own."

He grunted at that and continued to cross the room in those long, strong strides. He'd been keeping his distance from her since the shooting. No touches. No kisses. She'd caught him staring at her a few times, the same raw lust lurking in his eyes that she'd seen before Paul had screwed things to hell and back.

But the man had been holding on to a steel chain of control. And she was getting damn tired of it.

And tired of having both him and Santiago bunking on her couch.

There was more than enough room in her queen-size bed for Cain, and the man knew it.

So why the standoff? Miranda's patience was long gone, and she'd never pretended to have the control that the man before her possessed.

Time to clear the air.

She stood quickly, sending the chair rolling back behind her. "What the hell is your deal lately?" Grandma Belle had been a woman used to speaking her mind, and Miranda thought it was long past time she did the same.

Cain blinked, then lowered those glittering eyes of his to her throat. "Your bruises are gone."

"What?" Her hand lifted automatically and touched the no-longer-tender flesh. "Yeah, so—"

"The stitches came out this morning, didn't they?"

A stiff nod.

He smiled then, the smile of one very pleased cat. And his dimple curved. "Good."

The lust was in his eyes again. That need that had her breasts swelling and a ball of fire churning in her gut. She marched around the desk, angry he could arouse her with just a stare, angry that she'd wanted him all week while he'd kept that cold space between them.

Just angry, dammit.

Her arms crossed over her chest and the backs of her legs pressed against the desk. "What kind of game are you trying to play with me, Lawson?" Sam had told her about the background check he'd run on Cain. Until he was eighteen, her shifter had lived in Dallas, Texas. Then he and his mother had moved to Atlanta. He'd bounced around with the Bureau a bit after that, eventually winding up in Miami before he took his little retirement and headed to Cherryville.

Lots of big cities. And she was sure there had been *lots* of women in those cities. Cain was far too sexy not to have attracted more than his share of lovers. Hell, maybe the guy was too used to big-city life and the games that men and women played there.

Emotional games weren't for her. Her ex-fiancés could tell him that.

He stepped closer to her and lifted a hand to trail over her arm. "I'm not playing."

She swallowed, liking that touch far too much. And when the backs of his fingers rubbed lightly against her breast, she sucked in a quick pull of air. "Then—then what is this hot-and-cold mood? One day, you're acting wild"—*good word there*—"for me, the next—" He'd been completely hands-off.

And it had *hurt*. When she sure hadn't been expecting pain. She'd been rejected before. She was thirty-two, for heaven's sake. Of course she'd been rejected.

But this, it was different.

He was different, and not just because the guy could turn into an animal at will.

His hands clamped over her arms. He lifted her up and pushed her back onto the edge of the desk. Her skirt fluttered briefly around her flesh.

"What are you—"

His lips were on hers. Hot. Hard. Demanding and possessive.

Wild.

Just the way she'd been craving him.

Her fingers clenched into fists. She wanted to reach out and hold him, but she was *not* going to give in to her need, not until they settled a few things between them.

She wasn't some kind of itch the guy could scratch whenever he wanted. Good kisser—*oh, yeah, he was*—or not.

Miranda wrenched her lips from his, and Cain immediately began to kiss and lick his way down her neck.

Goosebumps rose along her flesh, and the urge to lean in to him was so strong.

"I had to give you time." He growled the words against her flesh. He pushed between her legs, shoving up the fabric of her skirt several desperate inches. The thick length of his erection was obvious even through his clothing.

He caught her earlobe between his teeth, bit lightly, and had her shuddering.

"I-I needed you too much." The words were almost a growl now and his breath blew over her skin in a delicious caress. "But my need . . ." Now his head lifted and his gaze caught hers. "It can be dangerous."

The jaguar flashed in her mind. Raging its fury in the night. Teeth. Claws.

"You'd been hurt enough." He caught a strand of her hair between his thumb and forefinger. Brought the lock to his face and inhaled. "I couldn't risk taking you while you were weak, and hurting you again."

So he'd pulled away. Her back teeth clenched. Men could be such jerks.

And damn, but they could make a woman want.

Want to kill them.

Want to fuck them.

"Next time," she gritted, "*explain.*" Before she went insane.

His eyes began to shine with the light of his beast. "I had to stay away from you as much as I could." His fingers released her hair. " 'Cause anytime I so much as caught your scent, I wanted to take you."

Didn't sound like such a bad thing to her.

"I held on to my control last time. I wasn't sure I'd be able to do it again."

"Who said I wanted you to be controlled?" She'd never

asked him to use kid gloves with her. The idea of having him, hungry and aggressive, it just turned her on all the more.

"You *needed* control. You were hurt. And *you're human.*"

He said the last like it was her fault. Her muscles tensed. Humanity wasn't exactly something she was going to apologize for.

The flare of anger must have shown in her expression because he swore softly. "You don't get it, baby. Being human, it means you're weaker than me. Than every supernatural out there. It means you can be hurt, *too easily.*"

So he'd been holding back because he didn't want to hurt her. She snorted. What utter bullshit.

And what a waste of time.

Her hands rose to grasp his shoulders. Curled into the muscles. "Stop worrying about hurting me." He should have realized after what they'd been through that she wasn't going to shatter with a bruise or a cut. "And focus more on making love to me." Because that was what she wanted. Right there. Right then.

The door was locked. Blinds were closed.

And she could tell that Cain was more than ready.

So was she.

When his nostrils widened, she knew that he'd caught the scent of her arousal. Hell, he'd probably known she was turned on the minute he walked into the room.

Her hands dropped to his waist. Caught the buckle of his belt in her fingers.

A tremble shook his body. "Ah, baby, you don't—"

The belt was free. She unsnapped the button at the top of his jeans, lowered the zipper, and stroked his erection through the thin cotton of his boxer shorts.

After a second, two, her fingers pushed the shorts down, and she took the length of his erection between her hands. Squeezed. Pumped. Root to tip. Again.

He was warm beneath her touch. And so strong. As she touched him, his arousal grew.

She wondered what he would taste like.

His hands were on her breasts now. Stroking her through her shirt and bra. Caresses that became harder in time with the movements of her hands. A growing demand to match her own.

A phone rang in the distance. Voices, muted, drifted to her ears.

She didn't care.

He jerked up her shirt. Shoved her bra out of the way, and those nimble fingers of his curled over her nipples. Squeezed.

Miranda bit back a moan and her hands tightened around him. God, but she wanted him inside and—

A growl built in his throat. Her gaze snapped to his and she found his burning stare flickering between a man's lust and an animal's wild need.

Then he stepped back, breaking the heated contact between them, and she could have yelled in frustration, could have—

"My way." The words seemed barely those of a man.

His hands were on her wrists and he yanked her forward so that Miranda tumbled off the edge of the desk. Her feet hit the floor a little too hard and she stumbled. But then he was holding her tight. Shifting her body, spinning her around so that she faced the scarred desk and—

"Brace your hands." A gritted order.

He was right behind her. Her body slid forward. She put her hands out automatically, palms slapping flat against the wooden surface of the desk.

"Cain, what are—"

Her skirt was lifted. No, shoved up. Cool air skated over her thighs. Then his fingers were between her legs. Stroking her through the damp crotch of her panties. Long, hard strokes that made Miranda bite her lip and rise up on her tiptoes.

Good, but not good enough.

"*Cain.*" A demand this time. His way, her way, she didn't care. She just wanted him.

His fingers slipped under the edge of her panties. One long finger pushed inside her, knuckle-deep. Her hips arched and she thrust back against him, needing so much more than that touch.

She needed deeper.

She needed *more*.

Miranda tossed back her head. "I need—"

With his left hand, he jerked the collar of her shirt to the side, baring her flesh. His mouth locked around her shoulder. The edge of his teeth pressed against her in a sensual bite that had her gasping.

His finger retreated. Thrust. Retreated. Then he was curling his hand over her panties and yanking them down.

The panties landed on her black sandals. She kicked off her strapless shoes—and the panties fluttered across the floor.

His mouth pressed tightly to the flesh of her shoulder. A warm swipe of his tongue. A kiss. His hands spread her thighs ever wider, and he pushed her farther over the top of the desk.

A rustle of foil reached her ears as he readied himself. Then the wide head of his erection pushed against the moist opening of her sex. A controlled thrust.

Not what she wanted.

And Miranda was damn sure that really wasn't "his way." She rolled her hips, rocked back, and took him in as deep as she could.

His hands slammed down next to hers. His claws were out, and they dug into the wood.

And he began to thrust.

Not so controlled.

Deeper. Deeper. Harder.

Miranda closed her eyes and tried to hang on for the ride.

The desk inched forward with his thrusts. Wood scraped. He was pistoning behind her, driving so fully into her that she felt totally possessed.

Joined.

He was all around her, his scent thicker, richer than before. His nails had dug deep into the desktop. His teeth pierced the flesh of her shoulder.

Not pain.

Just pleasure.

Not like Paul. God, no, never like that—

The climax caught her hard, spiraling through her body and stealing her breath as her sex spasmed.

His cock seemed to swell even more inside of her, and he thrust aggressively into her. The wild rhythm of their lovemaking continued, even as the climax rose, crested, his cock continued to tunnel deep into her flesh. So hard. So damn *good*.

Her hands lifted, caught the width of his forearms. Her breath was panting out, her upper body almost completely splayed over the desk, dangerously close to the edge of the computer.

And still he took her. In strong plunges, in demanding thrusts. Again and again.

When the second climax hit, their release erupted at the same moment. A hard ball of pleasure blasted through her, and Cain shuddered behind her, driving into her core one final time, then stilling against her.

A heartbeat was pounding, racing far too fast. Hers? His?

Miranda didn't know, and at that moment, she didn't really care. Her head dropped onto the desk and her hands fell from his.

He wrapped his arms around her then. Kept his cock buried inside of her and nuzzled her neck.

And damned if the man didn't let out what could really only be called a purr. A very, very masculine purr of satisfaction.

A sound she felt like echoing, and would have, if she hadn't been struggling to catch her breath.

Umm. She rather liked doing things his way. But next time, she wanted to be in charge.

Her way.

Her head turned to the side, and she stared at his claws. Slowly, the claws shifted away, until only a man's hand, with close-cropped nails, remained.

Amazing.

"I should have gotten you naked." His voice was husky and the words were murmured close to her ear.

Naked. Now that would have been a good plan.

"I've been dreaming about those sweet breasts of yours, and I didn't even get a taste of them."

A feeling of heady power swept through her. "Maybe next time." Oh, but she did love the feel of that skilled tongue on her flesh. Teasing her nipple. Licking her.

"Or maybe right now." He slid out of her, and her sex tightened in an automatic reflex to keep him inside.

Too late.

He eased off her, and, taking a deep breath, Miranda pushed up and turned to face him.

His lips were parted, and she could just see the edge of his strong, white teeth.

She smiled at him. "You wanting to go again, Lawson?" Talk about a dream man.

The back of his hand caressed her cheek. "Did you know"—he spoke softly, but with a trace of need that was undeniable—"that in the wild, jaguars can mate over one hundred times a day?"

All of the moisture in her mouth dried up. "Oh . . ." Impossible, for a man, surely, and there was no way—

He kissed her. Quick, but almost tender. "The need's not gone yet, baby. One fast time in an office isn't gonna cut it for me." A pause. "It'll take a hell of a lot more to satisfy the hunger I've got for you." His lips hovered over hers. "I want a big bed, I want you, and I want all night, for starters."

Sounded like a great plan to her. But—

"And once we get this asshole off our backs, that's just what I'm gonna get."

Ah, there was the *but.* The vampire.

Another kiss. A slow glide of his tongue. That soft rumble of sound from deep in the back of his throat that she was definitely terming a purr now.

She leaned into the kiss, loving the rich tang of his—

His head jerked away. "Dammit. Santiago's coming this way."

And she sure did love that superhearing.

Her fingers quickly smoothed down her skirt. Righted her shirt and the bra that was bunched all over the place. She searched, found her shoes and slid into them just as Cain ditched the condom and righted his jeans. She saw him wrap the condom in tissue, then drop it deep into the bottom of the trash can.

Her thighs squeezed together. She was damp, from him, from her—

"Here, baby." Cain put a tissue between her legs. Cleaned her gently.

His touch had her nipples tightening again. Her body responded like wildfire to the man.

Almost like—like she was in some kind of heat for the guy.

She'd sure as hell never responded so fast or so hard to any of the other lovers she'd had.

He snagged her panties. Started to hand them to her, then stopped and she saw his nostrils flare—

"Give me those!" She snatched them from him. They were still a bit damp, but she wasn't about to go around without panties for the rest of the day.

Okay, yeah, she'd just had great sex on a desk.

But she needed her panties, dammit!

A knock at the door sounded seconds after the panties were in place.

"Lawson? What the hell are you doing in there?"

Her cheeks heated as Cain opened the door. "Strategizing with Miranda."

Oh, was that what they'd been doing? Jeez, but she hoped the agent didn't catch the scent of sex in the air.

Santiago grunted and sauntered inside as if he owned the place. Sam would have said since he was a Bureau boy, he thought he did. Santiago pointed a finger at Cain. "You didn't give me a status report on the last couple of feeding rooms you checked out."

Feeding rooms? Some of her passion began to cool. What in the world was a feeding room?

Cain slanted a glance toward Miranda. "No sign of him at the rooms within a hundred-mile radius."

"What," she asked quietly, but with a pretty strong suspicion already in her mind, "is a feeding room?" Miranda shifted a bit. Wet panties were *so* not comfortable.

"Vampire paradise," Santiago answered. She'd learned over the past few days that although the agent was human, he'd apparently picked up quite a bit of supernatural knowledge while he worked with Cain.

And the longer she was around Cain, the more knowledge she was picking up too. Her rose-colored glasses had long since broken.

"They feed there," Cain said, looking perfectly normal and at ease. As if he hadn't just had wild sex. Well, his cheeks *were* a bit flushed, and his gaze held a faint, heated gleam when he glanced her way. "They take humans. Blood and bodies." He shrugged. "Figured if I checked out the nearby rooms, I could either find the bastard or get a lead on him."

Her eyes narrowed. "So that's where you've been going each night?"

He gave a quick nod.

Huh. She'd heard him creep out for the last two nights, only to return hours later. He hadn't left her alone. Oh, no. Santiago had always stayed at the house, though usually when she'd snuck down the hallway, Miranda had just found him sleeping on her sofa.

Well, great. "And these vampires in these rooms." From the way he described them, feeding rooms sounded basically like vampire bars to her. "Uh, how do they feel about a shifter coming into their territory?"

A sharp laugh escaped Santiago's lips. "They *hate* it when he comes to play."

Oh, she just bet they did. "You think going in those rooms, *alone,* is really a good idea?" No sane person would think it was. Did he have some kind of death wish? Just walking into a den of vampires?

In. Sane.

"You knew I was hunting," he told her, voice expressionless.

Yeah, and she was liking this hunting of his less and less.

"There's another place in Miami that we can try tonight. A feeding room at the beach."

One close to her profile's fictional home. "I'm coming with you."

His jaw tightened. "The hell you are."

"The vampires aren't going to tell you anything—"

"Trust me, baby, I've got some pretty good methods of persuasion." His lips peeled back in a smile that showed his sharp teeth.

"They'll tell me more." A human, a woman, they'd never think she was a threat. "I'll go inside, tell them I'm looking for my lover." She shifted her legs, ignoring the faint ache between her thighs.

The growl that broke past Cain's lips had the hair on her nape rising, but Miranda held her ground. "I can get more information with my cover story than you'll get by threatening it out of the vampires." Yeah, okay, the prospect of strolling into a vampire feeding room made her mouth dry up, but it was better than doing nothing.

"You go in there, you can get yourself killed."

She lifted one brow. "Well, I guess you'll just have to do a damn fine job of watching my ass, won't you?"

His teeth snapped together. "Baby, watching your ass is already one of my top priorities."

So he'd proven very well minutes before. Her gaze darted to Santiago. Did he know—

"What the hell?" Sam's disgruntled voice called out as he pushed past Santiago. "Who said it was okay to have some kind of damn party in my office?"

Technically, it wasn't *his* office, but Miranda refrained from pointing out that obvious fact. Sam had his eye on the sheriff's position, and, sooner or later, the office probably would be his.

"And what the hell happened to my desk?" He ran his hand over the deep groves that Cain's claws had created. "Looks like some jerkoff took a knife to it." He cursed under his breath. "McMillan is goin' to be pissed."

Miranda kept her eyes averted and hoped that her cheeks weren't flaming too much.

The chair squeaked as Sam threw his body onto the leather. "What's this shit? *Miranda.*"

She finally glanced his way, only to see that Sam was glowering at the computer screen. "I'll be damned," he said.

Cain stepped forward. "We never did get around to talking about just what you were doing in here."

Sam looked up at him, brows raised. "I'll tell you what she was doing, Lawson. Setting a trap for Roberts, with herself as bait."

The heat from Cain's eyes seemed to scorch her flesh. "No, she wasn't."

"Uh, actually"—Miranda cleared her throat—"I was." She jerked her thumb toward Santiago. "The FBI took my computer, so I had to use Sam's. I made a profile, one guaranteed to snag Paul's attention." If he were still hunting on that site, and her gut said that he was. He'd already chosen three women from those Web pages.

"We've tried making profiles before." This announcement came from Santiago. "The guy won't bite—"

"He bit me." On the Web and in the flesh. "And I can get him to take another bite. Just give me some time."

"I don't like this plan," Sam said very clearly.

Yeah, but what was new with that? If there was any chance of danger to her, Sam would never be on board with her idea.

But he wasn't the one making the call on this. Miranda held Cain's gaze and waited.

After a moment, he gave a slow nod. "You'll have your time, Miranda."

"What?" Santiago barked. "But we've had plants on—"

"Miranda's the real thing, Santiago. If we don't track him in the feeding rooms, and he goes back online to find prey, he'll find her." A pause. "And we'll be waiting for him."

Sam snorted. "Like you were last time? 'Cause that worked out so well."

Cain turned his stare on him. "He won't get away from me again." A vow.

Miranda believed him.

"If you're going to Miami," Santiago said, "you'd better hurry and get your asses on the road."

The feeding room was waiting.

Cain moved until he stood at her side. "Are you sure you're up for this?"

Hell, no. Her lips parted. "Yes." It felt like she'd been living most of her life on the sidelines, watching others live and take chances.

Now it was her turn.

Cain lifted his hand. "Then let's go, baby, and I'll show you a whole new world."

Of blood and death.

She placed her palm in his, lifted her chin, and pretended that her knees weren't shaking as they left the station and headed for hell.

Seven

Just after eleven p.m., Miranda walked past the doors of one of the biggest feeding rooms in Florida. Her head was held high, her walk was confident, a little cocky even, her skin pale, and her skirt a bit too short for Cain's peace of mind.

The guards stationed at the doors didn't hesitate. They waved her right inside, as they'd been doing with all the attractive human women he'd seen in the last hour.

Time for him to make his move.

Cain sauntered across the street. Headed for the door. The place wasn't located in the trendy, tourist area of Miami. It was hidden on the broken backstreets, in a building that looked like it could be torn down by the city at any moment.

The male guards stiffened when he approached. Their scents marked them as humans, and if he played his cards right, the guys wouldn't realize he didn't belong in their little death trap until it was too late.

He flashed fangs, just the edge of his teeth, and never slowed his steps. Closer inspection would show the differences between his shifted teeth and those of a vampire.

But he wasn't going to give the humans time for that inspection.

He grabbed the handle of the door and stalked inside.

The security at the place was shit. Most feeding rooms had a hell of a lot better protection to keep the "undesirables" out.

Undesirables like him.

Miranda was at the bar. Already, several vamps were glancing her way. His gaze focused solely on her, and he cut a quick path through the crowd of humans and vampires.

The humans were there because they liked the thrill of walking with death.

The vamps were there because they either wanted to screw the humans or to drain them.

Miranda's back was to him. He reached out, grabbed her shoulder, and spun her around.

Her breath jerked out and her eyes widened. "What are you—"

"Dance with me." Cain didn't give her time to refuse. Holding her wrist tightly, he pulled her behind him and onto the small dance floor. He could feel the gazes on him now, the awareness. A vamp's sense of smell was much more acute than a human's, and all the vampires there would know that he was different.

He'd once heard that shifters smelled like animals. Maybe they did.

Either way, the vamps would detect that smell and know he was different, and because he'd claimed Miranda's sweet body earlier that day, some of the older vamps might even be able to catch his scent on her.

"Uh, Cain?" Her nails dug into his shoulders. "This isn't exactly part of the plan."

Damn, but the woman felt good in his arms. "Plan changed a bit." He lowered his head, nuzzled her neck. He loved the way she smelled there, at that sweet spot where her pulse raced. The vampires were watching so closely, their stares weighed on him.

But at least now they'd understand why his scent was on Miranda. They'd attribute it to the dance.

And not to the sex.

"I'm gonna kiss you," he told her, lowering his hands to her hips and bringing her flush against the arousal he always seemed to have when she was near. A band played near the far back of the building, a drumming beat that matched the fire in his blood.

Her eyes were so damn blue. And her honeysuckle scent was calling to him like a beacon in the room that reeked of blood.

"This isn't the way to get the vamps to open up and talk to me."

His head lowered toward hers. He could already taste her. "No, but I want your mouth." So bad he was starting to ache. "And in about thirty seconds, when you slap me as hard as you can, you'll have the undivided attention of every vamp in the room."

Her eyes widened right before he took her lips. His tongue thrust deep. Slid over hers. The light flavor of her filled his mouth. Oh, yes, this was exactly what he wanted. Her nipples stabbed against his chest, pebble-hard and tight, and the creamy scent from her sex rose to tease his nostrils as—

Miranda jerked her mouth away from his. Shoved her arms between them and broke free of his hold. Then the lady did just as he'd directed. She drew back her hand and hit him.

He heard the gasp from those who'd been watching. Tension hummed in the air. Some knew what he was. *Shifter.* He'd caught the whispers moments before.

The vamps would be hungry for his reaction. Would he strike back? Turn tail and run?

Neither. Cain lifted his chin, smiled at her, and said, "Baby, if you thought screwing with an animal was bad, you don't know what's waiting for you." His voice was pitched to carry across the crowd.

She shook her head and threw herself into the little drama they'd created. "I know what's waiting." Her hand swept around the room. "And it's gonna be a damn sight better than what I had."

His eyes narrowed at that. Okay, so his little human was a good actress. He'd held back on warning her about this little scene because he hadn't wanted her to waste time worrying about what would happen. Or trying to analyze and plot out her performance.

In his undercover situations in the past, he'd found that a fast, gut response always came across as more genuine.

He hadn't realized that Miranda would shine so in the spotlight.

"Now, if you don't mind," she said, and her voice could have dripped icicles, "I'd like for you to get the hell out of my way."

His gaze held hers. Hunger beat at him because the woman was just so beautiful standing there, head thrown back, face taunting and angry.

Oh, yeah, damn good actress.

As he took a deliberately grudging step out of her way, he realized their little show had taught him a lesson he hadn't expected.

He didn't want Miranda to look at him with anger.

And he sure as hell didn't want to ever have to step aside so that she could go to another.

Shifters weren't designed to give up their mates. Not without one hell of a fight.

He snarled and slunk away into the shadows as the beat of the music flared harder.

By the time she got back to the bar, two vampires were waiting for her. Miranda's heart rate sped up at the sight of the men. Both were blond, pale, and wearing smiles that made her blood ice.

"You were right to leave him," the one on the left said, letting his gaze sweep over her body. He licked his lips, thin lips that, paired with his angular face and hollowed cheeks, gave him a harsh, almost cruel appearance. "Their kind doesn't know how to treat human women."

Like vampires did? 'Cause having her blood sucked out of her was just exactly what she'd imagined for her dream date.

"Have a seat." The second guy indicated the bar stool between them. "I promise, we won't bite—yet." His face was a bit softer than the other vamp's, but his eyes were already in that creepy black mode. *Hunting mode*, that's what Cain had called it. He'd said their eye color darkened to black when they were about to fight or feed. Or fuck.

Since she was supposed to be into the scary shit instead of disgusted, Miranda smiled at the men and strolled forward. She eased onto the bar stool and let her skirt drift up an inch or two.

They were undead, but they were still men.

The hunger that lit their faces told her they were men who could still be stirred by a woman.

"I was actually supposed to meet a friend here tonight," she murmured, tapping her index finger to her lips. Slowly, she swung around on the bar stool until she faced the crowd. Her gaze shifted around the room, as if she were searching for someone—

And found Cain's bright stare locked on her.

She swallowed and kept her expression light and flirtatious. He was watching out for her, guarding her back.

And looking like he'd seriously enjoy ripping the vampires apart.

"Another friend like the bastard shifter?" asked the blond on the right with a trace of disgust.

"Oh, no." She turned her gaze to him but then glanced quickly away. Cain had warned her to be careful with the vampires. Apparently, the older ones could use some kind of hypnosis thing called Thrall to control humans and some of the Other. "Paul is a vampire." Tossing them what she hoped was a secretive smile, she admitted, "Paul Roberts is the one who turned me on to vampires."

"Then you must have a serious taste for pain, my dear." The deep voice, accented with an Irish brogue, came from a few feet away. Miranda jerked her gaze over to the stranger. A tall, muscled guy with brown hair and sky-blue eyes stared back at her, arms crossed over his chest. "Paul Roberts is a twisted prick who gets off from torturin' women. Human women." A pause. "Now is that really your idea of a good time, Miranda Shaw?"

Oh, hell, he knew her name.

His stare shifted to the vampires. "Leave."

Two against one, like that was going to work—

They left. Irish smiled at her then, flashing those vamp teeth. He took the stool next to her and brought his legs close to hers, so close she could feel the muscled threat of his body. "The performance was very good, you know. Fooled most of the idiots here."

As fear began to trickle up her throat, Miranda studied the vampire before her. Handsome. Classically so, really, but with eyes that seemed to be ancient.

And maybe *he* was.

"Ah, here comes our brave bodyguard, rushing to the rescue."

She didn't look, but she knew Cain was on his way.

The vampire smiled at her. "Why are you really here, human? Not for the fucking. And I don't think you like the idea of yourself as food."

No, she didn't. Not one damn bit. She dropped her act and got down to business. "Paul Roberts attacked me a little over a week ago." The guy in front of her might not particularly give a damn about her attack. Hell, he probably couldn't care less. Were all vampires sadistic killers?

"Um . . ." He turned slightly on the stool. Gazed at two women who were dancing nearby.

No, he didn't look overly concerned.

"He's killed four other women." Christie's still face flashed through her mind. "I want to stop him."

The vampire turned his attention back to her. "Do you now? Easier said than done, I'd wager." He reached out and touched her cheek. "Even for a tempting one like you."

"Get your hands off her, Sullivan." Cain stood beside them, body tense.

"Ah, relax, shifter. I'm not going to hurt your pretty." Taking his time, he withdrew his hand.

"What the hell are you doing here, Sullivan? I thought you went back across the damn ocean—"

"I did." A little shrug. "Got bored." A brow lifted. "And I

thought you had given up the crime fighting? What happened? Did you decide life without the kill just wasn't worth living?"

Okay. She didn't like the sound of that. Miranda stood, placing her body between the two men. "He decided to save my life."

"Um. A life certainly worth saving."

Yeah, she liked to think so. "We're trying to stop Paul Roberts. Do you know anything that can help us or not?"

"Not," Cain snapped. "The vamps stick together, he's not—"

"What have I ever done," the one called Sullivan asked, cutting through Cain's words, "that makes you think I condone the killin' of innocent women? Vampire, I may be." A delicate pause. "But unlike other of my brethren, and *yours,* I might add, I don't get my jollies from tormentin' the helpless."

Cain just stared at him.

Sullivan shook his dark head. "And I don't drain my prey. A sip here or there." He shrugged. "But no murders. My conscience is clean on that."

"So you'll help us?" Miranda pressed. She didn't know if she believed the guy. Cain seemed damn antagonistic toward him, so no telling what kind of history was between the two men. Now that Cain had crossed back to her side, they were getting either suspicious or downright hateful looks from the other vampires in the room, and some of the humans who were picking up on the tension were starting to throw them dirty stares, too.

They'd need to get the hell out of there, soon.

But first . . .

"You won't find Roberts in any of the rooms in Miami, or any other city." The vampire seemed absolutely certain of that.

"Why not?" Miranda asked.

A smile that showed a lot of fang. "Because the prey here are willing. They want the bites." His teeth gleamed. "They want it so bad many of them will do anything to feel the plunge of fangs into their flesh." Sullivan shook his head at her doubting stare. "It's not always painful, you know. Some of my women have found great pleasure in my kiss."

Kiss? Is that what he was calling it?

His gaze held hers. "Perhaps I can show you."

"Sullivan, you're begging for a beheading," Cain warned.

"Sorry. Forgot she was taken."

But Miranda didn't think the guy had forgotten anything. He just seemed to enjoy pissing off Cain. She tried to get both men back on track, before Cain's claws decided to show, saying, "If we won't find him in a feeding room, just where is Roberts?"

"Looking for prey, I'd imagine. He likes to take those who are unwilling. Humans who don't know just what he is." He turned a bit to the side, and his fingers tapped against the bar top. "It's the fear, I think."

"What?"

"He likes to see the fear in his victim's eyes right before he takes the bite. It turns him on. Makes that first taste of blood all the sweeter."

The vampire sounded way too knowledgeable about Paul's killing technique. She wasn't aware that she'd eased back from him until she bumped into Cain's chest. His arm swept over her shoulders and he held her tight.

"You're not speaking from experience, are you, Sullivan?" Cain asked.

The vampire shook his head, and some of the intensity faded from his gaze. "I told you, that's not how I get my nourishment."

But he sure seemed to know an awful lot about a killer's motivations.

Takes one to know one.

"My sire was like him," Sullivan said, still drumming his fingers on the bar. "Sadistic bastard. Best move I ever made was to incinerate his ass."

Her eyes widened at the almost casual statement.

"Hope you find Roberts and do the same to him, before more innocents die." He inclined his head. Rose to his feet. Hesitated. "Word is he likes to find his women online. Fancies himself a Casanova of sorts. Picks the best prey, and they never see him coming until it's too late."

The vampire tilted his head to the side as he studied Miranda. Then his gaze met Cain's. "Is he linked with her?"

She felt Cain stiffen behind her. *Linked?* She didn't know exactly what that meant, but she sure as hell didn't like the sound of it.

"If he is," Sullivan continued, "he'll always be able to get to her. *Always.*"

Miranda bit back the questions that sprang to her lips, knowing now wasn't the time. But the minute she got Cain out of that place . . .

"Good hunting, shifter," Sullivan murmured and cast her a last, hooded glance. Then he disappeared into the crowd and Miranda took her first deep breath since she'd approached the two blonds.

"Cain." She turned to face him.

"We need to get out of here, *fast.*" He was already moving, dragging her with him and making a beeline for the door. "The natives are about to get damn restless."

"What?" She was nearly running to keep up with him and her shoulders bumped into people left and right. "Cain, what's happening—"

A vampire stepped in front of Cain. One of the blonds. His eyes were black. His teeth were sharp and glinting. "Not leaving already, are you, shifter?"

Hell.

"And certainly not with my new little friend."

Miranda stepped to Cain's side. Offered a tight smile. "Changed my mind. Decided I'd like to stick with the animal after all."

His eyes became slits of black rage. "Too damn bad. I've decided I want a taste and—"

Cain moved in a blur. Wrapped his right hand around the vampire's throat and lifted him off the floor. "I'm not in the mood for this shit," he snarled and tossed the vamp across the room.

The music stopped. All eyes flew to them. There was a rough scraping as chairs were shoved back. Vampires lurched forward and—

"Let them go." Sullivan's voice. Ringing through the crowd.

Miranda craned her neck, straining to see him. Where was—

There. He was sitting at a table, two women on either side of him. One, a redhead, had blood slowly dripping down her neck, and she wore an expression of pure ecstasy. He leaned toward her, licked up the drops, then his head lifted again. "For tonight, and only tonight, they have my protection."

None of the vampires moved and Miranda realized that the Sullivan guy wasn't just your average vamp. The guy had power, a lot of it.

Then Cain was dragging her outside—jeez, again with the dragging. Like she wouldn't have gladly run out of that pit of hell on her own steam.

The fresh air hit her face, driving out the scents of booze and blood. Their car waited just feet away. They jumped inside. Cain revved the engine, and they raced down the street.

Paul Roberts watched the taillights disappear down the road. His Miranda had joined with the shifter. A pity.

Now she was trying to hunt *him.* That wasn't the way the game was played.

No, not at all.

Miranda was prey. Food. Not a hunter.

He should have killed her that first night. If only that damn animal hadn't come running to her rescue.

But the shifter wouldn't be able to protect her forever. No, there would be a time when she was alone. Vulnerable. There always was.

And he'd strike then. Make her beg for death.

Then he'd go after the animal. It was rumored that shifter blood was more powerful than anything else on earth. Because of the two spirits the beasts carried. A man's. An animal's.

He'd find out if that rumor was true when he sank his teeth into the shifter's throat and gorged on his blood.

Oh, but death could be so wonderfully sweet.

Time to start *his* hunt.

And he knew just where to begin.

* * *

Miranda and Cain didn't drive back to Cherryville. Instead, they returned to the hotel room that Cain had booked for them. The minute the bellman closed the door and exited the room, Cain sucked in a deep breath. He knew what was coming.

"Just what the hell," Miranda gritted, "was that vampire talking about? *What* does it mean to be linked? And whatever it is, you'd damn well better tell me that I am *not* linked to Paul."

Oh, but the woman was beautiful. Cheeks flushed. Eyes bright. He wanted to kiss her.

Strip her.

Take her.

But first, well, first he was going to have to piss her off, and probably scare her. "I didn't want to worry you," he began.

"Worry me?" Her voice rose several octaves and she began to pace around the room, pausing to toss her bag onto the king-size bed. Oh, but he had plans for that bed. And for her.

"Miranda . . ."

She shot him a fuming glare. "I've got some kind of psychotic vampire killer on my tail. Trust me, I'm already worried."

Yeah, but there was being worried, then there was knowing-that-a-vampire-could-peek-into-your-mind-at-any-time worried. "When a vampire drinks from a human, it gives him a-a certain amount of control."

She stopped pacing and spun to face him. "What kind of control?" Almost instantly, her eyes widened. "You said that only the ancient vamps could use Thrall, and Paul isn't—"

"He can't use Thrall on you." His voice was firm. No, the vamp couldn't use that method with her. "But once he took your blood, he did form a connection of sorts with you."

Her lashes lowered a moment. Lifted. "I don't like where this is going, Cain."

He wasn't thrilled, either. "If the blood link is strong enough, he'll be able to glimpse into your mind. See memories." And if the guy had enough power and he deepened the link, he might even be able to control her.

The hard sound of her painful swallow grated on his ears. "Are you telling me that bastard is in my head?"

"I'm saying he could be."

Miranda sat down on the bed, hard. Her bag fell to the floor. "How do I get him out?"

He was working on that. *They* were working on that. But there was really only one way to sever a blood link. "We kill him."

"Easier said than done," she muttered.

His hands clenched. He'd been holding back the truth about the blood link because he'd thought Miranda had already been through enough.

He truly hadn't wanted to freak the woman out any more than absolutely necessary.

"And just who the hell was that Sullivan guy?"

Ah, Liam Sullivan. "He was an agent with the Irish government. Came here years ago on a case, wound up staying as a liaison."

"So how'd he end up fanged?"

"Wrong place. Wrong time." Simple words to describe the carnage that had taken out Sullivan's team and left him alive—sort of, anyway.

"I thought he was one of those ancients you'd talked about. Why'd the other vampires listen to him if he's still . . . I don't know, young to them?"

Because most of the vamps in the bar were considered the fresh Taken. Taken—an apt term for the vamps who'd once been human but had lost their mortal lives with an exchange of blood. Yeah, those assholes in the bar hadn't been blood vampires—the fierce creatures born onto the earth already having full immortal strength. Instead, the feeding room had been full of amateurs, vamps who'd been changed in the past few years.

Those guys had kept silent because they were still new to the game, and because Sullivan had a reputation for being one tough bastard. "He's made a bit of a name for himself in the vampire world." Sullivan, and the female, Maya, a vampiress who lived on the West Coast. Both were former humans who'd once held jobs protecting humans.

Now they both walked in the darkness and killing, well, they'd become very, very good at meting out death sentences to their enemies.

It was always a shame to him when protectors became Taken. "Don't make the mistake of thinking that Sullivan is harmless, Miranda."

She snorted. "Yeah, like that's what I was thinking."

"If you cross him, he'll come after you with fangs and claws—"

"Just like you would," she finished softly.

Her words had him faltering. "I would never hurt you."

Her stare was direct. "But what about those who cross you, Cain? Do you show mercy to them?"

In his thirteen years in the Bureau, he'd found that few individuals truly deserved his mercy. Not that he had much, anyway. "Some folks—they don't particularly deserve mercy from me."

"So you've killed, haven't you?" Her husky voice asked the question that he'd been dreading for days.

Every muscle in his body seemed to harden. "I'm not some perfect human choirboy, baby—"

"No, you're a shifter. A very strong, very dangerous shifter, and you've spent a large part of your life working in law enforcement." She licked her lips. "Did you have to use deadly force, in the line of duty?"

He gave a jerky nod but didn't speak. Because it hadn't just been in the line of duty.

"There's more, isn't there?"

Why did she have to push? He'd wanted to keep that dark part of his life separate from her.

Shit. He'd tried so fucking hard. Leaving the Bureau. The monsters—men and beasts. Buying the house in the middle of damn nowhere so that the jaguar could run free in the night and even swim in the water like the cat loved to do.

Then the vampire had come hunting in *his* territory.

And he'd realized that leaving the city hadn't really changed things for him.

Things would never change for him.

"Supernaturals, they tend to live in the big cities." His voice sounded hollow even to his own ears as he walked toward the windows and pushed aside the curtains. "Easier to blend that way."

"Were you tired of blending?"

His fingers tightened around the silky fabric. "I was tired of the dying." The demons. The shifters. Witches. Fighting. Dying. Right alongside the humans. "Jaguars—we aren't exactly the easiest breed to get along with. We like our space. We're territorial." Serious understatement. Hell. How many times had he gotten into pissing matches with cougars and coyotes? Matches that had too often turned violent.

Because that, too, was his nature.

"I can pretend to be like humans. To be just a man." He turned to face her, because he wanted to look into her eyes and make certain she understood this. "But I'm not, and if you go around thinking I'm a man who can turn into a beast, well, you'll be wrong. At heart, what I am is a beast . . . who just happens to be able to turn into a man."

A beast who'd made his first kill when he was eighteen. When the bastard with a gun had broken into his home and threatened his mother because he knew what she was. When the gun had pointed at his mother, and the asshole's finger had tightened around that trigger, he'd attacked.

And he'd never regretted his actions.

Cautiously, Cain walked toward Miranda, watching for any signs of fear or disgust. She'd given him her beautiful body, let him taste heaven, and he was very much afraid she was going to turn from him.

"I've killed in the line of duty, yeah. But I've also killed as a civilian. I've tracked beings you don't even want to know about. I took them out, because I was the only one who could." Again, no regrets.

What point was there in regretting? There was no way to change the past.

He stopped inches away from her. Wished that he could read the emotions behind her solemn stare. "Maybe I should have told you this from the beginning." After her attack. When she'd realized the world didn't work quite the way she'd thought. "But I'm a greedy bastard, Miranda, and I wanted you and—" Hell. He wouldn't say the rest. Wouldn't say that he'd been afraid she'd turn from him in disgust. It had happened before. Right after he'd graduated from college.

He'd told his human girlfriend the truth about his existence. The relationship had been getting serious, and he'd thought she deserved to know just who her lover really was.

Even now, he could still see the disgust on her face.

No regrets. The mantra slid through his mind once more. That was the way he lived his life.

He drew in a hard breath, caught her heady scent, and repeated, "I wanted you."

"And I want you."

Want, not *wanted.* His heart raced as hope raised its stubborn head.

Her hands reached for him. "I told you before, Cain, I'm not afraid of you. Not of what you are, and not of the creature you become."

Okay. Sandy had been running from him by this point.

Miranda didn't look like she was planning to go anywhere.

But looks could be deceiving. Hell, he knew that better than just about anyone.

His fingers caught hers. Tightened. "We're one and the same, baby. You've got to understand that—"

"I do."

He'd just told her that he was a cold-blooded killer. Why did she still look at him like—like—

Like he was a good man.

Oh, damn.

At that moment, he knew he'd just lost a battle he hadn't even realized he'd been fighting.

Miranda.

No fear.

Want.

Need.

His.

Cain swallowed back the lump that rose in his throat. "I need to be with you." Truer words he'd never spoken. And he didn't mean just for the night.

Forever.

Her lips curved in a smile. "Then what are you waiting for, lover? We've got a bed, a room, and all night long."

He felt it then. A strange warmth in his chest. Something he hadn't really felt in so long that it took him by surprise.

Happiness.

His lips lifted as he stared down at her. "That's just the answer I was hoping for." Then he took her mouth with his and tasted the honeysuckle on his tongue.

Cain pushed her back onto the bed, his cock already swollen with hunger.

When he'd walked into that feeding room and he'd seen the vamps sizing Miranda up like she was some kind of dream meal, a flash of possessive rage had burned through him. Then when those two blond jerks had cornered her, it had been all he could do not to unleash his anger.

Possession. Jealousy. From the man and the jaguar.

His fingers tightened around her hips as he thrust his cock against her. They should take it slow now. They had the bed. Soft mattresses. Sweet-smelling sheets. Yes, now should be the time when he took her like a gentleman. Kissing every inch of her body, murmuring those sweet words that women liked to hear.

It should have been the time, but it wasn't.

Possession.

Still kissing her, he fumbled for her shirt. Only managed to rip off one button. Okay, two. He shoved the edges of material aside. Touched her breasts through the cups of her lacy white bra.

It had been far too long since he'd tasted that plump flesh. She arched against him, and his hand slid under her back. He yanked the hook of her bra, and the garment loosened in his grip.

Perfect.

Cain ripped his mouth from hers. Kissed a hot path down her throat. Suckled her skin. Marked her lightly with his teeth.

The bra fell away. Her breasts rose up, nipples pink and tight, and he bent his head, catching one areola with his lips. Laving it with his tongue, then pulling her breast deep into his mouth.

When she moaned, his cock jerked in hungry response.

But he wanted to taste more.

He kissed his way to the other breast. Showed the nipple the same sensual attention. And let her feel the edge of his teeth.

Her breath shuddered out.

Then her hands were on him. Jerking off his shirt. Her nails skated down his spine. Scratched.

Now *he* was the one moaning.

Her fingers crept around his waist. Unhooked his pants with quick motions and freed his cock. She gripped him in a firm hold, squeezed, pumped—

Ah, *damn*. Cain realized that he was seconds away from coming in her hand.

Not gonna happen. He planned to come deep in *her*.

Lucky for him, she was wearing another skirt. One that showcased the legs that he loved so much.

His hips pushed between her thighs. Her legs spread, and he reached up, rubbing his knuckles over her panties and pressing against her clit.

She choked out his name. Her hands slipped away from him. Gripped the sheets.

He yanked the panties out of the way. Snatched the condom out of his back pocket. Tore open the packet with his teeth.

He didn't want to use the rubber. He wanted her. Flesh to flesh.

And if he made her pregnant, all the damn better.

It would make things a hell of a lot easier.

His fingers shook as he positioned the condom. Much as he might want to go bareback, he couldn't take the choice from Miranda, he—

Could thrust straight into her tight, wet sex. It would be so hot. Feel so good.

His.

Her lashes lifted and her stare met his. He saw the lust. The need.

The trust.

Fuck.

With one hand, he rolled on the condom. Soon enough, he'd take her the way he craved.

Flesh to flesh.

For now, now, he'd take what he could fucking get.

Cain drove balls-deep in one hard thrust.

His teeth were burning, stretching. The beast was always so close to the surface during sex. Fighting or fucking, the jaguar liked to play.

His nails were lengthening into claws. He caught Miranda's hands, pinned them against the mattress, careful not to cut her.

She twisted beneath him. Hips bucked. Breath jerked out.

The bed began to squeak in time with his thrusts. The mattress to dip.

Their bodies grew slick with sweat as they fought for climax. Her sex gripped him, squeezing so tight he thought he'd go out of his damn mind.

Heaven. So good.

He pulled his cock nearly out of her, plunged deep again. And again.

His mouth locked on hers. Tasted the need and the stark lust. Tongues met. Lips pressed.

Her breasts were against his chest. Nipples tormenting his flesh. Her legs clamped around his waist. Her hips met him thrust for thrust. Her sex closed around him, fist-tight, flexing, hot, perfect, and—

He felt the hard contraction of her climax along the length of his erection. His mouth lifted from hers. He gazed down at her. Saw the flash of pleasure on her face, watched those blue eyes go blind.

He drove into her creamy core once more and let the same powerful release take him. The pleasure exploded through his body, shooting from his groin and through his entire body in a burst of heat and passion.

In his mind, he heard the jaguar roar, even as a growl of pleasure escaped his lips.

His.

He licked her shoulder. Now was the time to hold her, to feel her warmth and pretend that he was just a man lucky enough to be with the woman he wanted and—

His cell phone rang. A hard, shrill beep followed by the muted sound of the vibrating cell.

Shit. Not now.

The phone beeped. Vibrated.

He withdrew from her body, swearing. Oh, but somebody had just made his shit list.

Cain fumbled for the phone, knowing he had to take the call, especially with Roberts out loose in the night.

"Lawson."

Miranda was silent beside him, face tense.

"We've got contact." Santiago.

Tension had his gut clenching.

"I logged onto Miranda's online account. Checked out her profile and e-mail."

"The bastard's already taken the bait?" An Internet sting had never worked that fast for him in the past. Never. Red flags shot up in his mind.

Had Roberts used the blood link to figure out what they were doing? Was he trying to trap them? Cain couldn't ignore that very real possibility.

"Oh, he's taken it," Santiago said. "An e-mail was sent

from the same account Roberts used before. Traced the IP address back to one of those free computers at a coffee shop just outside of town."

Figured. The guy was smart enough to cover his tracks.

"He's jonesing hard for another victim," Santiago muttered. "In the message, he starts talking about their shared love of antiques, then the asshole cuts to the chase. Says he doesn't usually do this, but he'd love to meet her for dinner, since they're both in the same area."

Slick asshole.

"Says she can meet him at a place called Mancini's Grill at seven tomorrow night."

A public meeting. One designed to make the woman feel safe. And she would be safe, until she made the mistake of letting Paul get her alone.

Then there would be no more safety.

"Tell him I'll be there," Miranda whispered.

His hold on the phone tightened. "*We'll* be there."

They'd have the place surrounded by cops and Bureau men and women. Roberts wouldn't escape again.

The bastard had let his bloodlust bring him down, and Miranda had been right; she was, indeed, the perfect bait.

Bait that Roberts would wish he had resisted.

Cain ended the call. Glanced at Miranda. She was clutching the sheets tightly to her breasts, her skin was flushed, and when she shifted, just a bit, he caught sight of the faint mark on her shoulder.

His mark. From their fast and furious lovemaking session in the sheriff's office.

"Do we need to go back to Cherryville now?"

He wrapped his arms around her. Inhaled and caught her scent. "Soon." But not that exact moment. He wanted to hold her first.

Stay with her.

Pretend that a devil wasn't waiting just beyond the door.

"Soon," he repeated and pressed his lips to hers.

The damn devil could wait a bit longer.

Eight

"You'll be monitored every moment," Cain told her the next evening, right before her promised meeting with the vampire. Cain bent and gave her a quick, hard kiss. "Plainclothes deputies and some cops will be in the restaurant. Santiago and Delaney will be watching from the kitchen."

"And where will you be?" Not too close, or she knew the vampire would catch his scent.

He smiled at her. "Baby, I'll be watching your every move; don't doubt it for a minute."

Her lips curved and she nodded.

"Once you can confirm that the guy waiting is Roberts, then you give the signal." They'd gone over the signal so many times that she almost rolled her eyes. "There's a chance this isn't our guy. We need you to verify ID before we bring hell crashing onto him."

"Right." Ah, jeez, but the butterflies in her stomach were doing some kind of wild dance. And her palms were wet. And her heart really, really needed to slow down.

It was almost showtime.

He caught her hands. Brought her fingers to his lips and pressed a hot kiss against her flesh. "It's going to be over soon."

Thank God. No more serial-killing vampire on the streets of her town.

"I'll see you at the restaurant, baby." His gaze was warm, tender.

And worried.

"See you then," she repeated and felt her smile melt away. For her protection, two deputies were still stationed outside of her house. And Sam was on his way. He was going to be her tail to the restaurant.

Cain opened the front door. Hesitated with his hand on the knob. "Don't drop your guard with him."

"I won't." Not that she particularly needed *that* reminder.

He looked as if he wanted to say more but then he turned away and pushed open the old screen door. He called out a quick greeting to the men stationed near the foot of her steps as he hurried to his car.

Miranda stood in the doorway, her hands gripping the hard wood of the door. This was it. The time they'd been planning for had finally arrived.

She just hoped she could hold everything together.

Cain sped down the drive, disappearing in a faint cloud of dust and the flash of red taillights. After a moment, Miranda nodded to the two men and pushed the door closed.

She'd change. Put on a short black dress, as if she were going to meet a lover. A wig was waiting in her bedroom, the perfect piece needed to make her become Angie Phillips.

If things went according to plan, Roberts would be spending the rest of his night in a jail cell. Then the Feds would take charge of the vampire the next day. Cain had told her that the vampire wouldn't burn in the daylight, but he would be weak.

The weakness would make him much easier to handle.

Miranda stepped toward the bedroom.

A floorboard squeaked behind her. It was all the warning Miranda got.

She spun around and found Paul smiling at her.

"Guess I won't be making our date tonight, eh, love?" he whispered and licked his lips. "But neither will you."

Oh, God.

Miranda screamed as loud as she could, hoping to alert the guards, and then she turned and ran.

He laughed. "Oh, dear, scream all you want. Those poor humans out front can't help you now."

Shit. Shit. Shit. He'd set them up.

"It was so easy to slide into your mind," he snapped, sending the words flying after her. "So damn easy."

The sadistic bastard had been on to them all along.

Had he killed the deputies? No, please no.

Her heart felt like it would rip from her chest. Paul was running down the hallway behind her now. The heavy thump of his feet hitting the wood echoed in her ears.

She shot to the left, dashing for the kitchen. The back door was close. A few feet away.

More laughter. Too close.

Now she knew his plan. Wished she'd figured it out sooner. A setup. For her, not him. Paul had just wanted to get her alone.

And now he had.

Her fingers fumbled with the lock. Managed to twist the deadbolt. She jerked open the door, sprang forward—

He tackled her, his body slamming into hers and knocking her off the back porch and onto the ground with a thud.

Another scream burst from her lips. One full of rage and fear.

She squirmed beneath him, managed to turn toward him, and her nails went straight for his eyes.

He pulled back, and she gouged deep lines into his face, feeling satisfaction well in her at the sight of his bloodied skin.

"Like that, do you?" He licked his lips, catching a drop of blood that had trickled onto his mouth. "I thought you might." Then he brought his mouth crashing down on hers.

She bit him as hard as she could.

His head lifted and he *laughed*. "Oh, you'll do just fine."

"*Help!*" Another full-on claw with her nails. Then a hard punch with her fist.

He didn't even flinch.

Paul shifted slightly, and the weight of his body pinned her torso to the earth. The starlit sky was over them, the night seemed incredibly still in that moment, and—

She didn't want to die.

Her fist thrust up for another punch, right along that angular jaw of his.

Miranda didn't make contact. He caught her hands, the right one, then the left. Then he jerked her hands over her head and pinned them in the dirt.

"I planned to kill you." His breath was hot and rancid on her face. His eyes were as dark as the night. "That first time, I was going to drain your body dry."

His hold was so tight the bones in her wrists ground together.

Sam. He was coming. If she could just hold the vampire off, he'd be there. With his *gun.*

"Dying is easy." His voice was soft. Deadly soft. Goosebumps rose on her flesh. "I know. Flash of pain. Fear. Then it's over."

He smiled again, fangs bared. "It's not going to be that easy for you." His nostrils flared, and the smile tightened on his face. "I can smell that damn animal all over you."

"Then get the fuck off me and you won't have to!" she snarled, bucking beneath him.

"Ah, but this is going to be fun." He lowered his mouth to her neck. When his teeth raked her flesh, she let out a yell of rage and tried to jerk away.

"Relax." The whisper of a lover, from the mouth of the devil. "I've decided not to kill you."

Her breath caught and wild hope flared in her chest.

He pressed a kiss to her neck. She shuddered.

His head lifted and his eyes met hers. "Well, I guess you will *be* dead, but you won't stay that way. Not for long."

Oh, God. *No.*

"Tell me, Miranda, do you think your animal will still want you when you become the thing he hates most on earth?"

* * *

Something wasn't right. Cain gazed across the street at Mancini's Grill, aware of a sense of unease slowly trickling up his spine. A reservation had been made in the vamp's name, so Roberts *should* be showing up soon.

And walking straight into their trap.

But Cain didn't like the waiting. Didn't like not having Miranda in his sights.

Didn't like the feeling in his gut that things were slipping out of his control.

His cell phone vibrated with a silent ring. Never taking his gaze off the restaurant, he flipped open the phone, put it to his left ear. "Lawson."

Static crackled over the line. "Guards . . . hurt."

His body went stone-hard in an instant. "Sam?" he barked. "Sam, is that you?" The connection was piss-poor, as it usually was in Cherryville.

"Find . . . Mir . . . an. . . ." The line cut off.

Understanding dawned too late.

It was one hell of a fine trap all right, but not for the vampire.

For Miranda.

He took off at a run, the beast growling and the man fighting back his fear and rage.

Sam cursed and threw down his phone. The thing had never worked for shit, and he *would* be in his civilian car—with no damn police radio. He felt for the pulse on Deputy Forest's neck. Weak, thready. Just like Dunn's.

The men had been taken down, hard.

But they were still alive. Was Miranda? God, she'd better be.

The flickering porch light shone down on the officers. Their radios and phones had been smashed to pieces.

Taking a deep breath, Sam rose. He'd go inside, find Miranda, and they'd call an ambulance and some serious backup.

He wanted to shout out to her, but he knew better. Roberts,

because he knew that freak was behind this, had to be around somewhere and he sure didn't want to give away his location to the killer.

His gun was in his right hand. His left hand reached for the handle of the door. *Unlocked.* He glanced down, saw the faint scratch marks near the keyhole.

A scream pierced the night then. A scream that had him turning and running with his heart in his throat and his fingers tightening around his gun.

A *woman's scream.* His mom had screamed like that. Just before his asshole father had stopped her screams forever.

He rounded the corner of the house, gun up and ready, and found a man pinning Miranda to the ground.

"Sheriff's Department!" he shouted, and the guy's head jerked toward him. "Get the hell away from the woman, *now!*"

But the guy didn't move. He smiled and the bastard had something wrong with his mouth. His teeth—they were filed or sharpened or something.

They looked like an animal's. Light spilled from Miranda's open back door, throwing a glowing circle around the struggling figures. Miranda was fighting. Squirming. Ramming her head against her attacker. Swearing.

And the perp's smile was just getting bigger.

"I said get away from the woman!" He would put a bullet in the guy if he had to do it. He wasn't in the mood to screw around with some cracked-up killer.

"Make me." A taunting whisper.

One hand pinned Miranda's wrists to the ground. The other lifted to her throat and, Christ—were those claws?

"Shoot him!" Miranda screamed.

The claws swiped toward her jugular.

Sam fired. The bullet caught the bastard in the shoulder, and his hand fell away from Miranda's throat.

"Again!" she yelled. "Keep shooting, keep—"

The man leapt away from her. Bounded to his feet in a single move. The smile was gone. Black eyes glared at him. "That stung, asshole."

Stung? It was a bullet, not a bee.

"And it really, really pissed me off." His lips curled back as he snarled, and those freaky teeth of his looked even sharper.

Sam aimed his gun straight at the freak's heart. "Get on your knees. Put your hands on your head."

The man took a step forward. Christ, he really did look exactly like the photo of Paul Roberts. *So the bastard faked his death. You knew that already.*

The hair on Sam's nape rose. Something was off here. Way off.

Behind the perp, Miranda scrambled to her feet. "Don't talk to him," she cried out. "Just *shoot him!*"

That wasn't the way things worked, she knew that. He had a badge. The guy, well, except for the claws and teeth, looked unarmed. If he could take him down the right way, he would.

Sam sucked in a sharp breath. "On your knees!" he ordered again.

"I'm a god," the man, Roberts, snapped. "I don't kneel for anyone."

God his ass.

He saw that Miranda had grabbed a broken limb and was holding it like a bat. At any minute, he expected her to slam it right into the back of the guy's head.

"I'm countin' to three," Sam muttered, "then either you're on your knees, or I'm shooting." Ample warning. "One." His finger tightened around the trigger. "Two." Sam finally realized something weird was up with the guy's eyes. They looked far too dark.

Empty. Like a dead man's.

"Thr—"

He never finished counting. The bastard launched his body at him, growling. Claws raked over his face, slashed into his neck, and then Roberts's mouth came at him, teeth bared.

Sam's finger jerked, squeezing the trigger. Once. Twice. Three times.

Those creepy eyes widened. The guy's mouth went slack.

The bullets had been fired at point-blank range, and they'd thudded straight into his chest.

The claws fell away from Sam, and Roberts's body hit the ground.

"Sam!" Miranda stepped forward. Hesitated. "Sam, come over here, now!"

He bent next to the body, searching for a pulse.

"No!" Her bellow had his head jerking up. "Get away from him! He's not human, dammit, he's a vampire—and he's not dead! He's gonna get back up, so move your ass over here, fast!"

A vampire? He blinked at that and slowly rose to his feet.

Impossible.

Fangs. Claws. A supposedly dead man on the ground in front of him.

Oh, hell.

He ran to Miranda's side. Grabbed her left arm. Spared a moment to appreciate the pure bulk of the limb she was gripping with her right hand.

"We've got to get inside, call for backup."

She nodded. Her lips trembled just the faintest bit, but her eyes were wide and determined.

They hurried inside, each casting fast looks back at the prone body of Paul Roberts.

Sam hoped the bastard stayed down. But if he didn't, well, he had more bullets.

A *fucking vampire.* Christ. Just when he'd thought things in Cherryville couldn't get more screwed-up.

"I need an ambulance and more damn backup at 101 Lakeview Street! I need—*Shit.*"

Miranda's gaze snapped toward Sam. They were in her kitchen. They'd pulled the two wounded officers inside and barricaded the doors with her furniture. "Sam?"

His eyes lifted. "The line just went dead."

Oh, no, that wasn't what she wanted to hear right then. She

took three steps toward the window. She'd just make certain Paul was still on the ground—

Glass shattered. She and Sam ran for the living room at the same time.

But it was too late. The vampire was already inside. Paul crouched on the floor, shards of glass from one of her picture windows all around him.

Sam jumped forward, gun ready.

He fired.

Paul attacked. He was on Sam in less than two seconds. "I don't fucking like getting shot!" Blood covered his chest. Dripped from his mouth. Paul grabbed Sam's right wrist and twisted. The gun dropped to the floor with a clatter.

Miranda grabbed the limb she'd propped next to the couch.

Paul drove his teeth into Sam's throat.

"*No!*" She swung the limb straight at his back, hitting as hard as she could. Again and again and—

The vampire spun around, caught the limb with one hand. "Dammit, bitch, do you want your turn already?" Blood stained his teeth. His blood. Sam's.

He shoved Sam back against the wall and she heard the sickening thud of his head connecting with the Sheetrock.

"Leave him alone."

Paul shrugged. Sam's body slid to the floor. "Don't like the taste of men, anyway."

Fear had dried her mouth. She could see the blood trickling from the wounds on Paul's chest, soaking his shirt, but the vamp seemed just as strong as before.

So damn bad for her.

She grabbed a lamp and threw it at his head.

He ducked, made a faint *tsk*ing sound. "I'm getting real tired of your shit, Miranda."

It wasn't shit. "This is my *life*, asshole!"

"And I'm going to let you live forever." His eyes were so black. Soulless. "You should thank me. I've given no other this chance."

Paul was stalking her as he spoke. Mirroring each step she took. "I'm *not* thanking you for killing me!"

"Death is brief. A bare moment when you'll see heaven or hell and know that it has to wait."

A moan slipped from Sam's lips. Her head jerked toward him, and Paul struck. He grabbed her, pulling her tightly against him, drenching her clothes with his blood. His hand tangled in her hair, and he used his painful grip to yank back her head and bare her throat.

"We'll see if he wants you now," he rasped and his teeth sank into her neck.

She kicked him in the groin as a white-hot agony lanced her. Miranda twisted. Cursed. Scratched. Punched as hard as she could.

But he wasn't letting go this time. Paul drank deeply, and her body began to sway. Her hands dropped away from him. He was taking too much. Black lights danced before her eyes.

And the furious snarl of a jaguar echoed in her ears.

Paul's head jerked up, his teeth slicing across her skin. She blinked, looked over his shoulder, and saw a giant black jaguar leap through the broken window.

"*No!*" Paul spun toward the beast, and Miranda's knees gave way as she fell to the floor. She hit hard, landing right on her ass.

The jaguar caught Paul in the chest with his claws, digging deep, ripping flesh.

The vampire fought back, swiping with his own claws and managing to dislodge the jaguar with a fierce toss.

The cat rolled in midair. Turned. Landed lightly on his feet. His teeth were bared, ears back, tail down. Then he was lunging toward the vampire.

The vamp tried to run, but the jaguar caught him, locking those deadly teeth around Paul's leg and yanking him down. Then the cat's long pink tongue snaked out, rasping over the vamp's flesh, again and again, and Paul screamed.

A few swipes of that cat's tongue could peel the flesh right off your hand. Santiago's warning echoed through her mind.

Miranda swallowed and tried to fight the nausea roiling in her belly. She inched toward Sam. Maybe she could find his gun. Then she could help Cain.

Although Cain didn't particularly look like he needed help. He appeared to be giving the vampire one serious ass-kicking, for which she was damn grateful.

Sam's lashes fluttered open. "M-Mir . . . an . . . da?"

"It's all . . . right." Damn, but her voice sounded nearly as bad as his did. She cleared her throat. Coughed. Felt the strain as she rasped, "C-Cain's here."

His bleary eyes darted around the room. "Wh-where?"

The jaguar let out a fierce cry, an unholy, deep, rolling roar of sound that seemed to shake the house.

Right there. And he's really, really pissed off.

Her head was spinning and Miranda was worried that she'd pass out at any minute.

Not until I know Cain is safe and Paul isn't a threat. Dammit, I can hold it together! I can!

The jaguar circled the vampire. Paul staggered but held up his claws. "I'm . . . stronger . . . than you," he managed, panting.

Not from where she stood.

"I've . . . got . . . her blood." He seemed to straighten a bit, and Miranda tensed, worried that Paul was faking weakness in order to lure Cain in closer to him. "And . . . soon, I'll . . . have *her.*"

Cain sprang forward.

"Cain!" Her warning came too late.

The vampire leapt aside, raking the jaguar's back with his claws, then driving them deep into the black fur.

Then Paul was running, jumping through the window and fleeing into the night.

The cat's muscles tensed, his gaze locked on the window.

Then shot to Miranda.

In those wild, golden eyes, she saw his fury. And his fear.

For her.

"I'm all right," she whispered because she really couldn't

manage much more than a whisper. "Go! Finish . . . it." She didn't want to spend another night fearing an attack from the vampire.

The jaguar's head moved in the smallest of nods. The bright light shone down on him, and Miranda had one thought as she watched him.

Beautiful.

He was the most beautiful animal she'd ever seen. Dark fur. Powerful muscles. Eyes so wise and mysterious.

She'd thought him completely black the first time she'd seen him. Now, in the light of her home, she could make out the pattern of markings on his body. Large rosettes lined his fur, and the designs encircled smaller dark spots.

Absolutely beautiful.

His claws dug into her carpet. His back legs curled, and he leapt through the broken window, charging off to track the vampire.

Miranda sucked in a hard breath. Cain could more than take care of himself. He was a shifter. A freaking jaguar, but—

He was *her* shifter, and she was worried.

From the corner of her eye, she caught sight of Sam's gun. Her hand flew forward, only to be caught in a surprisingly strong grip.

Her gaze lifted. Met Sam's.

"Cain." Not a question.

She gave a slow nod.

He flinched. "Christ. I . . . don't need . . . this shit."

And now really wasn't the time for explanations.

"Take . . . it." He released her, and his hand rose to his throat. He touched the jagged wound and winced. "Make . . . certain . . . Cain gets the b-bastard."

She would.

Using the wall for support, she climbed to her feet. She was still dizzy, woozy as hell, but the black lights were gone from her vision.

And she wasn't going to give in to the numbing lethargy

sweeping through her body. Not yet. Not until she made certain Cain was safe and that the devil was dead.

When her hand rose, she realized she'd left a bloody handprint on the white paint. Miranda swallowed and curled her fingers around the gun. Aim and shoot. That's all she'd have to do.

If the vampire would just *stay down* . . .

Just what would it take to kill one of his kind?

She was about to find out.

But first, shit, first she was gonna have to crawl through that window, because there was no way she'd be able to move the furniture Sam had barricaded before her door.

I'm coming, Cain.

Nine

The pads of his feet pounded against the ground. He had the vampire in his sights. The world around him shifted into a deadly red hue.

Rage.

The jaguar had only one purpose then, to kill.

The scent of Miranda's blood was in the air, mixing with the vampire's. The stench of the undead killer burned his nose and had his whiskers jerking.

This time, there would be no escape for Paul Roberts. No mercy.

The jaguar had none, and neither did the man.

In one bounding lunge, he tackled the vampire, sending Roberts crashing to the ground with the crunch of bones and the thud of flesh hitting earth.

Roberts screamed in pain and rage, and twisted beneath him.

The jaguar let the vampire roll. He always liked to look into the eyes of his prey. The better to let the quarry know what hell waited.

The vampire's lips twisted into what probably would have been a smile. Blood dripped down his chin. "Five more minutes . . . shifter. I'd . . . have . . . ch-changed her. Th-then she would have been mine."

He snarled.

"Wh-what would you have done . . . then?"

Loved her anyway. The answer came from the heart of the man.

"I'll . . . get her." Cain's claws embedded in Paul's chest. The vampire coughed. Choked. "I'll . . . g-get free . . . go af-after—"

Never play with prey. His mother had taught him that.

Cain knew exactly how to kill a vampire. It was all too easy with his teeth and claws.

Roberts screamed again when Cain moved in for that final attack.

Then . . . silence.

He jumped away from the severed head and the body. Didn't look at the remains of the vampire's chest.

And he caught the scent of honeysuckle on the wind.

No, not now, not—

His head jerked to the right, and she was there. Standing in the light of the moon, her hair a dark, wild tangle around her pale face. Her lips were parted, and her eyes were on the vampire's body.

Or what was left of it.

Her right hand gripped a gun, one that was pointed at him.

She'd seen the beast kill. Seen *him* kill. He'd been so caught up in the red fury of bloodlust that he hadn't even sensed her.

Miranda had seen him as he'd never, ever wished her to see him.

Predator. Savage. Killer.

Her breath came fast and hard. Pounded in his ears as he crept closer to her, his head down. He wanted her to touch him. To look at him not with fear, but with—

Hell, *more.*

Her mouth trembled. The gun lowered and its nose hovered over the ground.

He needed to hold her. To pull her close and feel the

warmth of her body against his. For that, he needed to be a man.

The change wasn't pretty. It wasn't easy. It was, in fact, nearly as brutal as the act he'd just committed.

But she'd already seen him at his worst.

And she wasn't running, not yet.

Cain let the all-consuming fire of the change sweep through him. The crack of bones once again filled the air as his body shifted from beast to man. The fur dissolved. Dark, tanned skin reappeared. Claws returned to fingernails. The jaguar's lethal teeth receded, became those of a man.

His fingers pressed against the earth. His knees dug into the ground. And the whole time, he kept his stare on her.

When the transformation was finished, he rose slowly. Closed the last distance between them. He was naked and when he lifted his hand toward her, he saw the blood that still stained his fingers.

It had always been there. From the first kill.

Miranda hesitated. Carefully put the gun onto the ground. "Cain . . ."

He didn't know what to say, but he knew this was the most important moment in his life. If she left him now, there would be no coming back.

Sirens sounded in the distance. Humans always did have piss-poor timing.

His fingers curled into a fist. He wanted her so much, but she deserved better than an animal.

"He was going to . . . transform me." Her gaze darted over his shoulder to the vampire, then jerked away. Her voice was quiet, hoarse, when she said, "Make me . . . like him."

Cain's jaw clenched. "You could *never* be like him."

Tears clouded her eyes. "If you'd been . . . just a bit later. If you hadn't come . . . I would have been . . . a vampire."

Or she would have been dead. He'd met only a few female vamps in his time. Men transformed much easier, while the women usually had quick, brutal deaths.

"If he'd changed me"—she blinked her eyes, and the moisture eased a bit—"would you have k-killed me, too?"

"*No!*" He reached for her then. He had to touch her, simple as that. He caught her hands in his. Held tight. "Miranda, don't you understand? I would never hurt you—no matter what you are or—or what you become." If she'd been made into a vampire, she'd have experienced the bloodlust, the desperate thirst, but she wouldn't have become a sadistic killer like Roberts. That poisonous instinct just wasn't in her.

"But if I'd . . . been a vampire—"

"I would have wanted you just the same. *Loved* you just the same." Oh, damn, he'd said it, but there was no taking the words back now.

Miranda's eyes widened and he saw himself reflected with the moonlight in that stare. "Cain?"

"You're mine, Miranda. *Mine.* And I don't care what you are—human, vampire, it doesn't matter. You're mine," he repeated, growling the words.

Her lips lifted into a smile. "You mean that, don't you?"

With every bit of his heart. But he knew she didn't feel the same. Things between them were too new. He'd probably scared ten years off her life with his shifts and—

Miranda kissed him. A soft, open-mouthed kiss. Her arms curled around him, held on tight.

As tight as he was holding her.

Her lips lifted a bare inch from his. "And you're mine, Cain Lawson. The jaguar, the man—both of you are *mine.*" Another kiss, one that had his cock rising and his blood heating.

The sirens were dangerously close now and Cain could hear the murmur of voices floating toward them. He tasted her with a quick thrust of his tongue, then pulled back. "Miranda?"

"I love you, Cain."

The words hit him straight in the heart. "Are you—"

Now the smile reached her eyes. "I'm absolutely certain though I don't really think this is the best place for a declaration—"

Not with a dead body a few feet away and a pack of deputies about to burst onto the scene any moment.

"—but I wanted you to know." She brought his hand to her chest. Pressed against the heart that beat too fast. "You're in here, and I think you have been, from the moment you kicked down my door and saved me."

She didn't understand. She'd saved *him*. From a life alone. From the darkness that could so often torment his kind.

Miranda was offering him life, a real life with a woman of his own.

He wanted to shout his joy to the world. He wanted—

"*Shit,* Lawson, did you have to leave such a damn mess?" Santiago shoved through the brush and he threw a pair of jeans at Cain. "Hurry up, the county folks are goin' to be crawlin' all over this place in the next two minutes."

Cain reluctantly broke away from Miranda and jerked on the jeans.

Santiago was frowning at the body. "How the hell am I going to explain this mess? I mean, I know the head had to come off, but—"

Footsteps pounded close by. Cain forced a shrug, wishing he and Miranda were alone and far away from the stench of death. "Just say it was an animal attack." The truth was sometimes the easiest way to handle these situations. "That story worked well enough before for him, didn't it?"

Miranda swayed next to him. Cain grabbed her, scooping her up into his arms and hoisting her high against his chest. Her lashes lowered. "S-sorry," she muttered, "this looks . . . weak as . . . hell . . . but I think . . . I'm gonna . . . fai . . ." Her head sagged back against him.

Too much blood loss. Cain cursed. He was such a damn idiot. He should have taken care of her sooner—

The deputies burst onto the scene. Not quite two minutes.

Santiago started shouting orders. "All right, we've got an animal attack here. Stay on guard and—"

Cain turned away, kept his hold firm around Miranda, and

headed for the houses. "It's all right, baby," he whispered, bending to press a kiss against her cheek. "I've got you."

And he was never planning to let her go.

Cain had Miranda out of the hospital and back at his place in near record time.

The next evening she found herself naked in his bed. Cain was curled possessively around her, and Miranda realized she was feeling almost, well, human again.

"Sam told me it didn't happen, you know," she murmured the words as she turned in his arms. God, but she loved the feel of his arms around her. The steely muscles, the warm skin.

She and Sam had shared a hospital room for a blessedly brief time. "He told me he was delusional, that he only imagined Roberts was a vampire."

"And how'd he explain the jaguar?"

Her lips pursed. "He figures in light of the attack, the cat part was real. The cat *wasn't* you, of course, just—"

Cain grunted at that, and his fingers stroked along the base of her back. "What? Some wild cat? A jaguar out prowling the countryside?"

Miranda stretched beneath his touch. They'd already made love once, but she wanted him again. "Something like that." Yet despite Sam's blustering words, she'd seen the real knowledge in his eyes.

It was a knowledge he didn't want to deal with, not yet. She didn't particularly blame him. The world was a bad enough place just with the screwed-up humans.

When you threw monsters into the mix, things truly went to hell.

"What does the deputy really think?"

Ah, he'd read her so easily. Miranda sighed. "I think he believes it's best to keep pretending, for now."

"He can't pretend forever." A quiet warning as his fingers stilled on her spine.

"No." No one could. She stretched and kissed the rough line of his jaw. "I didn't thank you before."

"Baby, you said you loved me. Trust me, that was thanks enough to last me a lifetime."

And she knew he meant those words. Miranda swallowed. "Where do we go from here, Cain?" Could a shifter settle down with a human? What would happen? Would he go back to working with the FBI while she taught high school students?

"I was thinking maybe an engagement," he said and his fingers skated over the curve of her ass. "You know, third time being the charm for you and all."

Her lips parted in surprise. Okay, she hadn't imagined his confession in the middle of all hell breaking loose. *He loved her.* "That is what they say." Grandma Belle had often said those words. *Try it again, sweetie. Third time's the charm.* Grandma Belle's soft voice seemed to whisper into her ears.

"Not too long," he murmured. "Don't want you to change your mind on me like you did with the others."

Never going to happen. She loved him so much there was no room for any doubt in her mind. "Not too long at all," she agreed.

"We'll get the rings, book a church, and then you'll be mine." He kissed her, one of those kisses that made her feel like she was the most desirable woman on earth.

God, but she loved those kisses. She moved, shifting so she straddled his hips. His bare cock brushed against her sex. Already erect. Warm and hard.

Miranda rubbed over that length, teasing him with the folds of her sex. "Will you keep working for the FBI?" Dangerous, but he was used to danger, and she wasn't going to ask him to stop being the man that he was. She would fear for him, but she would accept his choice.

A muscle jerked along his jaw and the fingers that had been caressing her now clamped over her hips in a steely grip. "No." His gaze dropped to her lips. Then her breasts. "Took the last case for you. I'm done."

Another slow glide of her sex against his aroused flesh. The cream from her core coated the hard line of his shaft. "What will you . . . ah . . . do?" Though right then, she didn't really give a damn. He could sell shoes for all she cared.

She just wanted to keep feeling that firm flesh pressing between her legs.

No, she wanted more. Wanted him inside. *Deep.*

Flesh to flesh. Finally.

"Gonna teach . . . criminal justice . . . community college . . ." He barely got the words out before her mouth crashed onto his.

Enough talking.

The guy had offered her marriage. Love.

Time for some serious celebrating.

His tongue drove into her mouth just as she angled her hips against him and impaled the length of his cock in one fierce move.

She moaned around his tongue, loving the hot feel of his flesh inside her.

No barriers.

Sex to sex.

Man and woman.

Perfect.

Miranda rode him hard, driving faster and faster. Sweat soon filmed on her body, on his. His mouth moved from her lips to her breasts. Sucking. Licking. Biting with rough care.

Her sex tightened around him. The telltale clench right before orgasm.

Cain twisted, rolled hard and fast, and Miranda found herself staring up at him. His face was taut, etched into stark lines of lust, but his golden eyes were blazing with love.

His fingers pushed between her legs, strumming her hungry flesh, and Miranda came with a gasp as the pleasure blasted through her.

Cain held his body perfectly still as her sex contracted with her release. She could hear the rough sound of his ragged breathing in her ears, and when she finally opened eyes that she didn't remember closing, his stare—glowing now with the power of the beast—was locked on her.

"No . . . protection . . ." The words rasped from him.

Miranda shook her head.

His jaw clenched and he started to withdraw.

"No." Her legs clamped around him. Her hips arched. "I want all of you this time."

His lips parted on a breath of surprise and she caught sight of his sharp teeth.

Then he was driving deep and fast. The rhythm was wild, and Miranda held on to him as fiercely as she could. Her head thrashed against the pillow, her nails dug into his shoulders, and when he came, exploding in a white-hot wave inside of her, she held him even tighter.

Then she waited, letting her heart slow, and finally heard the soft sound of his purr.

She smiled and pressed her face against his shoulder.

Damn, but she loved her shifter, and though their life together might not always be easy, well, that would be okay. Grandma Belle had told her once that the good things never came easily.

And Grandma Belle had been one smart lady.

Cain pulled back a bit and stared down at her. "A very, very short engagement, baby."

Happiness made her lips curl. "Agreed."

The sooner, the better. She couldn't wait to spend all of her days and all of her nights with the man who'd saved her from death, who'd given her pleasure, and who'd taught her that it wasn't always the beasts that a woman needed to fear.

Miranda stared into his eyes and whispered, "You know, I've really always been a cat person."

He laughed and lowered his head to nuzzle her throat. "Good, baby, because this cat has claimed you, and you're not getting away."

And neither was he.

Life with him would be one hell of an adventure.

Jaguar. Man. Lover.

Hers.

Sometimes life could be very, very good.

If you like your heroes
SUPERB AND SEXY,
then grab this newest Jill Shalvis book,
out in stores this month from Brava . . .

"Maddie," he said with shocking calm. A furious calm, if she wasn't mistaken, but still.

"I'm on leave of absence," she reminded him, not telling him that it looked like it might be permanent. Hell, she could hardly think it, much less say it out loud. "As in—I'm not currently working for you. So what's happening in my life is none of your business."

"That might have been true a few minutes ago. But now we're related."

"Stop it."

"No, you stop it." Yes, definitely fury. "What the hell is this all about, Maddie? Who was that asshole on the phone?"

She wasn't moved by much, but him standing there in that tall, muscled package, wrapped by all that raw and dangerous male beauty made her swallow hard. "You wouldn't believe me if I told you."

"Try me."

Try him? That had been her greatest fantasy up until Leena had shown up and Maddie's entire world of glass had shattered. Before that, she'd wanted to try him every which way possible, but that was going to be just a fantasy now, a remote one. She reached for the front door, but before she could open it, he placed his hand on the wood, effortlessly holding it closed above her head.

Facing the door, she eyeballed his arm, taut with strength. The fingers of his hand were spread wide. He had long fingers, scarred from all the planes he'd rebuilt. They were capable fingers, always warm, and the clincher . . . they knew how to touch. He'd held her face that time she'd kissed him, and if she closed her eyes, she could still feel his fingers on her jaw. She'd spent a lifetime schooling herself against feeling too much, against giving away too much of herself, especially to men. But the men she'd been with didn't make her nerves sing and her pulse jump by just looking at them.

Brody did.

"Maddie."

"It was nice of you to visit. But as you can see, now's not a good time."

He lifted his hand and traced a finger over the exit wound on the back of her shoulder. "Are you feeling okay?"

She loved his touch. Way too much. "Yes." Unfortunately, the man was a virtual mule when he wanted to be, unmovable, staunch in his opinions. On her best day, she might have gone toe to toe with him, no problem, using that voice of honey she'd perfected, her smile of ice, and the argumentative skills she'd honed well over the years. She was every bit as stubborn as he, and she would have won—she'd have seen to it.

But this wasn't her best day, not by far. In fact, it was quickly gearing up to be one of her top three worst ever. "Don't make me kick your ass out of here."

"I think I can take you."

With a sigh, she dropped her forehead to the door and just breathed. Not easy with well over six feet of solid, warm muscle encroaching into the personal space behind her.

And he was encroaching.

Not that her body minded. Nope, it had apparently disengaged from her brain and was making a break for freedom.

But then he did something that made it all the more difficult. He stepped even closer so that she actually felt his thighs brush the backs of hers. His chest did the same to her back, and then, oh God, and then she felt his breath on her temple.

She had to close her eyes. *Don't turn around because then you'll be in his arms, and you just might be stupid enough to kiss him again, get lost in him . . .*

He slipped an arm around her waist, hard and corded with strength. Adrenaline and something else, something much more dangerous to her well-being, washed through her veins, followed by a high tide of stark desperation.

If she pushed back against that body, she could rub all her good spots to his. No.

Yes.

You've got to get a
HOT DATE,
the latest from Amy Garvey,
new this month from Brava . . .

This was absurd. She was just excited, a little nervous, high on possibility and the idea of a fresh start, even if she'd never imagined starting over back in quiet, boring little Wrightsville, the town she'd been dying to leave ever since she'd been old enough to understand that roads led away from it.

As she leaned against the VW, breathing in the air's cool bite, she watched Nick direct the SUV around the tangled vehicles. She'd thought a lot about what moving home would be like, about old friends and second chances and possibilities she'd never considered.

But she'd never really thought about temptation, at least not with Nick Griffin in the same sentence.

By the time Nick moved the squad car to the shoulder, and started up the chugging, shuddering VW bus to move it, too, he'd recovered from most of his surprise.

Okay, maybe not *most*, but a lot. Some, at least. And then he stepped out of the ancient bus and turned around to look at Grace, leaning against a tree trunk on the riverbank, her dark curls blowing around her face and her eyes hidden behind a pair of sunglasses, a sucker punch of shock hit him in the gut all over again.

Grace Lamb was the last person he ever expected to see in

Wrightsville apart from her obligatory Christmas visit to her dad. But here she was, live and in living color, the epitome of trouble on two legs.

Two legs, he realized, that had somehow gotten a lot longer in the years since he'd seen her last. Long, slim legs in faded jeans, with ridiculous bright pink boots on her feet.

He caught himself with a cough. Grace was his best friend Tommy's little sister. She didn't have . . . *legs*. Well, yeah, of course she had legs, but not . . . *legs*. Not like that, anyway. That had definitely changed sometime in the past couple of years.

Running a stop sign and smacking into a police car, though, that was the Grace he had always known.

"Impulsive" was her middle name. Along with "reckless," "fearless," and, well, "distracted by whatever shiny new thing came along." Which wasn't a single word, but whatever. It was still the truth.

Grace had once set her backyard on fire when she tried to start the grill to make lunch for her father. Another time she'd decided to try ice fishing on the pond, only to sink into the water once she started cutting through the pond's frozen skin. She'd tried to go blond, but she'd used household bleach on her dark curls, nearly choking herself on the fumes in the process.

And that was all before she was eleven.

The girl was a walking disaster and always had been. Except she wasn't a girl anymore, and judging by the suitcases and boxes he could see through the VW's windows, she planned to be back in town for a while. Which was just frigging weird, because the one thing that Grace had always been was restless, most of all to get out of Wrightsville.

"Billy will be down any minute," he said as he walked back to her.

She tilted her head, looking up at him quizzically. "Billy?"

"Down at the precinct," Nick explained, settling his hips against the hood of the cruiser and crossing his arms over his chest. "I can't write up my own report, since I was involved."

"There's going to be a report?" She took off her sunglasses and turned horrified brown eyes on him. "It's just a little fender bender! Hardly worth mentioning, really. I can pay for the damage and no one even has to know . . ." She trailed off when he stared her down, arms still folded over his chest, immovable.

Leave it to Grace. Yeah, he'd taken care of the Great Microwave Disaster of 1988, and the time she'd lost the two Pomeranians she was dog sitting, but this was a little different. It was an official police vehicle, not his own battered Jeep, and Grace, well . . . he shook his head. As far as he could tell, she had never really learned to anticipate consequences.

Like wearing jeans that looked molded to her hips, and a white blouse that didn't completely hide the outline of a lacy bra.

Not that he was looking. Definitely not. He swallowed back a growl of arousal, and turned toward the VW, gesturing vaguely. "What is all that, Grace? What are you doing here?"

He'd forgotten how blinding her smile could be, and it surprised him all over again. He was still blinking at the brilliance of it when she said, "Coming home, of course."

His eyebrows nearly shot off the top his head. "You're . . . moving back here? To Wrightsville?"

"You don't have to say it like I just announced I'm having an alien love child and going on the talk-show circuit." She frowned, the light in her eyes turning to smoke the way it always did when she was mad at him. Boy, was that look familiar.

"Doesn't Robert work in New York?" he asked, glancing at the old bus again. And why on earth was Grace driving that thing? He didn't know Robert well, or really at all, but he did know he wasn't the vintage hippie chic type. "Commuting to Bucks County is an awful long trip."

"Robert won't be commuting." It was Grace's turn to fold her arms in front of her, but Nick was surprised to realize she didn't look upset. Instead, she was calm, almost peaceful.

"Robert is moving to Chicago, to work for The Museum of Contemporary Art."

If his eyes widened any further, they'd probably roll out of his head, Nick realized with a start. "And you're . . . ?"

"Not," she said simply, and gave him another smile. The sun gleamed on her hair. "I'm starting over, Nick. I'm getting a divorce, and I'm going to figure out a career, and I'm going to do it right here in Wrightsville."

Just when he'd convinced himself Wrightsville was getting a little boring, Nick contemplated as he restrained a groan, Grace back in town, at loose ends, looking for work and maybe romance?

They were all doomed.